WINIFRED PECK
THE WARRIELAW JEWEL

WINIFRED PECK (1882-1962) was born Winifred Frances
Knox in Oxford, the daughter of the future Bishop of
Manchester. Her mother Ellen was the daughter of the Bishop
of Lahore.

A few years after her mother's death, Winifred Peck became one
of the first pupils at Wycombe Abbey School, and later studied
at Lady Margaret Hall, Oxford. Returning to Manchester, and
under the influence of Christian Socialism, she acted as a social
worker in her father's diocese, as well as starting out as a
professional writer.

After writing a biography of Louis IX, she turned to fiction in
her early thirties, writing over twenty novels, including two
detective mysteries, *The Warrielaw Jewel* and *Arrest the
Bishop?,* now republished by Dean Street Press.

She married James Peck in 1911, and they had two sons
together. James was knighted in 1938, and it was as Lady Peck
that his wife was known to many contemporary reviewers.

Bewildering Cares, a novel about the perplexing and richly
comic life of a parish priest's wife in the early months of World
War Two, is now available as a Furrowed Middlebrow book.

BY WINIFRED PECK

FICTION

Twelve Birthdays (1918)

The Closing Gates (1922)

A Patchwork Tale (1925)

The King of Melido (1927)

A Change of Master (1928)

The Warrielaw Jewel (1933)

The Skirts of Time (1935)

The Skies Are Falling (1936)

Coming Out (1938)

Let Me Go Back (1939)

*Bewildering Cares: A Week in the Life of
a Clergyman's Wife* (1940)

A Garden Enclosed (1941)

House-Bound (1942)

Tranquillity (1944)

There Is a Fortress (1945)

Through Eastern Windows (1947)

Veiled Destinies (1948)

A Clear Dawn (1949)

Arrest the Bishop? (1949)

Facing South (1950)

Winding Ways (1951)

Unseen Array (1951)

MEMOIR

A Little Learning: A Victorian Childhood (1952)

Home for the Holidays (1955)

HISTORY

The Court of a Saint: Louis IX, King of France, 1226-70 (1909)

They Come, They Go: The Story of an English Rectory (1937)

WINIFRED PECK

THE WARRIELAW JEWEL

With an introduction by
Martin Edwards

DEAN STREET PRESS
A Furrowed Middlebrow Book

INTRODUCTION

WINIFRED PECK'S achievements have perhaps been over-shadowed by those of other members of her astonishingly gifted family. Yet her career as an author lasted for almost half a century, and her work has enjoyed considerable popularity. Less than a decade ago, a reprint of her novel *Housebound* (1942) earned enthusiastic notices; Michael Morpurgo, for instance, described it as 'beautifully written ... supremely funny'. When Peck died in 1962, *The Times* said that "she showed a marked talent for sharp characterization, amusing dialogue and an ability to condense a life history into the minimum number of words."

Peck was a versatile writer. She published a life of Louis IX in 1909, when she was 27, and turned to writing novels in her late thirties. Most of her books can be described as mainstream fiction, often written with a light touch that has drawn comparisons with the work of E.M. Delafield and Angela Thirkell. During the 1950s, she also wrote a couple of books about her childhood, but before then she had explored detective fiction. Her work as a mystery novelist, however, has tended – despite its quality – to be overlooked.

The Warrielaw Jewel and *Arrest the Bishop?* are detective novels that demonstrate the quiet accomplishment of her writing, but there are obvious reasons why she did not make a lasting impact as a crime writer. The books appeared more than a decade apart, and she made no attempt to write a series, or create a signature sleuth. The books had long been out of print and hard to find until Dean Street Press, which has unearthed a considerable number of long-lost gems, resolved to give them a fresh life. Their republication also gives a new generation of readers the chance to compare Peck's fiction with the more high-profile detective stories written by her brother Ronald Knox, who was one of the leading lights of "the Golden Age of Murder" between the two world wars, and a founder member of the legendary Detection Club.

The Warrielaw Jewel was first published in 1933, but the events of the story take place in the era 'when King Edward VII lived, and skirts were long and motors few, and the term Victorian was not yet a reproach'. Thus the novel represents an early example of the history-mystery, a fashionable sub-genre today but much less common at the time that Peck was writing. The setting is Edinburgh, which 'was not in those days a city, but a fortuitous collection of clans. Beneath a society always charming and interesting on the surface, and delightful to strangers, lurked a history of old hatreds, family quarrels, feuds as old as the Black Douglas. Nor were the clans united internally, except indeed at attack from without. Often already my mother-in-law had placidly dissuaded me from asking relations to meet, on the ground that they did not recognise each other.'

The story, narrated by the wife of the legal adviser to the Warrielaw family, encompasses such classic Golden Age elements as murder, a trial, a valuable heirloom, and a mysterious curse. The quality of Peck's prose lifts the book out of the ordinary, and in a review on the Mystery★file blog in 2010, Curtis Evans argued that it is 'an early example of a Golden Age mystery that, in its shifting of emphasis from pure puzzle to the study of character and setting, helped mark the gradual shift from detective story to crime novel.'

Pleasingly, Peck makes use of one of the game-playing devices popular with Golden Age novelists, a formal 'challenge to the reader', at the end of the twelfth chapter:

'STOP. THIS IS A CHALLENGE TO YOU. At this point all the characters and clues have been presented. It should now be possible for you to solve the mystery. CAN YOU DO IT? Here's your chance to do a little detective work on your own – a chance to test your powers of deduction. Review the mystery and see if you can solve it at this point. Remember! THIS IS A SPORTING PROPOSITION, made in an effort to make the reading of mystery stories more interesting to you. So – don't read any further. Reach your solution now. Then proceed.'

The mystery writer most closely associated with explicit challenges of this kind was the American Ellery Queen, but the device was also employed by a range of British detective novelists, including Anthony Berkeley, Milward Kennedy, and Rupert Penny. It was a way of making explicit the fact that the whodunit essentially involved a battle of wits, dependent on the author playing fair by supplying (although often disguising) the clues to unravel the puzzle.

Having entered so wholeheartedly into the spirit of Golden Age detective fiction, Peck promptly moved away from the genre, and did not return to it until after the Second World War, by which time tastes in crime writing, as well as much else, were changing fast. *Arrest the Bishop?* appeared in 1949; set in a Bishop's Palace, the story made excellent use of her first-hand knowledge of ecclesiastical life. This is another history-mystery, written in the aftermath of one world war, but relating events set in 1920, not long after the end of another.

As a bonus, the book is also an example of that popular sub-genre, the Christmas crime story. The murder victim is, as so often in traditional whodunits, an unscrupulous blackmailer, and again Peck makes use of tropes of Golden Age fiction such as a timetable of key events, and a list of prime suspects itemising their respective motives, opportunities for committing the crime, and instances of their seemingly suspicious behaviour. The result is a good old-fashioned mystery: Peck's gentle humour ensures readability, and in the twenty-first century the book has added appeal as a portrait of a vanished age.

Winifred Frances Knox, born in 1882, was the third of the six children of the fourth Bishop of Manchester. She had an older sister, Ethel, as well as four brothers. The eldest son, E. V. Knox, became well-known as editor of *Punch*; he was also responsible for a splendid parody of the Golden Age detective story, 'The Murder at the Towers'. Dillwyn ('Dilly') Knox became a legendary code-breaker who worked for British Intelligence during both world wars, while Wilfred Knox earned distinction as an Anglican clergyman and theologian. The best-known of the four brothers was Ronald, a man of extraordinary talents, who was also ordained an Anglican clergyman before converting to Catholicism; he proceeded to carve a considerable reputation as 'Monsignor Knox'. Amongst many other activities, he was a popular broadcaster in the early days of the BBC, one of the first Sherlockian scholars, an expert on word games such as acrostics, and creator of the Detective's Decalogue – ten jokey commandments for crime writers that were adapted into the initiation ritual for new members of the Detection Club. Suffice to say that these supposed rules of the game were honoured, by Knox as well as by his crime writing colleagues, more in the breach than in the observance.

Winifred shared, *The Times* said, 'her brothers' lively wit and sharp minds, and was well able to hold her own in the complicated verse games they played among themselves. It was the family custom to spend the summer holiday in a furnished house, generally a rectory, where they amused themselves tracing the life of the absent incumbent as revealed in the photographs that were hung about his walls. In such stimulating and imaginative company she had every inducement to become a writer, where much of the material the novelist needs lay to her hand.' In almost any other family, Winifred's record as a high achiever could not possibly be eclipsed, but such was the brilliance of her quartet of brothers that even her niece, the Booker Prize-winning novelist Penelope Fitzgerald (whose father was E. V. Knox), made only fleeting mention of Winifred in her book *The Knox Brothers*.

Winifred was among the first forty pupils to study at Wycombe Abbey School, and proceeded to read History at Lady Margaret Hall, Oxford. In 1911, she married James Peck in Manchester Cathedral. James, described by Penelope Fitzgerald as "a small, quiet, reliable, clever and honourable Scotsman", was at the time Clerk to the School Board in Edinburgh. The couple had three children, and James became an increasingly influential figure in both local and central government; when he was knighted in 1938, Winifred became Lady Peck.

By the time Winifred Peck died, her detective fiction had become a footnote to her literary career. It was not even mentioned in her obituary in *The Times*. Present day readers of the books will, I think, agree that this is a pity. Her contribution to the golden age of crime fiction, although modest in scale, is well worth remembering.

Martin Edwards
www.martinedwardsbooks.com

CHAPTER I
THE JEWEL IS THREATENED

TWILIGHT HAD FALLEN and only the wood-fire illuminated my drawing-room when the big door swung open. The light in the passage cast the shadow of two figures on the wall as my maid, Christina, announced:

"Miss Warrielaw and Miss Rhoda Macpherson."

All newly-married people will admit that for a year at least their home has little personality of its own. A new house, newly furnished, has the insipidity of a baby; an old house newly furnished shows itself in queer unexpected lights when visitors appraise it.

It was in the year 1909 that I married John Morrison of Edinburgh, the younger partner of the well-known firm of Hay, Morrison and Fletcher, Writers to the Signet, and came to live in the monumental house vacated for us by his parents in Moray Place. Like everyone of my day who had been brought up in an artistic atmosphere in London, I had my drawing-room painted white, and replaced the stout, stuffy Victorian furniture and carpet by Persian rugs, antique chests and bureaux, blue and white china and gay cretonne-covered chairs and sofas. I was very proud of the result, but as the new guests entered and Christina switched on the lights, it looked suddenly bare and raw and lacking in solidity. When I asked John later if he had experienced the same sensation and, like myself, put it down to the Warrielaw personality, he merely replied that all he felt was his own folly in being caught in the tail of one of my At Home days. Brides had their Days in the Edinburgh of those far-off years, and John never ventured into the drawing-room till half-past five.

"Will I infuse some new tea, Madam?" asked Christina. Like all good Scottish servants she was a perfect register of social standing. Evidently she felt nothing but respect for the dowdy couple she had just ushered into the room.

"Not for us, please don't trouble for us," intervened the elder woman nervously. "I have had tea with Rhoda and we came late intentionally in the hope of catching dear John."

If I could tell from dear John's expression that the pleasure was not mutual, I was glad for Miss Warrielaw's sake that her hopes were fulfilled. The lights revealed nothing to explain Christina's respectful greeting in Miss Warrielaw's appearance or dress, but they did make it clear that this elderly lady, in her queer, rather pathetic efforts at finery, was worried and upset. To John's murmur of introduction to "My wife" she paid only the tribute of a watery smile before she sat down by him, on the edge of a big sofa, in a flurry of agitation.

"How you must hate coming to live in Edinburgh!" Miss Rhoda Macpherson took a chair beside me and spoke coldly and abruptly. "I felt very sorry for you when I heard John was marrying an English girl."

"But it's such a beautiful place!" I protested. Already I had discovered the fact that no one but Edinburgh people can ever safely abuse Edinburgh.

"Oh that!" said Rhoda contemptuously. It seemed to me rather hard that this prim, neat little spinster, sitting so severely upright in her grandfather chair, should meet my compliments so ungraciously. "The place is all right, but you'll find the people impossible. When you get to know the wearisome cliques and sets we all live in you'll wonder, as I do sometimes, if it's possible for anyone who's been born and brought up in a radius of twenty miles to have a wholly reasonable attitude to life."

Rhoda was, I felt, speaking with some justice for her aunt and herself. My eyes wandered to the sofa where Miss Warrielaw was pouring out an incoherent story to my husband, and Rhoda's gaze followed me.

"I'm sorry," she said, looking up suddenly, and for the first time I realized that her thin, pale little face, with its sharply pointed chin and tightly closed mouth, was redeemed from the commonplace by her eyes.

"I'm sorry if I'm too outspoken. The fact is that a rather curious, rather alarming thing happened in my aunt's house yesterday and we're all a little upset by it. They have such confidence in your husband—his family have looked after our affairs for generations—that Aunt Mary would come to him. We should really have gone to his office."

"Do go and join them," I said, moving a chair for Rhoda towards the sofa. "Don't bother to talk to me till you've consulted my husband."

My two guests, now that they were seated one each side of my husband on the sofa, leaving me to my observations, were much more interesting than they had appeared at first sight. They were queer and dowdy, but they represented some tradition or point of view intensified by the very narrowness of their outlook. Aunt and niece had, at first sight, little in common. Miss Warrielaw had clearly put on her Sunday dress to come to see me. To-day of course she would look a figure of fun, but twenty-four years ago she appeared only as one of a common type, the country lady who depended on the efforts of a little dressmaker. She wore a coat and skirt of that dismal fawn colour, so trying to an elderly, weather-beaten complexion; a small brown hat topped a fringe of fair hair streaked with grey; from her wrinkled forehead one of the thick brown spotted veils of the period entangled itself in her hair. On her forehead was a yellow mole which she rubbed so perpetually in any moment of agitation that a vague blackness over one eye was a characteristic of her appearance. A big Victorian locket of solid gold hung upon her fawn silk blouse and a variety of bracelets adorned her thin wrists. Those slender hands and wrists, and her long, beautifully shaped feet in their country brogues redeemed the heaviness of her stout shoulders and shapeless waist, and redeemed her appearance also from any impression of vulgarity. She was a country woman, one saw at once: one could imagine her best tramping across a field in tweeds followed by a string of dogs. Rhoda, in contrast, looked oddly urban. She was small and self-contained, and her neat, cheap, dark little coat and skirt and depressed little hat suggested only the efficient, dowdy little typist of that distant period. She was not in the least like her aunt, I decided, as I contrasted her narrow face, her pointed chin and air of cool competence with Miss Warrielaw's long, broad face and agitated double chin. And then both looked up at once, and I saw that they had one feature in common. Both aunt and niece had wide, round eyes of that queer hazel shade which varies between yellow topaz in certain lights, and the dull green of old glass in others. The colour was not only odd in itself; the eyes were conspicuous because, owing I imagine to some curious defect of vision, they had very small pupils which, I was to learn, rarely contracted or expanded. Later I was to hear and see a good deal of the famous Warrielaw eyes, but from the first I subconsciously noted that peculiarity.

My thoughts wandered from the point because the story suddenly caught my attention. I was not particularly interested while Miss Warrielaw was occupied in denouncing the doings of her sister Jessica. Her voice was curiously even and toneless, and I had only gathered vaguely that Jessica was outraging her sister and her family by the proposed sale of some family property, when Rhoda's voice broke in, clear and incisive.

"Don't bother John with all that again, Aunt Mary. John knows and we all know, since Cora Murray brought that lawsuit against Aunt Jessica, and lost it, that Aunt Jessica can sell all the family property but the house, and do what she likes with the fairy jewel and throw away the money as she pleases. I thought it was about this attempt at burglary that you came to see John."

I had only been married then for two months, and it was still entrancing to me to observe how impassive and non-committal my tall, dark husband became when acquaintances tried to get legal advice from him outside his office. It was, as he often complained, the favourite economy of his Edinburgh clients to extract an opinion from him in ordinary social life without wasting six shillings and eightpence. But at Rhoda's sudden turn in the conversation, a look of relief and interest crossed his face. The Warrielaws, I gathered, had used an old friendship for legal discussions unmercifully in the past, and any change was welcome.

"Why, Miss Mary," he asked, "what's happened? You know I've always told your sister you really ought to get some man into one of the lodges now that poor old Macdonald's had to go to the Infirmary for good."

Evidently, I gathered, the Warrielaws were yet another of those families, whom I met not infrequently, who were clinging with true Scottish determination and self-sacrifice to some place handed down to them by richer and luckier ancestors. That would explain Christina's obvious respect, for the possession of land is still the only certain criterion of gentility to the descendants of clansmen.

"It was only yesterday," said Miss Mary, her poor hands fluttering painfully, her sentences tumbling out confusedly in her dull, even voice. "And I don't think you can call it a burglary because nothing has been taken as far as we can make out, and of course this evening the house is shut up properly, but, as you know, most of our locks are out of order, and Jessica won't spend anything on repairs that isn't strictly necessary."

"What do the police think?" asked John briskly. "We haven't summoned them, John. Jessica said it was absurd when nothing was missing, and she never has liked our local man, Maclure, since his boys were found stealing apples from the walled garden among her bedding-out plants. Besides, it would hurt Effie's feelings so dreadfully as things are, and Effie has served us faithfully for thirty years!"

"Of course she should have called in the police at once," said Rhoda decidedly. "I urged it most strongly."

"Too strongly, my dear," put in Miss Mary with sudden sharpness. "You know how Jessica dislikes being dictated to."

"Suppose," John suggested patiently, "suppose you tell me just what did happen."

"Jessica didn't seem quite to approve of that," said Mary distractedly, "but I insisted that you should know, as our lawyer and estate agent. Then at least, I said, it will be in the hands of the Law!"

"I think I'd better tell you," said Rhoda, interrupting her aunt's incoherent sentences with her brisk, cool voice, "especially as I was the one to discover it. Yesterday I bicycled down to see Aunt Mary. I knew the Aunts were worried because there has been a good deal of trouble over Annie."

"Annie?" queried John. Apparently there were limits even to his knowledge of the Warrielaw establishment.

"Annie is Effie's niece," said Rhoda, hurriedly forestalling her aunt. "You know Effie has managed all the work in that big place alone since Aunt Jessica had this absurd mania for economy, which isn't really necessary, I'm sure." A note of enquiry crept into her voice, but my husband ignored it, and Miss Mary seized her opportunity.

"Effie's sister, Hope, was with us for years in my mother's day," she broke in; "such a nice sensible woman and then she ran off with a tinker. Surely you remember, John, in the old days when you used to come down to play at Warrielaw, with Neil and Cora and Rhoda, how Neil used to annoy Effie by singing—'She's awa' with the raggle-taggle gipsies, Oh!' Poor thing! She died leaving two daughters, one such a good respectable soul who married a gardener at Carglin, and one this poor creature Annie, who is—well I don't know how to describe it. She's a fine big girl and an excellent worker at times, but she's rather—well she isn't quite—"

"She's overdeveloped physically and underdeveloped mentally," said Rita with cold distaste. "She works well if she's told just what to do, but she's the intelligence of a child of twelve, and has violent fits of temper and sulkiness. I never thought her safe in that household, but Jessica insisted on keeping her for Effie's sake. Two days ago, however, she was discovered coming back from a funeral in Aunt Jessica's black hat and cloak—she's a passion for funerals, like all uneducated Scottish people, and that was too much even for Effie. So Annie had her notice, and I was really rather afraid lest she should have one of her queer turns. So I went down to Warrielaw. It was about five o'clock and, as it was dark and my bicycle lamp isn't up to much, I walked down the avenue very slowly. It took quite ten minutes, for you know how shockingly it's kept. From the first corner I noticed a light in Aunt Jessica's bedroom. I wasn't surprised, as I thought she might have gone up there to avoid me. You know, John, there's been a lot of ill-will in the family about this selling of our last real heirloom—the fairy jewel. Of course it's nothing to do with me, there was no question of my having it, but I'd felt obliged just once to remonstrate against its going out of the family. I went up to the house and then round to the back, to save Effie or Annie coming all the way up to the front door from the basement. The door into the kitchen courtyard was open, and so was the back door. I went into the kitchen and found it nearly dark—only a flicker from the fire in that dreadful huge range, and one candle guttering on the table. I was surprised, and looked down the passage to the rooms where Effie and Annie sleep, but they were in absolute darkness. Then I remembered that one or both of them often give the dogs a run across the gardens about that time, and as neither of the spaniels were barking, I supposed the maids were out with them, though I did feel it rash of them to leave the door like that. I stumbled up the basement stairs in the dark and found the big hall just lit with that absurd little oil-wick lamp Aunt Jessica likes. Then it occurred to me that I would just run up to see Aunt Jessica before I went to Aunt Mary in the library. I am sorry for her, you know, and I thought we might make friends. You can't help being sorry for anyone who makes herself disliked as universally as Jessica. There was no one on the stairs, and no light in the long corridor, except a gleam from her door. I knocked, and went in when no answer came. The window was wide open and nearly blew out the candle on the dressing-table. There was no one there, but I had a horrible shock to find the whole place in confusion. Aunt Jessica is as tidy as anyone can be who hoards so many possessions, and her room is always neat. But there lay all the contents of her drawers on the floor, tumbled about anyhow. Her dresses were torn out of the wardrobe, her bed was all crumpled and upset. It looked as if someone had turned the room upside down in search of something. I ran downstairs to the library and found the Aunts sitting there, each at her own end of the room, doing their embroidery as usual. Aunt Jessica had not been upstairs since tea-time, Aunt Mary had only run up for a minute afterwards, without a light she told us. I tried not to frighten them, but I had to tell them of course."

"Rhoda was most considerate," put in Mary confusedly.

"We were ringing the bell just as Effie came upstairs with the dogs. She'd been out alone—"

"Tit and Tat never cared for Annie. I always noticed that, though Jessica said it was nonsense," persisted Mary.

"And she hadn't seen Annie anywhere. We heard the girl's step outside while we were questioning Effie, but she was in one of her sulky fits—she's been crying ever since she had notice, Effie says, and wouldn't answer when we asked answer where she had been. We all went upstairs then to examine Aunt Jessica's room, leaving Annie downstairs howling like a baby. We looked through everything, and nothing seemed to be missing, but when Aunt Jessica looked at the little safe in the wall—the safe grandmother had made for all her jewellery—we thought there were the marks of new scratches on it. It can't have been opened, for nothing had been touched. But it did look as if someone, as if Annie, had been hunting for the key everywhere."

"It does," said John slowly. "Only I should have expected a girl of that mentality to have picked up a few odds and ends she coveted rather than jewellery, somehow—the magpie sort of instinct, you know."

"But she's cunning, very cunning," represented Rhoda. "And of course, you see, we can't fix the blame on to her. Someone may have got in at any moment when Effie was out in the garden. Effie herself thinks that Annie probably was out at the back lodge speaking to someone. One horrid part of the whole affair is that there are tinkers near just now, camping down in that bit of waste land by the burn. Effie owned to us then that Annie has been off with the tinkers once or twice since she left school, with her father's relations you see. She may have let one of them in, for all we know. It's rather a horrible idea to think of that camp so near that old, big, lonely, unprotected house."

"But you'll send the girl away at once?" I broke in. By this time I was shuddering at the vision of the solitary ill-lit barracks of a house with its rabbit-warrens of passages, and the three lonely old women huddled in the confines of its dark rooms, listening helplessly to every footfall, while down the passages wandered the big half-witted girl, intent on theft or revenge, or, at least, on some message to the caravans of her silent, dirty kinsmen by the desolate burn outside. I could see the picture present itself, though doubtless in much more sober colouring, to my husband, as he shook his head.

"You must have the police. For one thing, if they looked up the camp the tinkers would certainly be off. Tell Miss Jessica to put the police on to them and have the locks everywhere seen to and get rid of this girl at once."

"Jessica won't," complained Miss Mary. "She will not hurt Effie's feelings, she says, by letting the police suspect her niece. And she won't send Annie away till April because …"

"Because Ellen Hay, Annie's sister, is going to have her sixth or seventh baby," explained Rhoda, as Miss Mary broke off in confusion. "It's the only place to send Annie to, and Effie says it would upset Ellen dreadfully to have Annie back on her hands before the event takes place. Effie is to go off to help her at the crisis for a night or so and take Annie with her. If she murders the whole household before that, Jessica is responsible!"

"She must get rid of her and we must get the police on to the tinkers," repeated John. "Do you think if I ran down to see Miss Jessica …"

"That's just what we want, John," said Miss Mary eagerly. "The only effect of all this is to make her more determined than ever to sell the jewel, and I thought you might perhaps put in a word against that too. In any case you could reason with her about getting the locks seen to and disposing of Annie. I can hardly bear to see her big, silly, greasy face about the place any more, and I'm sure she knows something, for her eyes have that cunning look just now which Rhoda mentioned. I managed to get Jessica to see that we've been most remiss in not calling sooner on John's wife"—she turned to me with a faint smile—"and I persuaded her to let me ask if Mrs. Morrison would pardon the informality and come down with you to tea to-morrow. That would give you a chance to say something about repairs. Why there isn't even a proper snib to the French windows in the library!"

"But I hoped", said John, looking puzzled, "that the sale of the Raeburn last autumn would give her plenty of ready money for all necessary repairs."

"The Raeburn?" Rhoda said bitterly. "All that went to Neil Logan as usual. It paid for his visit to Italy and for the sort of amusements he enjoys in Rome."

This sudden addition to the personnel of the Warrielaw family puzzled me, and I started a little as John gave me a nod. Then I recalled myself and accepted the invitation to Warrielaw.

"At four," said Miss Mary, getting up at last and moving uncertainly to the door. "At least that's the time I like tea, but perhaps I had better say half-past as Jessica likes to get as much daylight as possible for digging in the garden." The bitterness of her tone suggested such an age-long feud over the details of life as often obtains in the establishment of two sisters. "But of course," added Miss Mary, recollecting herself, "it is really wonderful of her to keep the gardens as she does when she refuses to have any help. Good-bye, my dear. Good-bye, John. It is such a comfort to have an old friend like you to rely upon."

"Now my old friend," I said as John returned to the drawing-room after his farewells, "I rely on you to tell me the story of this extraordinary family at once. And don't be legal or cautious, as I've evidently got to be plunged into this affair socially!"

"I suppose you've got to know about them," said John. "You're bound to meet some of them in Edinburgh, Cora Murray at any rate. I'm surprised she hasn't come to-day to find out about this mysterious burglary. All the Warrielaws hate each other, but they always know everything about each other's affairs."

"Well, go on," I said, settling down beside him. "I know they're only big tin cases in your office to you, but I look upon them as History."

This story of mine is now I suppose historical. My own children apply the term to that period, so far away from modern youth, when King Edward VII lived, and skirts were long and motors few, and the term Victorian was not yet a reproach. Yet as I look back I see no very profound differences in modern youth and my own upbringing. Before I married I lived with a literary father and artistic mother in Kensington Square, and that life seems to me to have changed but little in essentials. But when, after my marriage, I went to live in Edinburgh, I did feel that I had stepped back definitely into history. I am not speaking of the stricter social and ceremonial proprieties, already undermined by the charming youth of the city. It was not these things which surprised me, but a deeper truth, unimagined by a post-war generation. Edinburgh was not in those days a city, but a fortuitous collection of clans. Beneath a society always charming and interesting on the surface, and delightful to strangers, lurked a history of old hatreds, family quarrels, feuds as old as the Black Douglas. Nor were the clans united internally, except indeed at attack from without. Often already my mother-in-law had placidly dissuaded me from asking relations to meet, on the ground that they did not recognise each other. In a book of Stevenson's, I had read of two sisters who inhabited one room in the Canongate, a chalk line dividing them and their possessions, and never spoke to each other for twenty years. Now clearly I had stumbled into the story of a clan divided within itself by internecine war.

Five hundred years ago the Warrielaw family were, it appeared, new-comers and parvenus in the Lothians. They came from the Borders with the money and cattle they had looted in raids upon England, and built themselves a small baronial manor in the safer meadows of the West Lothians, seven miles from Edinburgh. By purchase or marriage they added to their property until, by the end of the eighteenth century, they were amongst the largest landowners in the county. In the next thirty years coal was discovered on their estate: mines and shale-pits and the railway began to defile the pleasant fields and gentle woodlands and clear streams of the Lothians, but they brought to the Warrielaws hoards of gold in their grimy clutches. About 1840 the Warrielaw of the day transformed his little castle with pretentious Palladian additions, and since then the Warrielaws had spent their money and squandered their possessions with reckless persistence.

Now the owners of the property were two old maids, Jessica of whom I had heard, and Mary whom I had seen. In a corner of the great lonely old house the sisters carried on the Warrielaw name and tradition. "And the chief one is", said my husband, smiling, "that all Warrielaws hate each other. Just you notice to-morrow, Betty, how the old ladies love to tell you that 'all Warrielaws' do so-and-so. I don't know if all their generalisations are true, but the hatred certainly is."

"But do Mary and Jessica dislike each other?"

"Not fundamentally, I imagine, perhaps not! But they're always quarrelling."

"Why do they live together if they fight with each other?"

"Of course they do," said my Scottish husband, puzzled. "They're sisters. And as a matter of fact they'd have to, in this case, as Mary is absolutely dependent on Jessica."

"But why doesn't she set Mary up on her own?"

"Mary wouldn't leave Warrielaw," said John. "She adores it, and she's the next to inherit it. It's a tangled story."

"But I'd like it," I said eagerly.

Two generations previously, it appeared, the entail had been broken to exclude a tiresome elder son. To dispose of his property had been a task beyond Jessica's father. He had considered the claims of his wife and five daughters helplessly, and solved the matter by leaving everything to his wife. She in her turn waited till death claimed her some twenty years before, and then made a hurried will without legal advice, bequeathing the estate and house "to my daughter Jessica and to my daughter Mary on her death", leaving the survivor to dispose of her property as she pleased. The three other daughters had married, and all three were now dead. The eldest left one daughter, Cora, who married Charles Murray, the richest lawyer in Edinburgh ("though not", added John, "till she and her cousin Neil had got themselves talked about everywhere"). It was she who had outraged Jessica by questioning the terms of the very unbusinesslike will, and persuading her husband at last to go to law about it. For Jessica claimed that, while the estate was hers, everything in the house was at her disposal, and for years had been selling off family jewels and pictures and some wonderful furniture. Most of the proceeds went, everyone imagined, to

Neil Logan, and only when Cora married did she begin to object to this leakage. Hundreds of pounds were spent on the lawsuit as to the exact meaning of the legacy, and in the end it was decided in Jessica's favour. So the steady sale of family treasures proceeded and Neil's exchequer was kept filled.

"What's Neil Logan like then?"

"Oh, he's a queer fish. His mother was clever and rather mad, and married a parson who lives now in the South of France. I've never liked him and I don't trust him, and he's always behaved pretty brutally to Jessica who adores him. He's an artist, and quite a success here: it's rather fun to go in for new art in Edinburgh! He holds little exhibitions and wears a black hat with a wide brim and a long cape and side-whiskers, like some of the people in your father's house. You'll swallow him, I expect, but Edinburgh gapes at him. He talks like someone out of Oscar Wilde."

"And behaves like someone out of Jane Austen?"

"Lord, no, though I sometimes fancy he's not as hot stuff as he makes out. Still, he's very bitter about Philistines, like me, and has run through lots of Jessica's money with little to show for it."

"He doesn't sound much like Rhoda!"

"No indeed. Rhoda's mother married first of the five sisters, an odd literary fellow called Macpherson who died, leaving her with Rhoda and very little else. Years later she married a second cousin of her own and died with him in a boating accident. Rhoda, who was only just grown up, took charge of the little girl they left, and has been a mother to her. She defied all the Edinburgh conventions and got a job as bookkeeper in a smart little dressmaker's near the West End. The shop's done well and she's done well. She's practically manager now and comes and goes as she likes. She's a little house in Comely Bank and the stepsister looks after it for her. You must have Alison to meet your brother when he comes to stay in April. She's rather a dear and extraordinarily pretty."

"How do you know them all so well?"

"Well of course my people were hand in glove with the old Warrielaws over the estate, and as long as they lived all the sisters used to dump their families on them for months on end. I used to go out there for tea perpetually, and heavens! how they quarrelled! Neil and Cora were friends always, but Miss Jessica hated Cora, and Neil was always rude and unkind to Miss Jessica, who adored him. Everyone but Miss Mary hated Rhoda, and Cora, after she married, had a quarrel with Rhoda over a frock she ordered from her shop, which almost led to another lawsuit. They hated each other and worshipped Warrielaw and always called it home."

"I see," I said. "Neil the Rip and Cora the Siren and Rhoda the Business Woman and Alison the little Beauty. Shall I see them all?"

"You're sure to, pretty soon. Everyone knows everyone in Edinburgh."

My husband's prophecy was only too correct. The door opened once more and Christina announced, in a voice which marked her disapproval of so late a visit, yet condoned it in view of the visitor's social standing:

"Mr. and Mrs. Charles Murray."

John jumped up and made for the door in the other half of our big drawing-room, but he was too late. Mrs. Murray swerved from her polite advance towards me and ran to John, catching him by both hands.

"John my dear! What fun! We hoped you'd both be in if we came late! Please forgive me for being so long in calling on you, Mrs. Morrison, but I've been in town since Christmas. I can't stand Edinburgh when it's festive in January! Ever since I got back I've been longing to meet John's English wife. I'm sure my Warrielaw aunts call you that! No Charles! You're not to try to get John to sneak off to the library with you for a drink. I must see him."

Charles Murray evidently knew his place and sat down beside me without a murmur. He was a tall, fair, baldish man with a nice twinkle in his eyes and a tolerant smile. Evidently he adored his wife, and at first sight I decided that the Warrielaw type was at its best in its sophisticated members. Cora, tall, slender, restless and exquisitely dressed, her hair beautifully coiffured, her complexion carefully made-up, showed little trace of her race save her eyes. These were frankly in contrast to her manner, her languid airs and graceful movement. Long eyelids emphasised the wide, staring yellow-green irises, and out of them looked a spirit not exactly wild or dangerous, but with a suggestion of an untamed will, of red-hot determination to get exactly what she wanted from life. I had detected something of that sudden, almost animal shyness and fierceness in Miss Mary Warrielaw, but it seemed akin to her eccentricity and lonely life. Cora's eyes were as out of place in her exquisite modishness as a jungle tiger set down in Piccadilly. Certainly she was an arresting personality, and I watched her with pleasure, while Charles Murray congratulated me intelligently on my nice empty drawing-room and Chippendale bureau. All the time, however, he was watching his wife, and when I mentioned that Miss Mary had called that afternoon, he made some excuse of fetching a cigarette to go and stand by her chair.

"That's an excellent bit of staff work, Cora," he said. "How did you know the Warrielaws were here?"

Cora for a moment looked like a wild cat about to spring, and then like a small child detected in a falsehood. In an emergency, I judged, Charles Murray might have the upper hand.

"I saw Mary and Rhoda go past my window," she said sullenly. "As it was so late I wondered what they were doing and watched them cross the street and come in here. That made me guess they wanted to see John as well as Mrs. Morrison, and I wondered if anything was wrong!"

"Now you know Edinburgh, Mrs. Morrison," laughed Charles. "Cora, as you've betrayed your real reason for calling at this unholy hour, I think you may as well retire gracefully and come home."

"No, no! I really wanted to see Betty—yes, I'm going to call you Betty!" Cora turned to me gracefully with outstretched hands. "After all it's quite natural that I should like to know something about Warrielaw, now that I can't go there and Neil's away, and I've broken entirely with that dismal little Rhoda. Is anything the matter there? Do tell me, John."

"Oh nothing, nothing out of the usual!" John gave me so portentous a wink that I felt Cora's suspicions must be aroused at once, but her eyes were fixed on mine imploringly and I managed not to betray myself unduly.

"Is it the jewel, John, do tell me? Is Jessica trying to sell the jewel again? Betty, I'm sure you sympathise with me, don't you? Obviously you love pretty things and old things. Isn't it dreadful that Aunt Jessica should sell our family possessions right and left and that the law can't stop her! She should be locked up, John, and you should see to it, if she really means to sell the fairy jewel!" John politely said nothing. He has a real talent for this.

"My dear, leave it alone," said Charles impatiently. "If she doesn't sell it she'll leave it to Mary, and Mary will leave it to Rhoda."

"Would she sell it to us?" pleaded Cora.

John exercised his talent again.

"Don't be silly, Cora," said Charles. "You know she refused you the Raeburn on any terms."

"And then it went for a few hundreds," cried Cora passionately. "And the jewel's worse, far worse. Oh, I can't bear it to go out of the family! You must stop her, John!"

I was almost as embarrassed as the two men when Cora began to cry. After all, there are certain things any woman may cry for legitimately, like losing a cook or some teeth or an engagement ring, but not in front of strangers, and not as if her heart was broken.

"My dear," I said, wishing Cora wasn't too old to be spanked, "I don't believe there's anything in the world I'd feel worth crying for like that!"

"You English have no family feeling," said Cora, but to my relief she stopped crying and got out her powder-puff. "It's so different for people like us who've inherited nothing but a few traditions and heirlooms! I don't care about money, but this comes straight from my ancestors and I love it! It's part of my old Home."

"God preserve us from our ancestors," said Charles, rising decidedly. "You must come now, Cora. I'm getting her to the Riviera soon," he added in a lower voice to John as Cora went to look at herself in a long mirror. "Her nerves are going to pieces. She's really unhinged by worry over this tiresome family junk."

"Is there any question of an immediate sale, John?" she persisted.

"Miss Warrielaw has said nothing to me about it," replied John stiffly. "I shall send Charles a bill every time you ask me that question, Cora!"

CHAPTER II
THE MISSES WARRIELAW AT HOME

THE BITTER south-east wind was tainted with the sickly odour of oil from the neighbouring shale-pits as we approached the gates of Warrielaw next afternoon. Two heraldic and weather-worn animals on pillars guarded a deserted lodge, open iron gates, and an avenue overgrown with grass and pitted with ruts.

These were the early days of owner-drivers, and my heart bled for our new, immaculate Albion and its tyres. This generation will never understand the mingled emotions of early motorists, the care and affection we transferred from our horses, the pride of pioneers, and the interest in every other car. When John explained briefly that there was a better road by the back entrance, but that he wished to see if the place was in worse repair than usual, I sat in sympathetic silence as we bumped along. Warrielaw was seven miles from Edinburgh, a five-mile walk from the car terminus for the Misses Warrielaw. It lay with its village in an angle of country lanes: the house and gardens and back entrance abutted on a road which led eventually to Ratho. That I made out for myself, while John shook his head at the rank grass and broken railings and the smoke-blackened trees with rotting branches. Across the park we saw the melancholy stone front of the house banked on each side by rhododendrons and laurels; only from an angle did I catch a glimpse of the old house with its thick walls, deep-set windows and crow's-foot roof, sheltering behind the meretricious classical front like a little old lady with a moun-tainous toupee. A stone terrace with a cracked balustrade bor-dered each side of the curving steps and pretentious portico: beneath it the basement windows showed only a faint light from a cavernous kitchen. On either side of the terrace French windows revealed the long drawing-room and dining-room, unlit and swathed in brown paper and dust-sheets. The cold wind blew maliciously round us as we stood under the pillars waiting for the big door to open to us.

The old maid, whom my husband greeted warmly as Effie, belonged, I felt, by nature to the old, charming little house of the past rather than to the vast, dim entrance hall with its pitch-pine panelling and wide staircase, into which she ad-mitted us. She was small and solid, wrinkled and red-cheeked, cheerful and demure; she might have stood in a turret door of the old courtyard, I felt, as a model for any of those old women whose humour, patience and endurance shine out of the pages of Scottish ballads and stories. Cordially as she greeted John, and pleasantly as she extended her welcome to John's wife, she was not, however, I realised, free from the shadow of preoccupation to-day. She gave a keen and appraising glance to my dress and appearance, and could, no doubt, have acquitted herself triumphantly in an examination upon them afterwards, but there was a note of anxiety and worry in her voice which I felt alien to her usual manner.

"Come ben to the library," she said, leading the way through a swing door opposite the entrance into a narrow passage. Here we were evidently in the old part of the house, and the only light came from a window at the end, obscured partly by the shrubs outside, and partly by some panes of stained glass featuring the Warrielaw arms. "Ah, the ladies must be out!" She flung open a door on the left for us, after peeping in cautiously. "They'll be in the policies, maybe! Sit you down and I'll find them."

"Terribly overgrown, Betty, isn't it?" said John, strolling to the window. Outside was a small semicircular formal garden, bounded by the rhododendrons. Through it a narrow tunnel led into the walled gardens in one direction, and to the massive stable quarters in the other. Beech trees rose high above the heavy tangle of shrubs, so that the only light in this room, with its northern exposure, entered through the cross-bars of branches and the shimmer of evergreens; and it was the light, I reflected, of some dim cavern beneath the sea. Why the sisters chose to make this so-called library their sitting-room instead of one of the many rooms facing south, I never discovered. It was neither bright nor warm nor cosy. It would indeed have been spacious if it had not been so crowded and overwhelmed with furniture. At first sight it seemed a mere conglomeration of ottomans and chairs, as were so many old-fashioned rooms of the day: then, gradually, I saw a scheme in its madness. It was not one sitting-room, but two, divided in the midst by a long narrow table at which the Misses Warrielaw doubtless took their meals. There was a fireplace at either end, where economical fires burnt behind high brass fenders which were sharp with age and shining with polish. Around each fireplace was grouped a bureau, a sofa, an arm-chair and an old-fashioned work-table, replete with drawers containing the little reels and scissors, receptacles and work implements beloved by our grandmothers.

"They always divide the room like this," said John, noticing my amused surprise, "and each sister keeps religiously to her own half. Heaven knows why they don't have separate rooms, for I believe when there's a real thorough-going row on hand they don't speak to each other for days!" There were steps in the passage and the door opened again. Holding a lighted candle, someone entered the dim room.

"Well, John!" a voice said. "I'm glad to see you. Introduce me to your wife."

For a moment I was puzzled, and then I realised that it was Miss Jessica Warrielaw who was advancing towards me. Then, as Miss Mary followed her, I felt foolish for my momentary bewilderment. The sisters were not really alike, save in height and build and in the contours of their long, square faces. They had much the same weather-beaten complexions and they shared, of course, the famous Warrielaw eyes. As in the case of so many sisters, it was possible to take one for the other when she was alone, though impossible when they were together. Jessica was taller, stouter, more alert, slightly darker in colouring and, above all, a much clearer and more definite personality. Nothing, I was to hear later, irritated the two Misses Warrielaw more than to have any resemblance between them noticed. Ten years ago, when the likeness was probably more easy to trace, they had left off a lifetime habit of dressing alike. Jessica had definitely taken to black, as befitted the elderly mistress of the house, while Mary varied the hues of her toilets between muddy fawn and chalky grey. But no variety in toilet was needed to mark the difference between Jessica's brisk, authoritative manner and Mary's nervousness and impression of incompetence. It was clear at once who was Mistress and who was Martyr, in that joint household.

"Mary," said Miss Jessica, "I'm sure you'd like to show John's wife your embroidery while I talk to John till tea comes."

Miss Mary cast one sidelong look of rebellion at her sister and then, seating herself on the sofa nearest the boundary-line table, handed me a vast album containing photographs of the west, east, north and south fronts of the Cathedrals of Northern France. Neither of us made much attempt at conversation. Mary was intent upon Jessica's confidences to my husband, and I was absorbed in noting the decorations of the room: the description would embellish so joyfully my next letter to my father. Never had I seen so much furniture crowded into any apartment, and never surely was such a mixture of rubbish and of treasures. On each mantelpiece was a hideous carved overmantel; into Miss Jessica's was set a gracious, smiling Raeburn, and into Mary's a faded, lovely Romney. Round the Raeburn was a crowded collection of mementoes in pottery and china of various watering-places: Mary's shelves were covered with revolting china animals. On a priceless old cabinet stood a sewing-machine with endless dusty volumes and pieces of knitting. There was a grand piano smothered with photographs. There were marqueterie chairs with horsehair seats, and a rocking-chair with a plush cushion. A Ming bowl stood on a case of stuffed trout: a Sheraton bookcase bulged with parish magazines and charity needlework. The walls were hung with invaluable proofs before engravings, framed texts, Cosway miniatures and Mary's water-colour sketches. You could spend hours disentangling gems and rubbish, I meditated, when Miss Mary suddenly turned upon me.

"Here is my embroidery," she said. "Jessica and I are very fond of *broderie anglaise*. Are you fond of any sort of needle-work?"

Incredible as it must seem to this generation, not only the Misses Warrielaw, but many of my own contemporaries spent hours over this peculiarly fatuous form of fancy work. With meticulous care we would pierce holes in white muslin and carefully embroider their edges with white thread till the hole was barely visible. My efforts in that direction had been confined to the corner of one handkerchief, still unfinished, but Miss Mary had been working for years, I imagined, at the large, grimy bedspread laid out before me, punctured inch by inch with embroidered holes.

"It's lovely," I said sycophantically, bending to make out the pattern, "and what a beautifully fitted work-table this is."

"I'm getting on with it very well. I hope to finish it by the spring. Jessica was ahead of me, but she's some other work on hand just now. We are both of us great workers. My mother, you see, was devoted to her needle. She had two worktables like this. Jessica of course took the one with mother-of-pearl fittings and gave me this one: they are only ivory."

With that bitter memory evidently encouraging her to rebellion, Mary turned her attention again to Jessica and my husband, and I listened too, for John was speaking.

"I'm glad you take the whole affair so lightly, Miss Warrielaw, but honestly I think you should speak to the police. These tinkers are a rough lot and they're too near an unguarded place like this for safety."

"The tinkers! There! That's Rhoda again I'm sure!" said Miss Warrielaw triumphantly. "She's been making the most of this affair to get back into the house, mark my words. As a matter of fact the tinkers broke up their camp last night and have gone off without leaving a trace."

"Taking nothing, I hope?" asked John.

"We haven't found anything missing, and I went through the silver this morning. But I'm quite aware that she means to haunt the place by making a fuss about nothing! She didn't let Mary come home alone last night—lest she should feel nervous in the rhododendrons, of course! I soon sent her about her business."

"Come, come, Miss Jessica!" John had told me that he always adopted this expression of his father's when he dealt with intractable clients. "I'm glad you're not alarmed, but there do seem to have been some rather queer happenings here the day before yesterday."

"Nothing to make all this fuss about," protested Jessica stoutly. "As a matter of fact, Effie came to me this morning, and said that Annie had played this same trick on her once before, and had done it in the old days, too, when she was a little girl at home. It's quite a common form of vengeance for the slightly wanting, I believe, to fling things about on the floor. As for the scratches on the safe, I think we were all a little hysterical the night before last and that made us imaginative. Rhoda made the most of it, you may be sure!"

"But if Annie is as mad as that, Miss Jessica, you should really have her medically examined and got into some home. Has she owned up to it?"

"No, but Effie is going to keep an eye upon her till she leaves in a few weeks," said Jessica indifferently.

"It's all very well to talk like that now, Jessica." Mary leant across the border table and spoke with surprising venom. "You were as frightened as any of us on Thursday, and last night you came to my room because you thought you heard noises. You're only pretending to make nothing of it all because you dislike poor Rhoda!"

"Mary!" Before Jessica's voice Mary's sudden courage failed. She turned to me suddenly and produced another album full of Warrielaws, who all, I noted, irrespective of age or sex, looked at me with those queer, round eyes with narrowed pupils. Then she asked me hurriedly if I liked walking and if I were fond of dogs and especially spaniels. "All Warrielaws like walking and dogs," she added, and had just murmured that she feared John's wife was a little town-bird when Effie entered with the tea.

A truce obtained as we sat round the table, and Miss Jessica asked if I were fond of embroidery and turned from the tea-table to show me her own large, grimy, hand-worked bedspread.

"I've some other work on hand," she said, pointing to a pile of fine linen handkerchiefs. "I'm embroidering these initials for my nephew Neil, but I shall lay them aside till I've finished my bedspread. My sister and I have been working at them for a year, and I mustn't let her get ahead of me! The handkerchiefs can wait, for Neil won't be back till the end of March."

Evidently Miss Jessica had heard her sister's remarks, for she cast a glance of unkind triumph in her direction. Near the immaculate handkerchiefs lay a dirty little square of the cheapest cotton. That was evidently good enough for Miss Warrielaw herself, and somehow the contrast between the dowdy old lady and the spoilt nephew, for whom no equipment could be too perfect, made my eyes smart suddenly. Here at least was a Warrielaw who loved another, however unworthy he might be! There was no further chance for sentiment, however, as Miss Jessica dropped the subject suddenly and turned to my husband.

"Well, the result of all this, John, is that I've finally determined to take the fairy jewel up to London and sell it to that American dealer, Elves, when he comes over in the spring. We have corresponded about it already. I shall be glad to get rid of it, and the responsibility of such a valuable, and all this ridiculous quarrelling about it. After all, Neil would only sell it himself when he inherits it. Now John, if you've finished tea, come up and look at the scene of the burglary, and you come with us too, my dear," she added, turning to me. "I should like John's wife to see the jewel before it goes to other hands."

I was not a little sorry for Miss Mary as I followed Jessica meekly down the passage and through the swing door back into the big hall.

It was only the lower rooms of the front of the house which were deserted, for the Misses Warrielaw chose to accentuate the inconvenience of the place by inhabiting two large bedrooms on the first floor. Jessica's was at the eastern extremity of the long gallery, above the drawing-room, and

Mary's at the opposite end, looking west. So Jessica told me as she led me into her room and produced a small bunch of keys from a black ribbon tucked into the front of her black blouse.

"I always keep the jewel locked up, my dear," she explained. "It is of great value and unique historic interest."

Whatever historic or financial value the jewel might have, I would, I decided then, have sold it and spent the proceeds, not on the unknown nephew Neil, but on doing up the bedroom. I was to see other rooms on this floor of this house in months to come, and all alike were supremely gloomy. They had been furnished, when the addition was made to the house, with all the Victorian respect for suites of furniture. This suite was of yellow satin-wood, but it was unpolished and grimy with age, and lest it should have produced any sense of cheerfulness, so alien to the spirit of the decorator, the carpet was of a dingy brown and red pattern, faded with wear, and the hangings of the be-canopied bed and window curtains were of a dismal olive-green chintz. Vast gloomy representations of scenes from the Scriptures glared out of black frames, and over all the available space swept a spate of photographs and little bookcases and china ornaments. Jessica, standing, black-robed and tired, sullen and lined, by the safe, fitted perfectly into the room, and so did the battered leather case which she extracted. But the story and the jewel itself belonged to another world.

Long, long ago, it appeared, when the Warrielaws inhabited a border fortress in the days of James II of Scotland, the black Laird of the house strayed out into his black woods by moonlight and met a fairy. He had carried the little, fair, glittering lady off to his castle and married her, with priest and bell and book. All the dowry she brought him was the jewel she wore, straight from the dim caverns of elf lands, but he was a devoted husband and she was a dutiful wife. She bore him ten sons and daughters and bequeathed to them all her fair hair and gold-green eyes—"for before those days, my dear, we were all black Borderers," said Miss Warrielaw, with a fine contempt for Mendelian questioning of the laws of heredity.

She took the jewel out of the case as she spoke and held it up to the window. This was the only occasion on which I saw the famous talisman at close quarters, and the original treasure seemed to me frankly disappointing. It was nothing but a lump of dull amber, interesting no doubt to an antiquarian, suggestive to the family of their queer optical legacy, but in itself, like the house to-day, dull and dead. But history in the interval had given life and colour to the legacy. A gay Warrielaw had been in the embassy which fetched Queen Mary of Guise to Scotland from Italy. He had employed a Renaissance workman to set round the amber a design of emeralds and pearls and exquisitely worked enamel. Two hundred years later a Warrielaw, before he set out on the journey after the Prince of Highland hearts which led him to Tower Hill, had invested half his fortune in five marvellous diamonds which hung pendant to the Renaissance frame and added incredible value to its beauty. It was a strange, piecemeal, muddled thing, but it was marvellously interesting.

"It's lovely!" I said reverently.

"Yes, it's well enough, but I see no point in hoarding relics," said Jessica detachedly. "It's supposed to bring a curse on its owner too, and we can do without that. But its value is undoubted. I've had absurd offers for it from America. It's the only fairy relic, you see, except that absurd flag in Skye, and the Yankees like that kind of thing. My niece Rhoda brought an American medium here, who held it, and chattered about little green men on a hillside and tiny swords clashing and little red wounds. Oh yes! it's interesting, specially to people with no history. We have really quite enough behind us without bothering about relics, and it would remove a cause of family dissension if it went. There's not one of them", said Jessica, closing the safe firmly, "who wouldn't steal it if they got the chance, except Neil. Now, John, what do you make of the safe? I can't see anything very convincing about those few scratches."

The little safe was let into the wall near the window. The ebony panel, and the huge dressing-table with its branching candlesticks, suggested a vision of some magnificent Victorian lady standing in her crinoline, selecting her jewellery, while the house blazed with light and warmth to welcome an assembling party below. Now the shadow of Jessica's scraggy hand waved oddly on the walls by the light of her candle when she took the jewel from me, replaced it and slammed the door, as if assailed by a sudden suspicion of my honesty. John offered no very definite opinion about the scratches on the plate round the key, and was merely murmuring that at least the lock had not been forced, when Jessica raised her head in sudden annoyance at the sound of a voice downstairs.

"That girl again!" she said fiercely. "Why can't she leave us alone?"

She hurried out of the room so unceremoniously that she was half-way down the stairs before John and I reached the top. In the darkening hall we saw a little excited group of women, and one of them came forward suddenly towards John.

"If you please, Sir," said Effie, "I've been thinking that I'd be glad, now you're here, if you'd take a look round the basement. I know well enough what some have in their minds, and if you'd been through my things and poor Annie's there'd be nothing left for Miss Rhoda to say. I'd be glad if Miss Jessica and Miss Mary were to see for themselves in your presence that it's no thieves they've been harbouring in their house." She turned defiantly to her companions as she spoke and I saw that it was Rhoda who stood there, beside Miss Mary.

"Come, come, Effie," said my husband with an involuntary glance of longing towards our car in the drive. "I'm not the police, you know. That's hardly my job."

"But you represent the Law, John," said Miss Jessica briskly. "Of course you do. It's a very good idea of Effie's. It may teach Rhoda to hold her tongue and leave us alone!"

Across the silence of the hall there reached us suddenly the distant sounds of sobbing, the loud, unrestrained sobbing of a perplexed, ill-used child.

"She's been at it again ever since she saw Miss Rhoda's bicycle in the drive," said Effie miserably. "Mr. John, I'd be unco' grateful if you'd come." Jessica led the way through the swing door, and without a word we all followed her and passed through a doorway opposite the library, down the stone stairs to the basement. I was last of the group and realised that my presence was unnecessary, if not unwelcome, but on no account would I have remained alone in the gloomy library.

At the bottom of the stairs the sisters turned to the left, and, followed by Effie and the unwilling John, went off to the maids' bedrooms. The sound of Annie's sobbing filled the damp, musty stone passage as Rhoda turned swiftly to the right and pushed open the big kitchen door. From within came the only glow of warmth and light in the house, and, hesitatingly, I followed Rhoda, unobserved, and sat down in the shadow. Rhoda had already walked firmly up to the table where the victim, or the cause, of all this disturbance sat sobbing, her head in her arms. At Rhoda's voice she looked up and so, for the first time, I saw Annie.

Twenty-five years ago the study of psychology was still, comparatively, in its infancy. The line between the normal and sub-normal intellect was far less clearly defined, and probation officers, rescue homes and mental specialists themselves had no very definite theory of treatment for the class to which Annie evidently belonged. No doctor could have certified her as mentally defective, and yet, as she got up mechanically at Rhoda's approach, and stood there, big and defenceless before her, she inspired me at once with that slight repulsion most of us feel towards the not wholly normal being. Her big, stupid, unhappy face, smeared with the traces of coal and greasy fingers, her small sullen eyes and big open mouth filled me with vague distaste rather than pity. She was of that type, big and clumsy, well-developed yet childish, uncomplaining yet helpless, which arouses even in the kindest and most patient of instructors a strange instinct to bully and browbeat. In the charge of firm, competent little Rhoda she would find no mercy, I imagined, and yet, in answer to some command of Rhoda's which I had missed, her face grew sullen and her eyes cunning and she left off sobbing to mutter rebelliously:

"No, I'm no going down that passage, Miss."

"Oh yes, you will," replied Rhoda. Her voice was almost casual, her back turned to me, but I recognised in her a strength before which Annie would be powerless. The girl's eyes fell, she turned uncertainly, her figure casting an ungainly shadow on the wall, and opened a door leading from the far side of the kitchen into yet another warren of stone corridors.

"Stop crying," said Rhoda, with a cool self-assurance which suddenly reminded me of some showman of wild animals in a circus, and the sobbing ceased.

Left alone, I crept up to the range with its smouldering coals, in the hope of attaining some little warmth at last in that cold draughty house. The big room was lit now only by the fire, and its reflection in the array of polished copper dish-covers which had presumably sheltered vast joints and entries at the great parties of bygone years. All the contrivances for the cooking of a vast country house and rows of deal chairs surrounded the wall, but by the range stood only a small table covered by a pastry-board, two cracked tea-cups, a penny novelette and Effie's knitting. I was thinking with almost passionate longing of the warm cosy kitchen in my old home, when I was startled by a sob so violent that it seemed like the howl of an animal in distress, and Rhoda's voice from the further passage reached me.

"Stop that at once," she said. "This is just what I expected."

I looked down the passage curiously. From a low doorway Rhoda had just emerged with a candle, her short upper lip curled in fastidious disgust.

"Whom have you kept in there, Annie?" she demanded. "No, it's no use for you to say you've been sleeping there! There's a shaving-brush by that filthy basin and that's a man's cap on the door. Who's been here? You've been sheltering someone and you'd better tell me the truth at once!"

Annie followed Rhoda out of the room, her hand to her mouth as if to repress her howls by force. Standing fascinated before the demure little figure, she broke into her story in the high, excited voice of a guilty child.

"It wasna what you think, Miss Rhoda. It wasna the tinkers. It was ever so long ago and it was my own sister's husband's cousin, Jock Hay, that I put in there last Hogmanay. He came all the way down here to be our First Foot at the New Year, and Aunt Effie was in her bed asleep and I couldna turn him out into the rain. I didna dare to tell Aunt Effie I'd put him awa', she's aye hard on poor Jock, so when he was awa' I just locked the door, lest she'd see, and hid the key in a press, and I couldna' find it again to sort it till I was at the press again on Wednesday forenoon and got hold of it!"

"But he was here again on Thursday evening? I may as well tell you, to keep you from any more falsehoods, Annie, that I saw a light down here on Thursday evening, and I knew well enough that no one ever goes near these old larders and boot-rooms. You were here then?"

"Oh aye, I was just here to sort the room when Aunt Effie was awa' with the dogs," whimpered Annie. "That's what I'm telling you. How could Jock Hay be here when he's a porter away over at Bathgate, and in the Edinburgh Infirmary just now with a grown-in toe-nail, and Miss Mary herself went to see him in his bed on Tuesday?"

There was a long pause. Rhoda was evidently reassembling and reassorting her facts while Annie moaned softly.

"Even if all this is true, that Jock was only here at the New Year, and you've not been near the room since, you've behaved very badly, Annie. If my aunts knew they'd turn you away at once and they couldn't give you any reference to a new place. People don't want servants who take men into the house for the night. You know that well enough. No, don't begin to howl again. I'm trying to think what is best for everyone. I do want to help you if I can. I don't think I shall tell the Aunts about this. They would be so sorry for Effie's sake, and there's nowhere to send you just now, I understand. If I keep this from them and from Effie, will you try to settle down and be a good girl?"

"Oh I will, Miss, I will!" Annie gasped and choked at the kindliness in Rhoda's quiet little voice.

"I think you know, too, that you should own up that it was you who left Aunt Jessica's room in that dreadful state. Now don't begin denying it! I expect you hardly knew what you were doing. You began in a temper and then ran off downstairs when you realised suddenly that Effie had gone out, and that you could get to this room and tidy it without being seen—"

"But—but—but—" Annie gasped out the words helplessly and no others seemed at her command. "But—but—" she repeated, tears falling helplessly, her grimy apron held to her swollen nose.

"There's no need to say any more, Annie. Go in there quickly and tidy the room and I'll do all I can for you with my aunts." Rhoda must have heard voices from the other passage, for she pushed the great clumsy girl into the room, and slipped back into the kitchen, as the search-party entered at the door at the other end.

"Not a thing!" said Jessica triumphantly. "Of course we haven't found a thing! I don't know how anyone had the heart to accuse that poor simple girl of theft."

"I've been talking to Annie," said Rhoda slowly. She looked at me a little curiously as if she felt uncertain as to how much

I had seen or heard. "She's practically admitted that she did untidy your room in a temper, Aunt Jessica, and she's promised to be good. I don't think you'll have any more trouble with her. These brain-storms don't occur very frequently as a rule, I believe."

"John, we must go at once," I said, with a determination that was almost a match for Rhoda's.

"Yes indeed," said John. "Well, well, Miss Warrielaw, I can say no more if you are determined to leave things as they are. Effie will keep an eye on Annie till you can part with her, and the less said about it all the better, I imagine."

"Yes indeed," said Effie unexpectedly. "The poor girl's been bullied from pillar to post enough these twa three days!"

Miss Jessica said nothing, but turned and led the way up the stairs. My husband followed her, Mary turned to speak to Effie, and I found Rhoda's arm laid on mine as I reached the bottom step in the darkness.

"I hope she's convinced—Aunt Jessica, I mean. I think so, don't you?"

"I haven't an idea," I said coldly. That silly heartfelt protest—"But—but—but—" was still echoing in my ears.

"I had to make the best of it, don't you see?" said Rhoda. "I've been so terrified lest she should begin to suspect someone else!"

"Who? Effie?" I asked incredulously.

"No, Mary! If everything hadn't pointed to Annie I really feared—"

"Her own sister! What nonsense!" I said hotly.

"Do you think so?" Rhoda stared at me incredulously. "My dear, you don't know the Warrielaws. And Mary had admitted that she was upstairs earlier!"

Anyone who climbed into our car to-day, and sat, perched over its crude gadgets, in a smell of petrol, and an incessant draught, would feel that they had strayed back into the Dark Ages. But upon that evening, I remember, our Albion seemed to me a gay centre of warmth and modernity and civilisation, as we drove homewards and left the gloomy house behind us.

CHAPTER III
A FAREWELL PARTY

"MY HERO in classical, or is it Biblical history, is Melchisedec," said Neil Logan. "He had, you remember, neither father nor mother. What ingenuity, what resourcefulness, that displays! To one like myself, harassed and bedevilled by relatives, the independence of his character is even more remarkable than his longevity."

Neil stood outside a bank at the West End of Princes Street as he made this oration, a unique and imposing figure. Eccentricity in Edinburgh tends to dowdiness, but Neil stood, in the fitful April sunshine, an eccentric and dandy of the Edwardian school. His black Mexican hat and a long cape falling from his shoulders proclaimed his artistic tendencies, but the cut of his suit was irreproachable, he wore a camellia in his buttonhole, and his shoes shone more emphatically than the sun. Beside him my brother Dennis looked a charming, overgrown schoolboy, though Dennis, who had just reluctantly left Eton at the age of nineteen, and come to pay me a long visit with some vague idea of looking round for a job, considered himself a man of the world. It was Dennis who had introduced me to Neil, but he seemed impatient of the artist's periods.

"Are you bringing my little Cousin Alison to tea at my studio to-day?" Neil asked, turning to him benignantly.

Two months had passed since my visit to Warrielaw, and the impression made by the family and the gloomy old house had faded from my mind. In the black frosts of February and the east winds of March I had sat shivering in so many other cold, overcrowded drawing-rooms as I dutifully repaid my calls. I had met many other sisters who disagreed, other clans who denounced their mutual relations with equal bitterness, other gloomy old places where penury or economy ruled supreme. The Misses Warrielaw had honoured me with no further invitations: no further word about the burglary had reached my husband. Rhoda was out at work when I returned her call. I met Cora frequently enough in ordinary social life, but she had offered no further confidences to my husband and myself. It was only, indeed, since Dennis had come to visit us that I had extended my acquaintance with the family.

"She asked me to come," replied Dennis. "Alison Warrielaw, you know, Betty."

Of course I knew. Dennis had only arrived a week previously, but in that space of time he had made more friends than I had in five months. Dennis is dark and slight and not very tall: he has no very obvious good looks, but he has eyes and a smile so engaging and so friendly a manner that already he walked through life picking up lovers, acquaintances and friends at every corner. He had met former friends at once in Edinburgh, and made new ones every day. Till his coming I had been naturally set up on a shelf amongst the married, as brides were twenty-five years ago, among John's older contemporaries and their parents. Now Dennis jumped me down with a laugh into the world of gay young people, and John smiled approval. But already Dennis's activities were becoming more concentrated. On his third day he had come to me with news of having met a new fairy—the real thing and no mistake—and since then he and Alison Warrielaw had run in and out of our house unceasingly. Dennis had been possessed by these wild enthusiasms since he was sixteen years old, and my mother had long ago decided to dismiss them as boy-and-girl friendships. Obviously Dennis was no entry for the matrimonial stakes as yet, but it did seem to me that Alison, so unprotected by life or her busy sister, might have her head turned: she was only seventeen, with the dewy, sexless beauty of a fairy child: after a nondescript education she had settled down as maid-of-all-work in her step-sister's flat: all the amusement she had ever enjoyed had been provided by Neil Logan, who was evidently the hero of her life.

"Melchisedec had no pretty cousin!" I said. It had been my reference to the Misses Warrielaw which began Neil's sermon.

"There are too many of us, however, and our eyes betray us," said Neil. "As Jessica would say: 'All Warrielaws have eyes.'"

"And queer ones!" I said, looking frankly at Neil. It was curious how the so-called fairy origin was impressed on the family. In Neil's case the squareness of the face was softened by side-whiskers, the high forehead by a drooping forelock, and the square sturdy figure by the artistic cape, but those queer eyes with contracted pupils and big yellow irises made me realise his likeness to his aunts. I could see it in Alison too, at the moment, as she came round the corner of Castle Street to meet us. When time filled out her slight form and thinned her wonderful golden hair, filled out the curves of her pointed face, and brought lines and disillusion to her dreaming eyes, she too would be a Warrielaw. That seemed a pity, for in her little green coat and hat in the spring sunshine she looked like a fairy who had wandered into middle earth.

"Alison's are queer," said Neil, greeting his cousin, "for they seem to dream of magic casements and they are really wondering how to do up yesterday's mutton. She has the face of Titania and the heart of Queen Victoria: that is why I adore her."

(And that, I reflected, is why Dennis dislikes you.)

"Now we have all met, Mrs. Morrison, you must, I insist, come with these young people to tea in my studio. If indeed Jessica consents to leave the bank at any reasonable hour. She would not let me cross the magic portals. She is breaking the bank by cashing a cheque to take her to London to-morrow."

"Then she's really going?" I said involuntarily.

"Yes, and when Rhoda and Cora know they will try to wreck the train. All Warrielaws hate each other, as Jessica would say."

"Neil, she adores you!" protested Alison.

"Alas, she does," agreed Neil, tapping his goldheaded cane on the pavement. "That is why I have had to endure a day of her, shopping. Oh, my God! buying stay-laces and fringe-nets and soap, articles one cannot apparently purchase in London!— lunching in the bleak desolation of a temperance hotel, walking on this side of Princes Street, greeting acquaintances. Are you as yet, Mrs. Morrison, one of us, the choice souls, the illuminati who always walk on the wrong side of Princes Street?"

"How that fellow does jaw! He is an outsider," muttered Dennis as Jessica Warrielaw came out of the bank, clutching her black bag. In the sunshine her square, wrinkled face, beneath her black pudding-bowl hat, was set in such suspicious dislike of her surroundings that she might well serve as a warning to her relations of the effect of bad temper, in advancing years, on the family features. The trivial bangles and lockets and earrings she wore seemed, like her tiresome mannerisms and affectations, to make her personality even more oppressive.

"Now, Neil," she said in her high nagging voice, "that's that. Oh, here is John's wife."

"And John's wife's brother," said Neil, "and John's wife's brother's friend. We are all coming now to my studio for tea. Let us hail a cab."

"Nonsense, Neil," said Jessica. "It's only a step, and all Warrielaws are good walkers. Besides, I want to order a cab at Small's to fetch me to the station to-morrow morning, and I must call at South's in George Street for a parcel."

"My car's just round the corner," said Dennis proudly. Dennis's single-cylinder Renault was the joke of the family; these, as I said before, were the early days of motoring, and few second-hand cars were available for owner-drivers. Dennis's was popularly supposed to be held together by strings and faith, and just now both were holding. "I'll take Alison."

"Mine, alas, is in the vile grasp of a garage," said Neil, "being nursed for a tour in England next month. Ah, here is a cab. This Warrielaw is a rotten walker."

Neil leant back in the cab in obvious relief and lit a cigarette. Miss Jessica wore one of those long, heavy black capes which were called Inverness cloaks in those days. It caught in the door every time she got in and out of the cab, but Neil made no effort to help her. "She has to do everything in her own way," he explained when she disappeared into South's shop. "She must order a cab from Small's because fifty years ago Small's father lived on the estate, and so a halo hangs over his business still. You, Mrs. Morrison, are reflecting that I am behaving very badly to my Aunt Jessica. She has been very good to me and I am an incredible ruffian, but I must plead for myself by explaining that she sets every nerve of my body on edge. These days on which I pay for my benefits are little short of torture. There are the confessions of a sensitive blackguard!"

Neil's home was as definite as his personality. He had taken a house in a forgotten, decayed square in the Old Town, and converted the upper floors into a studio. He was of course a modernist, and a picture by Gauguin, Egyptian sculptures, Japanese armour and Gothic gargoyles stared from walls striped in red and black and white. He had dabbled in his time, he admitted, in all sorts of work. There were eccentric ladies with one pink eye and green triangular bosoms, there were brilliant caricatures of old masters, his especial line, and there were some excellent portraits, including one of Cora Murray staring sullenly in a scarlet gown from a dark corner. A luxurious tea was laid on a green marble-topped table, and Neil reinforced it by numerous bottles from a wall cupboard. Even these failed, however, to make our party go. Jessica sat upright with a glass of sherry and a chocolate Eclair, a combination which Neil said, with some justice, made both food and drink seem unpalatable. Dennis and Alison retired to a distant sofa. I made suitable remarks about pictures, and Neil unsuitable remarks in the hopes of shocking us. I never know whether literary men create or portray the talk of their time. Did Elizabethans talk the bombast Shakespeare reproduced, or did they talk it in imitation of Shakespeare? Did young men—for Neil was, I suppose, about thirty then—lean against walls and fling off epigrams about sex before the novelists of the beginning of the century recorded them, or were they imitating Wilde and Shaw? Neil certainly originated or acted the part of the dissolute young artist with great success in his efforts to shock Edinburgh.

"You've been seeing Cora to-day," said Jessica abruptly, sniffing at a little scented handkerchief under the cushion of her chair.

"She came to me hot-foot to enquire about your visit to London." Neil's voice showed his annoyance at the question. "It was an unexpected and unusual pleasure."

"What's it to do with her?" flashed Jessica irately.

There was no reply. Before three of us, I imagine, rose a picture of the fairy jewel. There was such tension in the air that I rose to go. There is nothing more uncomfortable than the society of those who get on each other's nerves, and it was pathetically clear that this must always have been Jessica's lot in life. She was so clumsy and domineering and inapropos. She referred twice to recent gifts to her nephew: she demanded openly the affection he could never give. She gave me already that dreadful frayed feeling of irritation which I could see was Neil's sensation, intensified by years to something like hatred. I could have been sorry for him if I were not sorrier for Jessica, whose fate was so obviously to crave for affection and fail lamentably to win it.

"Can't Dennis run you down to Warrielaw?" I suggested, as Jessica also rose uncertainly.

"No, thank you, I want to have Neil to myself for a little," said Jessica with a frown. "And all Warrielaws—"

"Are fond of refusing lifts," put in Neil, wincing openly. I saw he could not bear that phrase again.

"Besides, I'm in no hurry to get home. Mary is having Rhoda out to see her this afternoon, and three is no company, you know."

"I thought you didn't allow Rhoda on the premises," said Neil, smiling rather unkindly at Alison. "I gathered that the door was locked upon her as well as on all undesirables since the great burglary scare."

"That was no laughing-matter," said Jessica severely. "Poor Effie has been worried about Annie ever since. She is taking her off to Carglin to-night, as we had a telegram just before I started to say that Ellen Hay would be glad of Effie for the night. Mary is using that as an excuse to keep Rhoda with us till to-morrow, I believe. You need not think I have my own way in my own house, Neil! The two of them are going to lunch with the Wises at Erleigh to-morrow."

"Is Rhoda actually leaving her shop then?" asked Neil indifferently.

"Yes, it's Good Friday, you know. It seems a strange thing that an English shop holiday should affect a Warrielaw! They have been trying to dissuade me from travelling on the grounds that the trains will be late and crowded. As if Easter holidays affected travel on the main line! The only crowd will be at Carstairs and that will not affect me. They are likely to have a far more uncomfortable time getting to Erleigh, unless they walk."

"But it's a long way!" I said. "Isn't it near Balerno?"

"About seven miles, but we think nothing of that. You young people with your cars have lost the use of your legs. Have you met the Wises, my dear?"

I rose to go as I assented, for the party was obviously languishing, and Neil's face was a study in boredom as he fidgeted idly with his monocle.

We made our farewells and escorted Alison home. It was not till we had parted from her that Dennis could express himself freely on the subject of Neil.

"The fellow's a bounder and a cad," he said vehemently, "and yet Alison says she loves him!"

"Hasn't he been very good to her?"

"Oh, he gives her a good time now and then, but he's not fit for a decent girl to talk to. Why, in front of her the other day he said to me, 'We must always remember, my dear fellow, that seduction is the sincerest form of flattery.'"

"Is he really pretty fast then?" I asked uncomfortably.

"No. Yes—well, I don't know. I think he may be mostly a poseur. All Edinburgh is thrilling about our naughty Neil, but sometimes I wouldn't be surprised to hear he'd only come in with the milk once really. Or he may be as black as sin for all I know. But you know, really, Betty, they are a queer lot, except for Alison! That old thing sitting there eating a chocolate eclair in a black glove and swigging away at sherry! She and Neil are a couple of lunatics!"

"Yes, I expect so," I said anxiously as we hurled round a curve excitingly. "But why are you coming the Jehu? Your string will come undone again!"

"I'm rather late. I'm motoring Carruthers out to Biggar, to his people, for that dance and staying there the night, you know. We're starting at 5.30 and it's after six now. I tried to get Alison to come, but she hadn't been asked, worse luck! She does have a poor time, poor darling. I do hate the Warrielaws!"

I did not disagree with him, and I didn't love Jessica. Yet all that evening I could not get out of my mind the picture of the poor old lady trudging along the road alone, leaving the nephew who hated the very sound of her voice for the sister and niece who were united against her. How the cold winds would buffet her and the lonely dishevelled old house frown at her as she struggled up the avenue!

CHAPTER IV
THE DEPARTURE OF
MISS WARRIELAW

EVERY SENSIBLE PERSON must feel the charm of Edinburgh, and learn to love it as a home, and yet there must be moments when a fleeting sense of exile assails the southerner who lives within its gates. One of these came to me on the day after the party in Neil's studio, when I stood in the Caledonian Station at a quarter to ten, watching preoccupied travellers and laden trunks make for the express train to London. It was the morning of Good Friday, April 13th.

That train still starts from the same platform at the same hour to-day, after the lapse of more than twenty years. Only one change, I think, marks the passage of time. In those historic years the express made its first stop at Carstairs, and was joined there by the Glasgow portion, whereas now the London expresses slip past that crowded junction disdainfully. In every other way the great railway system, however its internal organisation may change, keeps to its tradition, when it conveys the Scotsman on what Dr. Johnson called his favourite road, the road which leads to London.

In other ways human nature has not changed. Dennis had come up by car from London, a daring feat in those days, and especially so in a car like my brother's. He had sent his luggage by train, and he had arrived without my favourite fishing-rod, which he had been charged to convey to me in its wooden case. No man under the age of thirty, then or now, travels without losing something, and then, as now, it is his female relations who are sent in search. Dennis, before he left for his dance at Biggar the evening before, had charged me to enquire after the rod, and I obeyed him meekly. I had forgotten about the Easter holiday: the cloakroom and platform alike were crowded for the moment. I decided to wait till the express had gone, and strolled a little wistfully to look at it.

"Good morning." Miss Wise of Erleigh interrupted my meditations. She was a pleasant, energetic spinster, who, from her home in the country, came in daily to dominate the many charitable societies of Edinburgh. "You're not running away from us already, Mrs. Morrison?"

"Oh no, only waiting for the cloakroom. Have you just got in?"

"Yes, the early train is our most convenient. I'm really off for the whole day to leave Mother and Father to enjoy Mary Warrielaw at lunch alone. She's coming to us, and when no one's there the Edinburgh scandals of thirty years ago rise up and rustle. I fancied I saw Jessica Warrielaw getting into the London train, so I expect there's been a row, and my people will hear of it."

"I knew she was going," I said, looking still more longingly at the London train, as I reflected on the smallness of Edinburgh and its society.

"I only caught a glimpse of her," said Miss Wise. "She goes off like this every year or so, and makes no farewells and writes no letters, I believe. So very sensible! See if you can cheer her up."

Miss Wise hurried on, and I strolled doubtfully on to the platform, looking into the carriage windows till I saw Miss Warrielaw. No, I decided, when I discovered her. Jessica was not, in my maid Christina's phrase, apt for conversation. She was sitting, her head averted from the platform with an air of dejection and weariness which invited no comment. A gleam of sunshine shot through the glass roof of the station as I hesitated, and against the dark background of the cushions I saw clearly every white and gold hair in the curled, bristling fringe under its net and every line and mark of her pallid face. It was, I decided, the fact that all Warrielaws had light eyebrows and light hair which made their eyes so pale and startling. Then, as I gazed furtively, she suddenly pulled a black veil down from her black pudding-bowl hat and drew her black cape round her shoulders. Evidently she desired privacy, and as the carriage was empty so far, she would probably get it. At least I would not disturb her, and I went in search of my rod through the crowds hustling to less important trains.

"She did look wretched," I said to John at lunch. I had attended a Good Friday service in the interval, but the picture of the lonely old woman was haunting my mind. "I expect Mary was horrid to her if she really took that wretched jewel away to sell."

"Probably Jessica held her own! They're more than a match in a quarrel. I'd give Jessica odds on any day. And I expect Mary is repenting by now. Look here, Betty, I wish you'd run down to Warrielaw and cheer the poor old thing up this afternoon. Dennis could drive you down—"

"He won't be back, I expect. His car is sure to have had an accident! But, John, I'll walk down. It's only about five miles from the tram terminus, isn't it? And 'all Morrisons are fond of walking.' Then you can come and pick me up about six o'clock, and pat her back and say things are all right."

John smiled upon my energy, so soon after lunch I took a tram out of Edinburgh, and, at the terminus, got out and set off on my way, repenting a little of my errand. The night had been wet and stormy, but the rain had left off at mid-day and now the sun was shining, and a west wind was blowing clouds across the sky like the lambs chasing each other in the meadows. The road stretched between great fields with low hedges, and it was so uninteresting that I walked quickly. It was only when, at about three o'clock, I reached the ruined lodge which guarded the neglected open gates of Warrielaw, that I remembered Mary was lunching at Erleigh, seven miles away, and couldn't be back for another hour at least. I thought of turning to my left and walking all round the outside of the park, through the few houses which made up the village of Warrielaw, to the back gates. But these gates were, I knew, kept by a lodge-keeper, and from all I knew of the ways of the place, it was quite possible that they were locked or impassable. Only vans came through them after providing for the village, and to-day those vans would be few and far between. I was tired, and the lane looked long and dull, and I was not going to risk finding no entrance at the other end. I decided to walk up the long avenue to the front door, and take refuge with Effie till Mary returned or John came for me. And all these decisions I made as idly and carelessly as I had made my original plan of walking down, without the faintest premonition of the importance they were to have in so many lives.

Through the high budding beech trees of the rough avenue I soon caught sight of the front of the house. The threatening clouds behind it dwarfed and flattened the long, shabby, pretentious front and cracked pediment and porticoes. But for the open French windows, I decided, it would have been a perfect emblem of a dull, sallow, blind old lady scowling at the world. Everything was so quiet and dull that I started when a cock crowed in a distant cottage. It was easy to imagine, now the sun was obscured, that it was breaking the dawn in a sleeping world.

It was easier still when I rang the bell. There was no sound of Effie's feet scuffling along the hall, and the yapping of the spaniels sounded far away, as if they were shut up in the stables. I rang again and again, but there was no reply. Effie, like everyone else, was apparently out. I looked into the great drawing-room with its swathed mirrors and furniture, but all was silence. I meditated walking in and sitting down, but the Warrielaws were not people, I decided, who welcomed, or pardoned, informality. There was just a chance that Effie was in the garden getting vegetables, so I walked down the steps and round the front of the house. Here, on the left of the house, the carriage sweep dwindled into a path amongst a sea of rhododendrons: they were so thick that I could only just make out the path between them, and beneath their branching boughs, which led to a door in the great dilapidated stone walls surrounding the garden. It creaked open noisily, but within it everything was still. In front of me was a small area dug for vegetables and cultivated by Jessica: beyond was a tangle of broken pergolas, high waving weeds, colossal rose bushes and moss-grown paths. Through this garden, and a further walled garden distinguished by acres of broken-down glass-houses, the path led, I knew, to a gate in the main road, much used by the Misses Warrielaw. But that gate was probably locked, I reflected, and the gardens in their decay were unspeakably dismal, so I turned to go back. And it was at that moment that I heard the sound of a car starting at the back of the house, and it was then, I think, that I remembered that Effie had gone off the night before with Annie and presumably had not returned.

As I said before, cars were few and far between in those days on lonely country roads, and it was not likely that a van was at the door. There would be no one at the back to answer it, anyhow, and it was then I realised that the Warrielaws had fallen back into their foolish habit of leaving the house empty and unguarded. It was extraordinary to me that they should do so after the scare of burglary only two months ago. At that very moment a van driver might be exploring the back regions, though he would not, I imagined, find anything to steal in that parsimonious kitchen. Still, as I was here, it might be as well to show that someone was about, so I turned back from the gardens, down the rhododendron tunnel into the drive, made my way past the front of the house and plunged into the rho-dodendron and laurel tangle on the west side of the mansion. Here the shrubs grew close to the wall, pressing over the path, and I noticed the joining up of the Palladian front to the old house. Deep-set windows looked out under crows'-feet from the thick stone walls of the old building, with gables above them and a turret at one corner. It was strange to think that anyone could have tampered with that little sedate home of history; and then, as I emerged from the shrubbery, I saw again the nefarious work of the Warrielaw of one hundred years before. The distance between the house and the back drive was not more than a hundred yards, but a wide sweep to the left led to the stables, where Mr. Warrielaw's love for pomp and expansion had had its way. A great cracked yellow arch with a stone coat of arms lay between an empty lodge on one side and a coach house on the other. Within was a vast courtyard; and behind this showy, dilapidated front, around the ragged courtyard beyond the gates, lay a warren of stalls and laundry buildings and outhouses, all backed by a series of low out-houses, potting-frames and tool-sheds. A colony of the unem-ployed might have been housed in them: a colony of old tins and refuse was there already. And then I looked quickly from this absurd monument of past glories, for my eye was caught by the flash of something moving. The semi-circular sweep from the house to the stables swept on to the back lodge gates. Through them was disappearing the car which I had heard in the garden. It was, I recognised with the keen eyes of the owner-driver of the period, a Lanchester car of aristocratic origin: some caller must have arrived at the back before I had come myself, and shown at the back far more persistence than I had in the front. I had not heard anything as I walked down the drive, so for twenty minutes at least someone must have pealed the back-door bell. How like any old Edinburgh lady, determined to make her call! One trace, however, she had left of herself: as the car turned through the back lodge gates a pa-per fluttered from it. The wind caught it and swept it merrily towards the stables.

Girls who have grown up with brothers have as a rule one virtue to their credit. They learn to respect confidences and to regard correspondence as sacred. I walked to the stable-yard and picked up the paper. It was an envelope, innocent of stamp or address, but containing, obviously, some enclosure. If it was valuable the owner would return to look for it: if not, it was unnecessary to leave it fluttering about—though indeed a Bank holiday crowd let loose in it could hardly have increased the disorder of the stable-yard! Without bothering to consider the question seriously, I stuck the paper inside the nearest opening, on to the sill of a broken window in the coach house. It would be safe and out of the way there.

As I came away from the stable arch, I felt a sudden scud of rain. The wind dropped, and in a moment the clouds seized their chance and the drops fell in torrents. From the back lodge chimneys came a faint streak of smoke, and I ran there and knocked on the door, hoping for shelter. Never would I arrive unexpectedly at Warrielaw House again!

A hoarse voice bade me "Come away in," and I opened the door. "Our family boasts of one aged retainer"—so I remembered Neil had remarked. "She is a gate-keeper who cannot open gates." On a bed in perilous proximity to the fire, flanked by a table covered with dirty crockery, three broken chairs occupied by cats, and dim bits of furniture in dark corners which suggested rats, lay Mrs. Lee, the lodge-keeper. Her only greeting was an histrionic groan which seemed like the frowstiness and evil odours made audible.

"Hoots, Effie, I'm sair put aboot but I couldna get up to the hoose," said she, her head still averted. "My rheumatics have been that bad the day that I wasna fit to budge. The doctor was in this morning, as he'll tell you, and he's told my niece to come over to me when she's through with her washing. I'm real upset, but if a' the windows are open at the hoose, and there was thieves and robbers in every room, step up to it I couldna."

"It isn't Effie," I said, rather timid at introducing myself. "I came down to call and I couldn't find anyone in."

The remark fell flat. Mrs. Lee's further qualifications for her post were, it appeared, almost total blindness and deafness. She raised herself slightly in bed, from a marvellous assortment of flannel rags, to ask me to repeat my message. It took me several minutes to convey my story, and all she said at the close was that I must be weary of waiting, and if I'd join her in a cup of tea she'd be thankful if I'd take the pot off the hob. Turning from me, she buttered a bit of bread lavishly from the supplies on her table, and pointed to a dresser where I could find some very dusty cups. As no protests of mine could reach her, as the rain was streaming down and it seemed cruel to hurt the poor old thing's feelings, I dusted two cups surreptitiously, and sat down to the strange party with my face towards the window, my ears and eyes alert for any sign of John's car. Mrs. Lee seemed to enjoy company. She regaled me with a long tale of how Effie had gone off the night before to see her niece, who was expecting, with an interminable obstetrical digression on the subject of Effie's niece, Ellen Hay, and that daft sister of hers, Annie, who was just as well off the place. Effie had gone off the evening before; Miss Jessica was awa' by the early train. Miss Mary and Miss Rhoda had planned to be awa' early to Erleigh, walking, Effie had told her, and had urged her to go up after nine o'clock and see the house was closed properly, as the Warrielaws would never think of it. After a long disquisition from her on the folly of the Warrielaws' passion for fresh air, one which I could indeed sympathise with in the dreadful atmosphere preferred by Mrs. Lee, I realised that the rain was over. I looked at my watch. Mrs. Lee's recital had, like most Scottish sermons, dragged itself out for nearly half an hour. It was now nearly four o'clock, and I might surely expect my hostess or Effie in a few minutes. I got up and escaped, with profuse thanks from Mrs. Lee for the shilling I offered. At her request I pulled to the rusty old gates of the back entrance and locked them. Then I paddled round cautiously through the puddles and dripping shrubs to the front of the house. To my surprise the drive was empty no longer.

But it was not John's car which stood there, though it was one I knew. Large cars with handsome chauffeurs were even then in those days a common enough sight in Edinburgh, but the owner-driver was the cynosure of all his or her acquaintances. This small and elegant De Dion two-seater (it appeared elegant to me then) was well known to the inhabitants of Edinburgh. Cora Murray had, indeed, only driven it about the streets for the last three weeks, but they had been weeks full of surprise and terror for many nervous pedestrians and the entire staff of the tramways' companies. Her efforts had, as Neil said, lent a new fervour to prayers in the churches against murder and sudden death. It was wonderful to find that Cora had negotiated the drive safely, but still more surprising that she should be at Warrielaw at all. Jessica had forbidden her the place, and I could not imagine that Mary would remove the ban. Perhaps, however, like Rhoda, Cora found the younger aunt easier to manage. Meanwhile evidently she had felt no scruples about making her way into the empty house. Possibly Effie was home again, and I ran up the steps and rang the bell once or twice. But there was still no answer and no sign of Cora. The rain had begun again, so I opened the door of Cora's car and got in. I had no hesitation about treating her informally. Since her call in Moray Place we had met more than once and she was always friendly. I did not care about her; at the age of twenty a girl does not usually have much use for a nerve-ridden woman of thirty. But I admired her exquisite frocks and careful make-up, her charming house and indiscreet conversation, from a distance. And, as I thought of Cora, in the stuffy, scented atmosphere of her beautifully-lined car, I succumbed to a bad habit of my youth. For the first half of my life I was always able to fall into a comfortable doze if I sat unoccupied for more than five minutes. John disapproved of the practice, which was indeed exercised frequently in his Presbyterian place of worship, but I could not cure myself. To-day my head nodded almost at once and I fell asleep.

The hand of the clock had moved to a quarter past four before I awoke with a start, at an inrush of fresh air. Cora herself was opening the door of the car.

"Oh, I'm sorry I startled you," I cried.

It is alarming to find any human being unexpectedly not two inches from you, but the queer truth flashed across me vaguely that Cora's face looked white and her hands were trembling before she realised my presence. Then the colour rushed into her cheeks and her queer light eyes flamed in anger.

"What are you doing here?" she demanded.

I stammered out my story as I got out of the car, almost alarmed by the fury in her voice.

"How long have you been here?"

"In your car? Oh, about a quarter of an hour. What is the matter?"

"Oh, nothing," snapped Cora. "Only I'm dreadfully worried at home and I've come down here on a fool's errand. I had to sack my wretched little under-housemaid to-day and send her packing, and my own woman insisted on having the Easter week-end at home just because I'm taking her to Cannes next week to please my tiresome doctor. You know what servants are! They all seemed about to give notice at the prospect of managing the house for a week short-handed, the lazy, incompetent fools! I knew Annie had just left or was just leaving Warrielaw, and I also knew, I may add, that both aunts were out to-day, or I wouldn't have dared to put my nose into what was my mother's own home, my own home once, Betty! I felt it a chance, too, to have a look round!"

Cora's manner was thawing rapidly, as it always did on the subject of her grievances.

"But it's all gone wrong. First my beastly car stuck at the front lodge and I was hours getting it to start. And I've looked everywhere for the maids and there isn't a sign of them. And the whole house is unlocked and open as far as I can see!"

"Effie and Annie are at Carglin with a married niece, I believe. Miss Warrielaw said they were going there when I saw her yesterday."

"I might go there and get hold of her," said Cora. "Don't tell anyone you saw me here, Betty! I've been ordered off the place, as you know, and Charles would have a fit if he heard I'd been down like this. He doesn't understand that I have a feeling about it I can never have about anywhere else in the world!"

Cora was smiling quite amiably by now though her face was still white and her hands shaking. It was hard for me to imagine, I reflected, the intensity of the passion which the Scots feel for their own homes and possessions. Surely Cora had enough in her life, with her wealthy and devoted husband and her freedom from every sort of financial or social anxiety! In her exquisite red coat and frock with its rich astrakhan trimmings, and her little Paris hat of red velvet, she looked wholly out of keeping with the desolate and decaying house behind her.

"Well I must go! Remember to keep quiet, my dear!" Cora smiled at me ingratiatingly as she got into her car, but suddenly her face changed. From her arm slipped a red suede bag with an enamel clasp and monogram and a tiny lock after the fashion of those less trustful days. It fell at my feet on the gravel and as I picked it up I was reminded unpleasantly of Neil's phrase for his cousin—a panther in a Paris frock. Her eyes were blazing with passion and she snatched it from me as if I were a confirmed pickpocket.

"It's all right! It hasn't burst open!" I said.

I was surprised it had not, for the sides were distended.

"Of course not—it's locked!" she said.

"Take care," I said, as she put it down on a cream-coloured rug by her side. "It's damp and it's staining your rug with the pink dye."

Cora stared at the red mark spreading from the bag.

"Of course it's wet," she snapped. "I was out in the gardens in the rain looking for Effie."

There was nothing in Cora's dress or stockings, I noticed vaguely, to suggest that she had been walking in the rain. At the time, however, I only noticed these details vaguely as yet another proof of the erratic nature of the Warrielaws. It seemed wholly in keeping with their characters that Cora should be annoyed with me because her bag was damp, and should set off on a twelve-mile drive to get hold of a half-witted house-maid, just because that maid might give her roundabout in-formation of her own relatives. Cora was indeed a Warrielaw!

"Good-bye, Betty!" Cora started the car so suddenly that I nearly fell off backward from the running-board. "And don't forget! Just you keep quiet about all this!"

CHAPTER V
THE EMPTY JEWEL CASE

I COULD ONLY hope that Cora would not meet John in the drive as she started off, accelerating wildly. She might in de-cency have offered me a lift as there were still no signs of life about the house, but I was glad she had not. It was too tire-some to have to deal with people who kept their feelings so perpetually on the surface as the Warrielaws and grew emo-tional on such absurd provocation. Far the nicest of the clan was old Effie, their maid, I decided, as I saw her now on the front steps, looking out of the door.

Effie was desolated to hear of my adventures. She had only just got in, and came to the front because she thought she heard a car. I did not enlighten her about the visitor she had missed, and when she heard John was coming she insisted on taking me to the library to tea. "I'll infuse it now, Ma'am," she said, "for Miss Mary canna be long now. I've never seen her miss her tea. She'll be glad of your company, I'm sure, Ma'am, and Mr. John's, now she's left alone."

If so, Mary Warrielaw disguised her feelings admirably. A minute or two later, alone in the library, I turned from the study of a Sheraton cabinet where vases, labelled as presents from Margate, jostled with exquisite Chelsea figures, to see her approaching with Rhoda out of the shrubbery. They had walked in through the walled gardens and were emerging by the tunnel in the rhododendrons, which opened into the semicircle of flower-beds, in front of the library windows. Rhoda was wheeling a bicycle. She looked, as usual, alert and trim, and I noticed that she cast almost a proprietary glance over the flower-beds as if to assure herself that everything was in order. She would, I felt, be in command of affairs at Warrielaw during Miss Jessica's absence. That would be no concern of mine, for I was certainly not a welcome guest in her eyes. She frowned as she saw me and murmured something quickly to her aunt. Then, with a curt nod in my direction, she turned and wheeled her bicycle away through the rhododendrons towards the kitchen quarters.

"I'll just dry it down," she said to her aunt. "It got dreadfully wet in that last shower."

Mary walked wearily towards the window, dragging her feet in the last stage of exhaustion. Poor Miss Mary, I thought, poor, tired, defeated Miss Mary!

No one of my acquaintance in Edinburgh had ever seemed definite as to which of the two Warrielaw sisters had the upper hand. Gossip had hovered round the point for years, and there were some who held that Mary, in spite of her financial dependence, could hold her own with her sister in sheer obstinacy and bad temper. But to-day they seemed wholly wrong. In Mary's manner was all the exhaustion and depression of one who has lost in the last round, who has found out finally that life has broken her. For the purpose of her life had been to keep together the family estate and possessions, and now, presumably, the greatest treasure of all had been snatched away, taken off by the inexorable Jessica to London, or still worse, to American sale rooms. Mary was left to endure the loss of the unique heirloom, and doubtless, on Jessica's return, to watch yet another and another packed up and sent off into a cruel world where Warrielaws were unknown. So only I could interpret the glance of her glazed, weary eyes as she came into the room, her mouth half-open as if in thirst, her hands hanging limply as if in submission to fate.

"I have taken a long walk," she said, dropping into a chair. "A long, long walk, and I am very tired. I really hardly feel equal to visitors, Mrs. Morrison."

And it was at that moment that Effie, with the tea-tray, announced John and Dennis.

Mary Warrielaw was a lady in society, whatever curious social customs might prevail in private at Warrielaw. She brushed aside my hasty efforts to get my husband and brother away, and insisted on pouring out tea for us with swollen, shaking hands. Her own cup did its beneficent work on her: the dreadful pallor left her face. Dennis has an almost uncanny charm for elderly ladies, and she was actually smiling at his prattle when Rhoda came into the room. But before Rhoda's curt greetings and cold hostility it was impossible to do anything but rise and go.

"Wasn't it a funny coincidence," said. Dennis cheerfully as we said good-bye. "Peter Carruthers and I saw Miss Jessica standing on the platform at Carstairs. My car wasn't going very well and we hopped out to see what train we could get if the garage couldn't make it go, and there she was standing by her carriage near the London train. There was an awful crowd about, of course, and all sorts of holiday people and excursions, so she didn't see us, and she was some way off so we couldn't wish her a good journey."

I was moving towards the door as he chattered on, but next moment I had turned back as John gave a sudden exclamation. Mary had swayed by the tea-table and fallen back into her chair in a dead faint.

It was at that moment that Rhoda showed her efficiency. She issued her directions so briskly and clearly that in a moment John and Dennis were carrying the poor old lady upstairs, while I was despatched to the kitchen to summon Effie for a hot-water bottle. By the time I got up the stairs John and

Dennis were returning from laying their burden on Mary's bed, and John was offering to go at once for the doctor.

"No, certainly not," said Rhoda coolly. "Mrs. Morrison, will you go and give her the bottle and some water and loosen her things? She often has these little turns and she's only overtired herself. I'll go and get some brandy from Aunt Jessica's room."

Rhoda was less speedy on her own errand than I expected from her presence of mind. Miss Mary had returned gasping to consciousness, and was stammering out an apology for her foolishness before we heard Rhoda's step in the passage. The aunt's colour was coming back, but her breath came in hoarse gasps and I thought she looked dreadfully ill, when the niece entered the room with empty hands.

"It's gone," she said brusquely to Mary.

"Perhaps there's some downstairs," I suggested.

"What do you mean?" Rhoda turned from me coldly. "It's the jewel I mean, Aunt Mary. The key of the safe is on the table, the case is there, but it's empty."

I thought Mary would collapse again, but she struggled to her feet as Rhoda spoke and stood holding one post of the bed. It seemed so cruel to torment her at the moment that I interposed recklessly, in spite of Rhoda's obvious desire to get rid of me.

"But Miss Mary knew that. Why, surely that was why Miss Jessica went to London—to sell the jewel, I mean."

Something in my voice seemed to pierce Rhoda's preoccupation. She turned and looked at me, and made an obvious effort to recover her temper and her manners.

"Yes, of course, that was her original reason. But we hoped last night that we had persuaded her to leave it behind till she had got into touch with an intending purchaser. You see it's got rather an historic reputation: most dealers in jewellery have heard of it. And it did seem risky for one old lady to travel about with it in a handbag. She seemed to agree with us last night, and we assumed she had gone off without it. But I looked into the case when I was hunting for the brandy—I couldn't find any—And the case is there, but the jewel has gone."

"And the case is there," repeated Mary, dropping back upon the bed. Her breathing sounded laboured now, but her cheek was flushed with the shock.

"Oh dear!" I spoke thoughtlessly in my horror.

"I suppose she did take it. I hope she did! Do you know, when I got here, a little after three this afternoon, every window in front was wide open, and the lodge gates, and, I suppose, the back doors, just like that time you came here in February. Suppose some burglar got in …"

"But Mrs. Lee was to have come in and looked round," said Rhoda sharply.

"She was in bed with rheumatism when I went to shelter at the lodge. She told me she hadn't been able to come up as she promised Effie last night."

"Was there anyone about?" asked Rhoda. "Did you see anyone while you were waiting?" My heart gave such a sudden jump as I thought of Cora, of Cora's manner, and of Cora's vanity bag, that I felt I must have betrayed myself. I dared not mention the episode to these two pale, angry women till I had spoken to John or thought the thing out for myself, and an earlier memory came to my rescue.

"There was a car driving away from the back door just as I went round the house," I said. "But I hardly saw it. It wasn't a tradesman's van though. It must have been a caller, I think, for it was a landaulette. Shouldn't we let the police know at once?"

"Certainly not," said Rhoda sharply. "I see it all now, Aunt Mary. We were foolish even to think we could persuade Jessica. She must have taken the jewel out of the case at the last moment —it was a very big clumsy case—and put it in her suit-case. Yes, it was in the suit-case, Aunt Mary!"

Her voice was so vehement and threatening as she spoke that I moved uncertainly to Miss Mary's side. Rhoda was a panther-like Warrielaw, certainly, though her frock had never seen Paris.

"Let's consult John," I put in hastily. "I'm sure we ought to get the police on to it at once, in case a tramp—"

"Nonsense. Aunt Jessica always refuses to have the police mixed up in our family affairs," said Rhoda angrily. "We can write to Elves and those other people we dealt with before, Aunt Mary, and ask them to let us know if they hear anything about it."

"And of course you'll find out when Miss Warrielaw writes," I said, anxious to close the subject and let Miss Mary get to bed.

"Yes, of course, when she writes to us," said Rhoda, turning suddenly to the window. "Though as a matter of fact she's a very bad correspondent. We might not hear from her for weeks, or even months."

And at that Mary gave a groan and fell back again unconscious on to the bed.

"Betty!" called John's voice from below. "Are you coming? I think you ought to be going."

Rhoda was bending over Mary now and I ran to the staircase.

"John," I said urgently, "you must go and fetch a doctor at once, the nearest doctor. Didn't you say that the doctor they always had from Edinburgh has retired and lives in the old Manse in the village? Miss Mary has fainted again—at least I suppose it's a faint—but she's breathing so queerly and her colour is so odd that I'm sure she should have advice. Do go at once!"

Few Scotsmen like to do anything without due meditation, but John was newly married and obedient. Urging Dennis to look everywhere for brandy, I ran back to the bedroom.

"John's fetching a doctor," I said defiantly. "This isn't like an ordinary fainting-fit, I feel sure." Rhoda shrugged her shoulders.

"Very well, you look after her. I'll go and have another hunt."

"Miss Macpherson!" I said, outraged to the point of rudeness. "I do think Miss Mary's health is more important than any jewel."

"The only thing which would do her any good would be to say I'd found it," replied Rhoda with surprising meekness. "Will you bathe her head and see what you can do till the doctor comes?" There was really nothing to do, and I looked round me miserably. The room was so appropriate and pathetic a setting for the still figure on the bed. It had been furnished last, like Jessica's, when the front portion of the house was built, in the style we know so well from Leech's pictures in *Punch*. But the monumental suite of mahogany and the canopied bed were, like Jessica's, dull and tarnished with years and neglect, and the Axminster carpet almost threadbare. In such rooms as those of the two sisters, all over Scotland in the last half-century, families of daughters grew up to lonely and unhonoured spinsterhood, victims to the traditions and extravagance of the past. Outside, the sun was shining again on the budding trees, and the rooks were calling, but within, youth and spring had passed away irretrievably, leaving the poor wreckage of the past in Miss Mary's figure, on the bed. All I could do was to arrange her pillows and sponge her face, and try to bring her back to a world which held little happiness for her.

The doctor arrived unexpectedly soon, and, alarmed by John's report, had brought with him the district nurse, a pleasant, homely woman.

"I've been worried over her health for some time," he said. "I've been afraid of a stroke or a threat of one for a long time, and she took no precautions. She wouldn't diet, and she took an absurd amount of exercise. Now she must pay for it. She's lucky enough to have escaped a stroke I fancy, but she must lie up altogether for some weeks. I'll send a nurse down to-morrow, and you can stay with her till then, can't you, Nurse Howe. Ah, she's coming round now!"

It was with the utmost relief that I saw Miss Mary's eyes open and her breath become normal again. She frowned a little at the sight of the doctor and nurse, but grew tranquil as I whispered that Nurse had come to sleep with her and look after her.

"I'm glad," she said. "And, listen, my dear, don't let Rhoda come to see me again. I don't feel equal to it. Make it quite clear to Nurse and Doctor that I don't want to see her again. Perhaps you could give her a lift to Edinburgh. She means most kindly but—but I can't see her."

I whispered to the nurse as I bade Mary goodbye, and then followed the doctor out of the room, with Mary's message. Rhoda was standing at the top of the stairs, waiting evidently for our departure, and John and Dennis stood a few steps below, as puzzled and crestfallen as men always are in the case of illness.

"Now we must all be getting along," said the doctor cheerfully. "Miss Rhoda, you must come too. You're not to go near Miss Warrielaw tonight. She's to have absolute quiet: those are my orders."

"But I must stay to look after things here," said Rhoda impatiently. "Of course I won't disturb her till she's better, but there must be someone to arrange for the nurse."

"Now, now, we're none of us indispensable," smiled the doctor. "Effie will know what to do, and Miss Mary has sent marching orders to us all."

"And we'll drive you home, Miss Macpherson," I put in.

But it was John who won the day.

"What are you making such a fuss over, Rhoda?" he said with annoyance. "Why on earth are you so keen on staying down here when you're not wanted? Get your bag and gloves and come along."

"But I don't want a lift," said Rhoda sullenly. "I'll get my bicycle and ride home."

"Nonsense," said the doctor determinedly. "You've had a nasty shock and you're not fit for it, and I won't have you on my hands as well. Now, Miss Rhoda, you've done what I've told you ever since you had measles when you were a child of six. Get you into that car when you've fetched your things."

Effie was standing about in the hall, and gave a sigh of relief as Rhoda came downstairs with a parcel and got into John's motor.

"And see your windows are all shut, and the house safe," John called back.

"And the lodge gates kept locked," added the doctor. "You can't have the place too quiet for Miss Mary, and Mrs. Lee will have her niece to help her and take in orders by hand."

Effie nodded her assent, and as we started the noise of the shutting and bolting of windows and doors reached us. It was impossible not to feel that it was Rhoda first and foremost whom Effie was shutting out with such assiduity. Certainly I could have dispensed with her in our car, for there was so much I wanted to think over before I was alone with John. Mary's physical needs had kept my thoughts at bay for the time, but what was I to do, what was I to think, about Cora's behaviour that afternoon?

"I say," said Dennis, who finds silence for more than two minutes impossible. "I say, won't it be bad luck on Miss Jessica if she has to come tearing back from London as soon as she gets there because Mary's ill?"

"We can't let her know. We haven't Aunt Jessica's address," said Rhoda curtly.

"Oh well, she'll write, I suppose," said John easily.

"Warrielaws never write letters," said Rhoda in a voice so like her aunt's that Dennis choked.

"How queer that you saw her to-day," I reflected.

"Yes, wasn't it? Do you know, I wasn't sure that she wasn't going to get out of the train and double-cross everyone. She was strolling down the platform in the most *dégagé* way—that ass Peter said she was looking out for her young man, but of course he's an awfully low type of mind."

"You didn't see her left behind, then?"

"Lord, no. We were too busy looking after our own middle-aged party. Betty, I'm terribly afraid I'll have to have that radiator looked at after all, and I expect it'll cost a bit more than I like." Rhoda sat silent, nor did she pay any attention to Dennis's suggestion that he should blow in and see how Alison was getting on, what? She only thawed a little to John when he told her kindly that she and Mary must let him know if there was any business he could do for them. We all breathed a sigh of relief when we drove away from her grey demure little house in Inverleith. For although, as John said, no Warrielaws have hearts and no Warrielaws have manners—"except Alison," amended Dennis—"of all the heartless and mannerless young business women he'd ever seen Rhoda took the cake." I was glad to think that her presence, at least, was not darkening the vast, sad, threadbare bedroom where Mary Warrielaw lay alone.

CHAPTER VI
THE SILENCE OF MISS WARRIELAW

DURING THE WEEKS that followed the afternoon at Warrielaw we were each of us, it seems to me now, in the position of some musical ignoramus taken to his very first concert. How pointless to such an innocent would be the buzz of the gathering audience and tuning-up of all the instruments, how impossible to think that out of this there would come one full coherent melody, hushing every other incongruous sound into rapt silence. For the next six weeks nothing but queer and unconnected incidents were to sound in our minds over affairs at Warrielaw. Then indeed the main theme was to prove urgent and engrossing.

From the first I puzzled naturally over the events of that afternoon of April 13th, but most of my worrying was done in private. From our childhood Dennis and I have been rapt readers of adventure and detective stories; and so often had we applied their suggestions to everyday life around us, that any announcement on my part that I had noticed some very queer person or event in a London street was dismissed at once as a "Betty Ramp". That odious phrase was applied by Dennis at once to my descriptions and puzzles over those dreary hours at Warrielaw. John shared his scoffing amusement. What was there curious about a couple of old maids and their servant leaving their shabby old place unguarded one afternoon? Why was it strange for one old maid to go off to London, as she had done before, or take a breath of fresh air at Carstairs? Or why shouldn't the other throw a fit when she had overwalked herself all day and probably overeaten herself at lunch? Of course I could have changed their tone at once, I surmised, if I had told them about Cora's doings, but, about those, rightly or wrongly, I was silent. I had promised Cora to say nothing, and the boyish conventions of my childhood kept me silent till I had seen her and warned her that I could keep silence no longer. Often enough I faced the possibility of her having gone up to Jessica's room and abstracted the fairy jewel while I slept in her car. But even if Cora were a thief, even if it had been the jewel that distended her bag so queerly, one thing was quite clear. The jewel for the present was safe in her keeping. She would never sell it: she would never lose it: it was more sacred to her probably than any other Warrielaw. And if on the other hand she were innocent of the monstrous theft, it was terrible to think, of meeting her in Edinburgh for years to come after I had made irremediable mischief by accusing her. I had seen enough of feuds in this fierce Northern city to realise that for the rest of my life every party would be spoilt for me by trying to avoid Cora and her friends, every street corner would hold the menace of meeting her unexpectedly. If John knew, John would have to take some action, and all this trouble would begin. Meanwhile it was surely best to wait till a letter came from Jessica to prove whether the jewel was or was not still in its owner's keeping. So at least I reasoned for the next few days, and then John came home with the news that Charles had put his foot down at last and hurried Cora off to the Riviera. Her nerves had all gone to pieces, said Cora's unlucky husband, and he had simply packed her up and bundled her off in the charge of her favourite sister-in-law. I was not a little sorry for the sister-in-law, but I was delighted to be relieved from the chance of meeting socially one whom I seriously suspected of theft, and one whose enmity I had certainly aroused. Cora might be mad in some ways, but she was not careless. Wherever she was, the jewel was safe. It was safer by far, I felt, with her than it would be at Warrielaw within reach of Rhoda's covetous grasp.

For it was from Rhoda, to use my former simile, that we were first aware of the muttering of the orchestra from which the main theme was to come. Miss Mary had rallied wonderfully. She consented to see Rhoda when three or four days had passed by, though Effie reported gleefully that she had just given the new nurse a wee hint to stay in the room. "She's an awful genteel body," said Effie when Dennis took me to make enquiries, "and Miss Rhoda'll have to mind her manners when she's by." But Rhoda had achieved her object and seen Mary, and from that visit John's troubles began.

"The woman's mad!" said John when he came in one afternoon, announcing that Rhoda was coming to see him. "And yet if ever I imagined there was a business woman with her head screwed on the right way, it was Rhoda Macpherson. I really begin to believe all women have as undeveloped a legal sense as you, Betty."

"What's she being illegal about?"

"Well, Betty, what would you do if I suddenly went off to London and left you without a penny and didn't write for a fortnight?"

"I should forge a cheque and go home to Kensington," I said promptly. "All the Howards are good forgers."

"What sort of cheque?"

"Oh, ten pounds or so, I suppose. What are you getting at?"

"Well, you've more sense than Rhoda and Mary Warrielaw! Jessica's bankers rang me up this morning to say that Rhoda had come in and tried to cash a cheque for a hundred pounds on Jessica's account. The cheque was signed by Mary, and there was almost a scene, I imagine, when Collins very naturally pointed out that they couldn't make free with Jessica's money just because she'd gone off on a visit to London."

"But has she left Mary with no money at all?"

"So I gather! That's quite typical of her eccentric ways. She drew fifty pounds for herself and then went off with it. As a matter of fact, even though Mary can get as much credit as she likes from her ordinary shops, it was, of course, absurd to leave her with hardly a penny in her purse. If Jessica doesn't write reasonably soon, I can obviously arrange with the bank to let Mary have some small monthly sum for the management of the place. But to cash a hundred pounds was ludicrous! Collins tells me that Jessica draws about twenty pounds a month for all her expenses. I suppose Rhoda was simply trying to make hay of poor old Mary while the sun was shining! Well, I rang up and asked if she could look in, so of course she asked herself to tea and suggested that Dennis should fetch her and Alison. That saves her a lawyer's fee and twopence for a tram! Oh, she's practical enough in small ways!"

I was out when Rhoda arrived and absented myself till six o'clock, in the hope that all legal business would be over. But when I entered the drawing-room I found Dennis and Alison far away in the big window, and John still endeavouring to bring Rhoda to reason.

"That's all I can do," he was reiterating. "We can arrange for a monthly allowance, but it's out of the question to touch any capital, as I've told you again and again."

"But if we don't hear from Jessica?"

"Of course you'll hear from her." John was evidently weary of arguing round and round in a circle. "If not, as I say, we can do nothing till the law presumes death—and that's not for several years. But it's absurd to go on bothering about these things, Rhoda. No doubt she'll write in a few days."

"How is Miss Mary?" I asked, to rescue my husband.

"She's better, only naturally she's worried over all this. For all we know, Jessica may have lost the suit-case and the jewel in it."

"Yes, she must want to know Miss Jessica is all right." I could not help pointing out what seemed a curious omission in Rhoda's outlook.

"If she's really anxious, all we could do is to employ a private agent to get on her track," said John. "But it would be absurd when she's only been away for a week and presumably has the case with her."

"Nearly a fortnight. I do think we should make enquiries about the suit-case. It was the 13th of April when she went."

"Well, even so, it's rather doubtful whether we've any right to employ an agent to hunt for Jessica with Jessica's money when she doesn't want to be found! Do try to make Miss Mary understand anyhow that she can't touch a penny of Jessica's money as things are. Why should she want to get hold of capital so suddenly?"

Rhoda made no reply to his question. "There's another thing," she said abruptly. "Do you know what Cora's done? She's got hold of that half-witted niece of Effie's, that girl Annie, who gave us so much trouble in the winter, and installed her as under-housemaid."

"Christina said something about it to me," I admitted. "Why shouldn't she give her a chance?"

"Do you know how she got her? She motored out to Car-glin on the very afternoon Effie took Annie there—the day Aunt Jessica went away—and engaged her on the spot and motored her back with her to Edinburgh. Effie said she was in her uniform and about the house half an hour after Cora got back with her. Effie evidently felt it was a great triumph over me: she always seemed to think it was my fault that the Aunts got rid of Annie."

"It doesn't seem to me that this is a point on which I can give you legal advice," said John, rising.

"Except that it would be interesting to know what Cora was up to," said Rhoda severely. "I never knew Cora engage a maid out of sheer philanthropy before. I suppose she wants to have some sort of connection with Effie, so as to hear just what is going on at Warrielaw, but it seems odd to me, very odd."

It seemed even stranger to me that Cora had adhered to her plan when I remembered how white and ill she had looked that afternoon in the drive at Warrielaw. It was not a long drive to Carglin, a village near to Bathgate, but long enough for a nervous woman with a car which had given her trouble earlier in the day. Certainly she must have wanted to get hold of An-nie for information of some kind, but she must have wanted it badly before she introduced the clumsy, stupid, untrained woman into her immaculate servants hall. "Mrs. Murray took such a fancy to her from the first that she said Annie was to attend to her own bedroom," Christina had reported, but that I did not repeat to Rhoda.

"Annie's back at her sister's now, I believe," I volunteered. This seemed a harmless piece of information for Rhoda. "Cora sent all the underservants home on board-wages, Christina told me, when she went to the Riviera."

"And that was only a week later!" exclaimed Rhoda. She got up and stood by the window, her brows knit in thought. Then, recollecting herself, she spoke more lightly—"Well, Cora's really hardly responsible for herself, is she?"

"No Warrielaws are responsible for themselves or for anyone else," said John severely, when Dennis had escorted the two women to his car. "I don't mind her tricks or Cora's about this domestic system of espionage in which they indulge, but I do want to find out why Rhoda is trying to lay her hands on her aunt's capital."

Dennis enlightened us on that point when he returned. Alison, he explained, had told him long ago that Rhoda's whole heart was set on going to America and starting in business there, far away from the Edinburgh people who looked down on her and her sister and the family which was falling into decay. For years this had been her ideal, and she had more than once approached Jessica on the subject. She had, apparently, never really grasped through it all how useless Mary was to her as an ally, and she was proportionately disappointed now. She was still, Dennis reported with a grin, hoping to make John see reason, and she was playing with the idea of setting an enquiry on foot, though evidently in some ways the scheme displeased her. "But I think I can venture to promise that you'll hear from her again, soon, John," said my brother.

John seized upon the incident as text to a sermon on the impossibility of giving the vote to women, a subject which gave rise to much domestic wit in those far-off, forgotten days.

Rhoda certainly displayed the tenacity and fighting quality of a suffragette in her quest for money. We heard indirectly that she was trying to borrow on her very problematic expectations, with no success. It was she who evidently inspired Miss Mary to write off piteous, trembling letters with many crossings and underlinings, to ask to know exactly where she stood. Rhoda herself was busy getting other legal opinions, and John was maliciously glad to think she would have to pay for them. She was so preoccupied with her affairs and her visits to Warrielaw, where, however, she was still only admitted on sufferance to Mary's presence under the eye of the nurse, that Alison was more often in our house than ever. In her presence we could not discuss the family affairs; behind her back Rhoda's doings were a subject for jest. So that it was almost a surprise when John spoke seriously one day.

"You know, Betty, I don't like this business at all. Do you realise that it's a month now since Jessica went away?"

"May 11th—yes, so it is," I said, shivering in the cold wind. "I never realised May had come in like a lion already."

"It's a long time, really, you know, longer than I like. I rang up Neil Logan to-day to ask if he'd heard from her, and all the cold-blooded beast would say was that the longer it was before we heard, the better. Her loss, he added, is certainly our gain, and I was so angry that I rang off. I mean, seriously, Betty, she was pretty old to go wandering off alone to some doss-house in London, with a fabulous historic jewel tucked into her bag or hanging from her neck. She may have met with any kind of accident in the London streets and remain unidentified, or she may even have met with foul play. I've written to tell Rhoda that I think a few very private and careful enquiries wouldn't be a bad thing, and what's more, I've even thought of the very man to make them. You've heard me speak of Bob Stuart? Well, he's at a loose end just now—out of a job. If Rhoda and Mary agree to get someone, I shall approach him."

It was therefore in this manner Bob Stuart came into our lives.

Bob's relationship with John was one of those curious affairs which flourish in democratic Scotland. Old Mr. Morrison was a lawyer of the old type and sent his son to the most famous day school in Edinburgh, criticising severely those snobbish Edinburgh West End people who sent their sons to England for their education. John and Bob had fought their way up the school and played in the fifteen together: they had known every thought in each other's hearts, climbed every mountain in Skye together and risked their lives together on sailing boats in the Islands. But never once, as far as I could make out, had my mother-in-law asked Bob to her house, or John penetrated the Stuarts' house in Morningside. Just when John went to Oxford, Bob's father died, leaving his family penniless. Bob went into the police force and rose rapidly. He had been promoted to the detective branch and done excellently. For ten years he and John had maintained their friendship outside their homes and families. Then, just before we married, Bob had inherited a comfortable sum from an unknown great-aunt on condition that he should leave the force and go into some business. The interests of his family obliged him to accept, and at the moment Bob was looking out for some outlet for his activities. When I heard his story I suggested to John that Bob should come to see us in Moray Place, but such a breach in tradition was apparently impossible for either of them to contemplate. It needed the full force of the Warrielaw affair to bring him to the house, but when once he came, Dennis and I were determined not to let him go. It was only in a private capacity that John consulted him first, before he gained the consent of the Warrielaws.

Dennis and I sat and looked at the two men with the greatest interest in that first interview in the library of Moray Place. It seemed to me that we were looking at a page in Scottish social history. When the Morrisons handed over Moray Place to us, I made a revolution in the vast Victorian drawing-room and my bedroom, but I left the library untouched. The lofty dark walls were still covered with dark prints of legal luminaries and the family trees of the Morrisons and the families into which they had married, with college and school groups and trophies. The vast leather chairs and John's desk and tables were ugly but convenient, and the whole room was beautified by the view, from the big windows, of the Firth of Forth, far away over a grey haze of smoky chimneys, and the shadowy line of Highland hills beyond the sea. My tall, strong, silent husband (those were the days of strong, silent men) with his stern mouth and good-humoured eyes, his unimpeachable code of life and morals and his pleasant, casual voice, fitted perfectly into the background and traditions of two centuries of an Edinburgh legal family. Bob Stuart was a complete contrast: he was, I thought idly, the Highlander strayed into a Lowland fortress of conventions, Rob Roy brought to book at last. He was so slight and active that I could never imagine him in majestic blue, controlling the traffic: he had that delightful type of what Dennis called the bashed-in face, where the mouth and chin seem the most prominent features. His forehead was rather low, and if you had brushed his hair over it he would have looked a criminal type, and if you brushed it back he would look the twin of a famous actor. When he had lost his hair, Dennis suggested further, he would look very like a bishop. His lids drooped habitually over his eyes, but his glance was extraordinarily quick and penetrating. He could speak broad Scots, or ordinary English with only a slight Scotch accent, in alternate sentences. He had just enough of that personal magnetism we called charm in those days to make people fling confidences of every kind at him, while he himself sat in silence making the favourite Scottish comment of "Hmhm" at intervals. His clothes were cheap; he wore them badly and without interest. He would have been a glorious companion in an earthquake or shipwreck, and an interesting neighbour at dinner or on any occasion when you could settle down to talk to him. In a drawing-room at a tea-party he would be hopeless, not because he was shy, gauche or self-conscious, but because he would find no interest in social amenities. He would never, I think, have come to meet me save on business terms. He had his own world and John had his, even in the tiny universe of Edinburgh, and he had no wish to enter John's. In the Great War men found such intimate companionship irrespective of background, training and tradition, but it was, I think, only in Scotland, before that date, that men like these two had a capacity for intimate friendship with no interest in each other's surroundings. Our library was at that moment, it seemed to me, the representative meeting-place of all that is best in pro-

fessional aristocracy and independent democracy. For generations Scotsmen like these have realised that women with their
conventions and snobberies complicate social life for them,
and, ignoring them, persist in their own undisturbed mascu-
line friendships. I sat glowing with pride over the Country to
which I now belonged, while Bob was obviously feeling not
the slightest interest in me, though he took in the efforts of
Dennis's tailor and Dennis's boyish charm, with a glance of
pleasant interest.

"Well, if I can get their consent, and I'm pretty sure of it,"
said John, "will you take on the job for me, Bob?"

"I would if he won't, you know," said the irrepressible
Dennis. "I've always wanted to be a detective!"

"Hmhm," said Bob. "This is hardly the most exciting sort
of detective work though, is it?"

"Well, it won't exactly lead to the Riviera Express or Inter-
national Plots, but there's a Lost Jewel and a Missing Dowager."

"Let's hear all about them," said Bob, taking an appalling
pipe out of his pocket absent-mindedly, and then trying to
hide it. When I implored him to smoke it I think he felt that
John might have married happily after all.

One delightful attribute of Bob was that after every answer to any question he said "Hmhm," and then had that fact
securely fixed in his mind for ever. By the time John had told
the story of the Warrielaws, and Dennis and I had answered
every possible question about Jessica's departure, he knew all
there was to know about her up to the moment when she had
disappeared from Edinburgh's ken at Carstairs.

"I'll take on the job," he said slowly at last, after a long
meditative silence in the room; "partly because I'd like to work
with you, John, partly because I've had thoughts of starting an
Enquiry business rather than any other routine life, and partly
because I'll enjoy working a bit with the Force again if I come
across them—they're the very best of men. Also I agree with
you that it's as likely as not something has happened to that

poor old body. You say she hated most of her relations and wasn't much of a letter-writer. That's all very well, but I gather that she was fond of her garden, and I'm yet to meet the gardener who'd leave his seeds unpricked and his beds untouched in April without sending a card to give directions to somebody. So if the family will employ me, I'm on. Of course it won't be a cheap job. As far as I can see, most of my enquiries must be in London, and if I draw blank there it might even mean America and the dealers there. With fifty pounds in her pocket she might have got across. I gather it's her money that you'll draw on, but I suppose we have the consent of her heirs?"

It was Rhoda who gained the day over the question. For once she and John were in agreement. Neil remained incurably casual, and Miss Mary wrote protesting against the whole affair, but Charles Murray for Cora, Alison under Rhoda's orders, and Rhoda herself made a majority in favour of an enquiry. John sent off his instructions to Bob, and Bob disappeared on his quest, dressed, as Dennis said disappointedly, in no more interesting disguise than his own abominable ready-made suit of clothes.

It was a fortnight before we heard anything from him, and in the interval Rhoda rang up almost every day to ask if he had found the suitcase and why he was so long about it. She had the grace to sound slightly ashamed when John pointed out that it was Jessica's fate rather than the suit-case which was the origin of the enquiry.

"But of course," said Alison with large, innocent eyes, "she really didn't get on with Aunt Jessica and she does believe, I think, that Aunt Jessica may be keeping quiet just to annoy Aunt Mary. And she says Aunt Jessica is so careless that she'd be likely to lose her luggage. She was always absent-minded, and she's very unkind to Aunt Mary often, you know! And Rhoda can't help caring about the jewel. Not for its value, of course" (I tried to look politely acquiescent) "but she has second sight from our Highland grandmother, and thinks that we should find such interesting things from it if we took it to an American Professor in that sort of thing."

"But you don't want to go to America?" said Dennis jealously.

"Oh, no," said Alison, blushing very prettily. "I'd hate it, but of course I'll have to do what Rhoda does."

"Then I hope the suit-case and the jewel are lost," muttered Dennis.

But the suit-case was not lost. A wire announced that Bob was returning with it, though without any news, and John summoned Rhoda, as Mary's representative, to come to the office to go through its contents and hear the result of Bob's enquiries. Neil refused to join us. "The sight of my aunt's intimate toilet details would unnerve me," he said firmly.

It was nearly seven before John returned that evening, and I ran down as the door opened to find him in the hall with Bob. Both men were looking angry, and I was about to fade away when John opened the library door for me. "No, come in, you and Dennis. You've been in it from the beginning. You may as well hear all about it now. And you'll restrain our language a little, Betty! Bob and I have been saying exactly what we think about Rhoda all the way from Charlotte Square and we'd better get a little more temperate. Have a whisky, Bob?"

It was extraordinarily difficult at first to see why Rhoda should be angry. Bob seemed, to Dennis and me, to have worked miracles. It is not easy to set off on a quest six weeks old for a perfectly normal, middle-aged lady, in a black hat and cloak, who disappeared, presumably in London, of her free will. There had been no information of any sort after Jessica's start from any railway official. Small's office recollected her ordering the cab on April 13th, and their man remembered perfectly driving down to Warrielaw and taking her up to the station next day. He remembered that she was carrying a suit-case and a parcel, and that she had tipped him threepence for a six miles' drive. Miss Wise had caught a glimpse of her, and I myself had certainly seen her in the London train at the Caledonian; Dennis and Peter Carruthers had seen her at Carstairs. After that all was a blank, yet Bob, by systematic enquiries, had found from a cheap hotel near Euston that Jessica had, in a letter dated April 10th, ordered bed and breakfast for the night of April 13th. The room had been reserved, and Jessica had never come. He had set off on a tour of the best-known private jewel dealers in London, and discovered, in the hands of one of them, a letter from Jessica making an appointment for an important transaction on April 14th. She had failed to keep it. The probability seemed to be that she had not reached London at all, but Bob set out to track the suit-case. That at last he identified, unlabelled ("No Warrielaws use labels," I could hear Jessica say), in the lost property office at Euston Station. It had been handed in from the train which arrived on April 13th, but no one remembered if it had arrived in the van or in a carriage. Miss Jessica might have arrived with it and forgotten it, or she might never have arrived at all: that defied discovery. There was no trace of any parcel accompanying it, but Rhoda declared that her Aunt took with her a parcel of sandwiches and fruit, of which naturally no traces would be left. She had, however, paid little attention to the story of Bob's activities: her eyes were glued to the suit-case.

It was horrible, John told me later, to see it unpacked. Apart from the fact that Jessica was not distinguished for personal daintiness, there was something very dismal and sinister in watching her little odds and ends turned out for public inspection. Rhoda fell upon them like a fury. Jessica had a passion for little, rather grubby bags. Rhoda shook out a brush-bag, messy with odd yellow-grey combings, tore open a sponge-bag with a slimy sponge, a tooth-brush case, a bag containing a Bible, two shoe-bags and a work-bag. She shook each garment viciously as it came out, a best black blouse and skirt, black petticoats and mysterious, strangely-shaped woollen garments from which John looked modestly away. She tore at the case as if it were a rat, she rustled through everything again and again, she snatched open the bags in a fury, but at length the truth was undeniable. The suit-case was found, but the jewel, like Jessica, had vanished.

At that Rhoda broke into a passion. She practically accused Bob of theft, and in the next breath asked if he had put the police on to the guardian of the lost property office. She raged at John for putting off the enquiry so long: she declared that he knew nothing of his business, and that she would ask her aunt to put her affairs into other hands. She disgraced herself, in short, utterly and finally, and then cooled down and asked Bob for a probable estimate of his expenses if he followed the jewel to America. No wonder Bob and John found a good use for their time and language on their way back from the office.

"But, of course," said John, "Rhoda's of no more real importance than a yapping pom. What really concerns us is, what has happened to Jessica?"

"I don't gather that my licence is renewed," said Bob drily.

"Nonsense. As Jessica's lawyer I'm determined to get to the bottom of this. Mary and Rhoda can make arrangements for their share of the Warrielaw trust with a new firm, but Jessica's my affair. What do you make of it all, Bob? Did she ever get to London?"

Bob was quite candidly at a dead end for the moment. He would, of course, pursue again his enquiries at Carstairs; it seemed to him just possible that Jessica, anxious to escape altogether from her family, had always meant to go to America. Against that theory was her correspondence with London, but it remained possible that she might have been suddenly inspired to get out at Carstairs, and get into the Liverpool train, to sail thence to New York or Montreal. Her haste and confusion in such a case might well account for her forgetting the suit-case till it was too late to retrieve it. "But above all," said Bob, "I must go down to Warrielaw and have a good look round there. I want to know more about her, and I'd like to question her sister and the old maid. You see there's whiles when I wonder if she didn't just get out of the train and take the next train home after all?"

"But then we'd all know," I said. "I was down there that afternoon, and so was John, and we were all over the place, and saw Mary come home from her lunch party. Ever so many people would have seen her!"

"Suppose she got back that night of the 13th? Mind you, I've no support for this theory, but I want to explore every possibility before we set out on this American quest. It'll be long and costly."

"But that evening Mary was ill in bed with a nurse in charge, and Effie there, Effie who adores Miss Jessica! No, she can't have come on the 13th or later without our knowing about it."

"Well, I'd like to get down to Warrielaw," said Bob. "For one thing I'd like to get this garden clear in my mind, to see what she's been in the habit of doing and so on. I could almost tell from the look of it if she'd planned a speedy return, or was meaning to vanish for a bit. She may be odd enough to go off and leave her property for weeks or months in John's hands, but no one I ever knew would leave their garden without a thought to it." For the moment it seemed as if difficulties would be put in the way of the visit. Next morning Rhoda arrived at John's office with a letter from Miss Mary. In dejected and shaking writing Mary wrote that as she and Rhoda could not feel satisfied that John was administering the estate satisfactorily in Jessica's absence, and as Mr. Stuart's efforts had been so unsuccessful, Rhoda and she had decided to transfer all their legal affairs to the firm of May, Leigh and May for the future. "I am sorry indeed, dear John," wrote Mary pathetically, "to part with you thus, but Rhoda is such an excellent business woman and feels we should have more modern and up-to-date advisers behind us. You know how it hurts me to make such a parting, but I do hope that your dear little wife will come down to see me, to show that this does not affect our old family friendship."

The dear little wife was, conveyed down to Warrielaw in Dennis's car that afternoon, not so much in token of an unbroken friendship, as in John's desire to discover, unofficially, how far Mary was under Rhoda's undue influence. This question of transferring either Mary's claims to the estate, with the little money she possessed, or Rhoda's tiny capital to another perfectly reputable firm of lawyers, was of no importance. But it was important, if Miss Mary made a new will, that John should know what the relations between the two women were, and give a hint to her new lawyers.

Miss Mary did not receive me. Effie refused me admission most reluctantly, but she could not help herself. "The poor body's been so harried and worried by Miss Rhoda the last few days that Nurse and I just put our heads together and got the doctor to say no one was to see her at all. She was really getting up her strength a little till Miss Rhoda was at her the last few days. Nurse has never left them alone, but she says what she likes in front of Nurse now, forbye she's always trying to get at the bed to whisper to Miss Mary and such havers. Miss Rhoda's been set, as ye ken, on getting new lawyers instead of Master John, and him known from a child and his father before him, and she's been at Miss Mary to get the whole place tidied up, as though my poor lady were dead and buried and the heir walking into the estate. Miss Mary hasna given in that way yet, I understand, and now Miss Rhoda shan't get at her again, I promise you. But I don't see how I can very well let you in, things being so, Ma'am, though I'm sure a sight of you would do her good and stop her worrying."

"Well, give her these flowers and say Mr. John understands," I said. "I expect he'll ring up the doctor and see that Miss Mary isn't bothered any more. Besides, perhaps we'll soon hear from Miss Jessica!"

"Hoots and I wish we could," said Effie, sighing. "It's a' very weel for Miss Rhoda to say she didna write when she was awa', but she was always in the habit of sending me a picture postcard about the garden or the weeding now and again, and I'm just wearying for a word from her, Ma'am."

With that sole contribution to what Dennis called already "the Warrielaw mystery", I went home, to find, to my surprise, that Neil was waiting to see me in the drawing-room with John.

"This is a farewell visit before I go for my month in Paris, Mrs. Morrison," said Neil. He was exquisite and debonair as usual, but his manner was a little different. It seemed to me that Neil, even Neil, had something on his mind.

"Perhaps you'll find Jessica there," I said.

"Hardly in the Salon!" Neil seemed to find his usual casual style an effort. "I may try to get on her tracks in the dens round Bloomsbury where she used to riot on poached eggs under the shadow of the British Museum. But I still feel that her doings are her own affair. She was kind enough to leave me handsomely provided for, and I should like to leave her in return her liberty of action. However, I have just been assuring John that I leave all my affairs and hers in his hands with full trust in his discretion before I, too, lose myself in Paris." He rose to go, but he left John at the door and came back to me suddenly.

"Be nice to Cora on her return, will you, Betty?" he said in a low voice with more feeling in it than I imagined possible. "I have a feeling that when she returns she may need friends."

His words brought back to my mind with a shock all Cora's odd doings and behaviour on the afternoon of that 13th of April. Till then we had been concentrating so entirely on Jessica's disappearance from Carstairs that my visit had faded from my mind. Now I was left to live the afternoon over again and puzzle over my duty in the affair. "Be kind to Cora!" Neil had said. It hardly seemed kind to interrupt her convalescence at Cannes with the news that she was suspected of theft! It is the penalty of being a lawyer's wife that one can't hand over such confidences with the proviso that they must lead to no further action. If I told John every sort of publicity must follow. As far as I could see, also, Cora's actions could have no connection with Jessica's disappearance and that was the crux of the situation at present to all save Rhoda. Once again I decided to say nothing till Cora's return. Then I would screw up my courage and go to see her, and tell her outright that I must tell everything I had seen that afternoon.

But in the end my confidences were delayed again. Cora returned on May 31st, almost seven weeks after Jessica's departure. It was on that afternoon that Bob Stuart went down to Warrielaw, persuading Alison and Dennis to accompany him as a blind, while he made his investigations in the garden and saw as much as he could of the house and its inhabitants. They motored to the front and strolled round to the back, and Alison pointed out to Bob a way through the stable-yard into the wall gardens. Half an hour later they heard an exclamation from Bob, and next minute he came out under the archway with a grey face, and told Alison curtly to go indoors and enquire after her aunt. Dennis was sent off, puzzled and frightened, to fetch a policeman, and on his return Bob led the two men across the yard, to one of the low row of tool-sheds close to a rotting heap of manure which had been ordered doubtless by Jessica before her departure, and had lain there since, untouched, contaminating the air. One low door stood wide open, and at first they could see nothing in the dark, messy interior, but a heap of sacks. Then, following Bob's eyes, Dennis saw a ragged black ankle and the remains of a black shoe sticking stiffly out beneath one of them. Together Bob and the policeman had the courage to pull the heap of sacks carefully aside. There, in that miserable outhouse, within a stone's-throw of her house and the garden she loved, was all that was left of the body of Jessica Warrielaw.

CHAPTER VII
MR. STUART'S DISCOVERY

IT IS PERHAPS a humiliating confession for one who had been addicted to "Betty Ramps", that even after the lapse of so many years and all the horrors of the Great War, I cannot write down any description of what the three men found. I will simply copy a Press cutting:

"The deceased lady was recognised only by the clothing she wore, which was identified by her maid as that in which she set off on her fatal journey on April 13th. The Police Surgeon, who was called in at once by the officer in charge, examined the remains and summoned a famous specialist immediately. Dr. Hewetson, who was also present at the scene, offered his assistance. The doctors gave their opinion that Miss Warrielaw undoubtedly met with her death by violence. The upper part of the skull was almost shattered by a blow or blows from some blunt instrument, or, possibly, from some very violent fall: further the deceased had been stabbed to the heart with such violence that the weapon had broken upon the breast bone and was still actually embedded in the body. It is clear also that the corpse was conveyed, when already the stiffening of death had set in, to the shed in the grounds of her own house, where the gruesome discovery was made. From the fact that an unused ticket to London and a case containing a number of bank notes were found on her person, it seems clear that she met with her death on the day of her journey to the metropolis, and that the motive of the crime was not robbery. Inspector Ard, who is in charge of the case, is said to be already in possession of clues which should lead to remarkable discoveries. Miss Mary Warrielaw, sister to the deceased lady, is prostrated by the shock. The Warrielaw family is well known as of the most historic …

There was one part of the story which the reporters did not know. Alison had parted from Dennis, alarmed, and gone,

white and scared, into the library. Miss Mary, now fully con-
valescent, was sitting there, and at the sight of the girl's face
she got up unsteadily and hurried to her, asking her insistently
what was wrong. Alison supposed that she had heard the sound
of men's voices and knew the direction whence they came. In
spite of all Alison's entreaties, she tottered across the circular
garden, through the path between the shrubs, into the back
avenue, and thence to the stable-yard. It was just as the men
were facing their ghastly discovery that they looked round to
see Miss Mary, clutching Alison's unwilling arm, just behind
them. And as she glanced uncertainly at the shed, suspecting
something terrible, for she could hardly see what was within,
Mary gave a hoarse, strangled cry and fell forward, almost to
the door of the shed. When they tried to carry her indoors,
they found one side rigid and paralysed, and it was to the bedside of one sister that Dr. Hewetson went before he faced the
terrible remains of the other. His verdict in the former case
had no uncertainties. The stroke he had always feared for Mary
had fallen on her, the result of the shock, intensified by her
long illness. That it was fatal, or even necessarily dangerous, he
could not prophesy. All he could do was to summon another
nurse from Edinburgh on his return, and give his directions to
the nurse in charge. Alison had not been allowed to see her.
Bob, when at length he could leave the scene, found Alison
with Dennis, sitting with her hands in his in the library, too
stunned and overcome to speak. I rang up Rhoda on our return to Moray Place and got leave to keep the poor girl for
the night. Rhoda would, I knew, be hurrying down to Warrielaw—("Where the carcase is," said John brutally, "that eagle
won't be missing")—but we could trust Effie and the nurse to
keep her from poor Mary.

I put Alison to bed after I had coaxed her to have some
soup, and the first ghost of a smile Dennis could produce was
when I told him she was asleep. Dennis would not touch soup.
He was helping himself to whisky, which he dislikes, at a rate

which horrified me, and pouring out in a high, jerky voice all the most appalling details of the discovery again and again. John would not let me interfere: when Dennis grew incoherent he took him off to bed himself—"the only treatment, Betty, for a boy who's seen what he's seen. I'm not sure that I'd better not try it on you too. You look a ghost."

"No, don't send me to bed yet. It's too awful to face in the dark. John, I can't bear to think of Dennis—he's such a baby really, isn't he? And to think he's got to tell all that at the inquest."

Then I discovered what is known doubtless to the ordinary well-informed person. There are no inquests in Scotland. The police go about gathering information and taking statements from any person known to be connected with the scene of the crime and, when they have any definite reasons to suspect the author of the deed, lay their evidence before an official known in law as the Procurator Fiscal, but more familiarly by the populace as the Fiscal.

"In any case where there's a doubt as to the cause of the death, any question of suicide or accident for example, a Fatal Accident Enquiry may be held, but there's no question of that in this case. You and Dennis will have to tell the police all you know when they are collecting evidence, but Bob will see you through all that."

It was, I think, to restore me to some sort of composure that Bob, when he came in, drifted into a long discussion with John as to whether the English or Scottish procedure were the more effective. John, for once, was on the side of the English law, and Bob withheld him stoutly.

"Ah, yes, but there's another side to it. When an educated man like the Procurator Fiscal receives the report of the police and summons the witnesses to give their precognitions, they haven't the benefit of having their remarks considered by the jury composed of twelve men as slow and stupid as themselves. There have been cases where the Fiscal's own preconceived views tend to twist or colour their evidence. Take the case of Kelly in 1862—"

"But isn't there ever a public court at all?" I asked, bewildered. "Shall we really get out of giving evidence at all in public?"

John laughed.

"No, Betty dear. Trial in public by jury has reached even this benighted country! When the police have laid sufficient evidence before the Procurator to warrant an arrest the accused is brought before the Sheriff Court, just as a man's brought before the Police Court in England. In the case of murder the proceedings are usually formal and the accused reserves his defence. No witnesses are called then and he is remanded to await his trial. When the case is fully prepared by the Crown the accused is brought into the Sheriff Court again to hear the indictment against him. That again is formal: invariably he reserves his defence and his case is remitted to the High Court and tried as soon as it can be brought forward. But we're a very long way from that, Betty, if indeed we ever get there!"

"It won't be an easy case for the police," said Bob thoughtfully. "In fact, it's going to be as hard a business to collect evidence after all these weeks as it well could be. I'm afraid we shall have to rely as much on your evidence as anyone's, Mrs. Morrison, as to what happened at Warrielaw on April 13th."

"But what did happen?" I cried helplessly. "Was she there all the time? But I saw her in the train! Dennis saw her at Carstairs! Oh John—!"

"Hush, Betty dear!" John moved to my side. "You're not to try to think of this to-night. Go to bed!"

"That's very good advice," said Bob firmly. "I'm going too, John, when I've just settled with you exactly where I stand. I've done what I was engaged for, you see, so now I expect you wish me to withdraw from the case."

"Certainly not," said John warmly. "I represent Jessica's interests and it's in them to retain your services, as you know the little there is to know already. The Crown will have its work cut out and may want all the aid we can give. We've got to discover who did this monstrous thing and you've enough evidence already to help the police solidly. Of course you must go on with it, but Betty, I really think you should toss off some whisky and go to bed. I know you want to talk all this awful business out. I know, like the rest of us, that facts and suspicions are buzzing all over your head. But do have a drink and try to forget."

I did not drink, but my usual unromantic faculty stood me in good stead. Before I had managed to disentangle the thread of the story which had so completely changed its venue and its character, I had fallen asleep.

It is a dreadful thing to wake from a heavy slumber to know that when you climb up out of the pit of unconsciousness some horrible thought awaits, staring at you, from the top. On this morning, my memory and imagination alike conjured up such a ghastly figure that it seemed terrible to see that the sun was shining into the room. As a knock came on the door I wished to hide far down among the clothes and never emerge again into a world in which such unbelievable things could happen.

Christina usually usurps the work of the house-maid when she has any exciting news to bring to my bedside with my tea. I was not surprised to see her to-day, but I was surprised to see her flustered and too angry to gossip.

"Mr. John was awa' early, Ma'am," she said breathlessly, "and left orders you was to have your sleep out, and it's half-past nine now. But Mrs. Charles Murray was in the moment that ever his back was turned on the house, saying that she must see you at once. She's tried to get up the stair once."

"But I thought Mrs. Charles was abroad?"

"They got back last night, I heard from my niece, Bridget. I wouldn't let her in to you before, but—"

Christina started as the door swung open and Cora herself slipped into the room.

"Betty," she said, "forgive me. I couldn't wait any longer."

A long mirror opposite my old chintz-hung four-post bed reflected us both, as Cora feverishly pulled a chair to my bedside and Christina reluctantly went away. Her stay on the Riviera had not apparently done Cora much good. She was thinner than ever and her eyes had black lines under them: with her careless make-up they made those queer light irises larger than ever. She bent towards me in a marvellous French sports-suit of white and black, strained, exquisite, world-worn and tense, and the mirror showed me myself, ridiculously small and childish and tousle-headed in a frilly nightgown, looking like a fluffy duckling confronted by a strange, infuriated bird of paradise.

"Won't you wait in the dressing-room till I'm up?" I suggested.

"Betty, I can't wait! I'm in hell! I shall be until you promise to tell no one that you saw me at Warrielaw that day!"

"I can't promise. John told me last night I'd have to say just what I'd seen on April 13th on my oath, when I give my statement to the police. Anyhow I'd have to tell the truth when I have to give it to the Procurator Fiscal."

"But, Betty, not about me. Why should you? I thought Jessica was in London or I'd never have gone there. I'm still in a maze about this news. How did she ever get to Warrielaw if she was killed in London or at Carstairs? What does this man Stuart think about it all?"

"I haven't heard," I said stiffly. If Cora had come for information, she should not get it.

"Well, you know I'd nothing to do with it! How could I? You know it's absurd, Betty!"

"I don't suppose you murdered anyone," I said, gasping at this extraordinary conversation. "But there were some queer things done at Warrielaw that day, Cora, you know. I mean, I can't help guessing that you went to get something and you got it. You didn't only go to get hold of Annie—I'm sure of that."

Cora had been pale before: now all the skin round the rouge on her cheeks and lips went livid.

"All I wanted was my own," she said after a long pause.

"But the jewel wasn't yours," I said straight out.

"The jewel? Oh, you mean the fairy jewel." Cora's voice expressed nothing but genuine, or wonderfully simulated, surprise. "Betty, that had nothing to do with it, nothing! Listen! I see I'd better take you into my confidence."

"I'd rather you didn't," I said.

Cora leant forward and clutched my wrists so tightly and suddenly that I nearly screamed.

"I must," she said, "to make you understand! And if this ever comes out, I warn you I'll poison myself, so you can feel responsible for my death if you begin chattering. Listen! Probably you know that Neil and I always loved each other, long, long before I met Charles. We couldn't afford to marry and I was desperately, degradingly poor and when Charles turned up and wanted me at any price, I took him. How could I help it? I wasn't ever meant to be poor and I thought Charles and all he'd got would make me happy. Well it didn't, and I went on seeing Neil, and, what was worse, writing to Neil, silly, idiotic letters. And Neil kept them. I used to implore him not to but, Betty, you've never seen the real Neil. Only I know that and know how passionate and faithful and romantic he can be."

"Oh!" I exclaimed at this new interpretation of Jessica's nephew.

"Of course you don't know; you and ordinary Edinburgh people are taken in by his poses," said Cora scornfully. "But I knew. Only, then, Betty, a strange thing happened. Neil went away a few months after I married. Jessica sent him to America—(that was the time she sold the Gainsborough)—and when he was gone I was miserable for a little and then ... Then Charles was so good to me and he was there and I expect" (she laughed harshly) "that I'm just the type of kept woman who belongs to any man she's with. Anyhow I got to love Charles and I was ill, and when I got better Neil had just faded out of my mind. When he came back after a year I saw he'd got over it too, or nearly got over it, for he's never loved anyone else really. So we agreed just to be friends and I asked for my letters back, or rather, I think I told him to burn them. And then he had to confess that he'd lost them, that they'd gone! Jessica had been to his studio while he was away and got hold of them and ever since she's been keeping them over my head like a sword. She's never spoken of them to me because I haven't seen her since that lawsuit about the will, but I've always known she had them and might ruin me at any time by showing them to Charles. I was frantic to get them. I'd tried twice already. Then I heard, this April, from Bridget, that Jessica was going away on that Friday and that Mary was lunching out. So I went down, knowing I could get round Effie. I found no one in the house at all, so I went up to Jessica's desk and tried the drawers and there I found my packet. I stuffed them in—don't you remember, Betty, how full my bag was?—and I came down and found you in my car. I was furious to think that anyone had seen me, but last night I realised that everyone would be asking questions about that day after that horrible business yesterday. I did trust you not to tell about my visit before—I'm sure you haven't—but what you must see, Betty, is that it's more important than ever to keep it all quiet now. If any of this gets out, people will begin to ask why I went down, and what papers I wanted, and Charles will hear about it all and find out the truth. And that'll break his heart, Betty, for though I've teased him and worried him, he's always trusted me, but he never would again, never any more!"

Cora paused, tired out and on the verge of hysterical tears. She let her head fall limply on to the pillow beside mine as I sat up straight, touched and horribly puzzled.

"I'll have to say I saw you," I got out at last. "I'm sorry, Cora, but I can't leave that out."

"Well, you can let them think I just drove up to call and went away when I found no one. That's bad enough; it'll make people talk, but that must be all!"

"I'll have to say your car was there a little time," I said. "Don't you see, Cora, I'll be examined on my oath? I can't tell lies, or even suppress the truth, when they ask me. I can say you were never near the stables—I do know that. And I can say you told me you had been fetching something from Jessica's room and leave the rest to you, but honestly—"

There I paused in sudden horror. Cora had lifted her head and her face was close to mine. Her eyes were strained and bloodshot, and in them was a glare which convinced me once and for all that any Warrielaw was capable, in an extremity, of any crime.

"You won't, you little fool," she muttered. "You won't say anything of the sort. If you do—"

I cannot pretend to be proud of my own heroism as I met Cora's glance. I leapt out of the other side of the bed and raced across the room and cannoned at the door into Dennis, who was bounding up the stairs.

"What is the matter?" he asked. "You look like an angry chicken. Hurry up and come down. John and Bob are waiting for us."

I looked back into the room. Cora had strolled to the glass and was using her lipstick with trembling fingers.

"Just wait and see Mrs. Murray downstairs," I said. "Cora, I must fly to my bath. I'm so sorry. Good-bye!"

"Good-bye and don't forget!" said Cora in a low, dull voice.

The library looked extraordinarily safe, secure and legal when I ran downstairs. My mind was still preoccupied with Cora's story and the question of my responsibility to her, and it was only as I looked at Dennis's strained face that the full horror of the day before came back to me. John must have noticed the look I exchanged with my brother, for he rose from the big table where he and Bob were sitting before a pile of papers, and put his hand on my arm.

"Betty, we want you and Dennis to come and sit down here and go through all the details we can get together about this affair at Warrielaw. We've got to go back to that 13th of April again. The medical evidence refers us to that date approximately, and the clothes she wore, and their condition, make it clear that we must assume that it was the day on which she was murdered. I hate to ask you to dwell on all this, but it's inevitable."

"That's so," said Bob, "and let me tell you, Mrs. Morrison, there's no better cure for the mind after a great shock than to make yourself turn your attention to details. The best way to put your imagination to sleep is to set your wits to work."

I must confess at once that Bob proved to be right. In the detective stories I have read I used always to worry over the insensibility of the characters who discovered a murder. Everyone knows that the sight of death, apart from such horrors as those attending Miss Jessica's murder, shakes the human mind to its foundation, yet no such tribute was paid by my favourite characters in fiction. But from that morning I understood that, for those who are directly or indirectly associated with a criminal investigation, another human instinct overrides the first passionate reactions of horror and pity more rapidly than one cares to confess. Almost every human being likes a puzzle. There are few people who can resist the pleasure of sorting out and reconstructing a baffling sequence of events any more than they can resist crossword puzzles to-day. Some details certainly escaped me, but my story made me forget my horror a little already. By the end of it Bob had made out a fairly coherent time-table of the day.

April 12th, 5.30 p.m. Effie and Annie left Warrielaw for Carglin.
After 5.30 p.m. Rhoda arrived for the night. Miss Jessica returned to Warrielaw.

April 13th, 8.30 a.m. A cab from Small's called at Warrielaw, picked up Miss Jessica and her suit-case and drove to Princes Street Station.

10 a.m. Miss Jessica seen at the station by Miss Wise and Mrs. Morrison.

10.40 a.m. Miss Jessica seen at Carstairs Station by Mr. Howard and Mr. Carruthers.

At some early hour. Miss Macpherson and Miss Mary started out to lunch at Erleigh, a seven miles' walk or bicycle ride.

Warrielaw was left deserted except for old woman at the lodge who was bed-ridden and deaf. Back and front gates alike were open.

3 p.m. Mrs. Morrison arrived at Warrielaw. Walked about gardens.

3.30 p.m. Saw Lanchester car disappearing at back entrance. Rain began and took shelter in the lodge.

4 p.m. Returned to front of house and found Mrs. Murray's car (a De Dion) standing before the house. From the lodge Mrs. Morrison had overlooked the back drive, but could not see the front drive nor hear sound of car approaching. Time of Mrs. Murray's arrival therefore unknown.

4-4.15 p.m. Mrs. Morrison slept in Mrs. Murray's car.

4.15 p.m. Mrs. Murray emerged from house and after a short talk drove away.

4.30 p.m. (or a little earlier) Effie returned and took Mrs. Morrison into the house.

4.30 p.m. (or shortly afterwards) Miss Mary and Miss Macpherson returned from Erleigh.

4.35-5 p.m. John and Dennis arrived. Miss Mary taken ill.

About 5.30 p.m. Doctor and nurse arrived.

About 5.45 p.m. John, Mrs. Morrison, Dennis and Rhoda left the house. House closed securely by Effie. Back lodge locked up by new, capable keeper, niece of old woman, with large family of children.

"Hmhm," said Bob. "Well, let's look at our facts. The only solid evidence we have is that Miss Warrielaw left her house at 8.30, took the train at Princes Street at 10, and was last seen at Carstairs. Before three o'clock that afternoon, when Mrs. Morrison reached Warrielaw, she had been murdered and put into that tool-shed next the manure heap in the yard."

"But where was she murdered? There or at Carstairs?" I asked desperately.

"That's what we've got to find out."

"Weren't there any footprints in the shed?" asked Dennis. "Or finger-prints? Or anything to catch hold of?"

"There were no footprints, for the ground had been carefully scrabbled over with a rake, presumably one hanging on the wall. After seven weeks you can't hope for footprints outside or fingerprints on the latch."

"But on the body?" I ventured. Dennis turned away suddenly and Bob shook his head.

"Better not ask details. All that is clear is that the weapon was thrust into the heart just below the sternum and was broken off against it, presumably as it was removed hurriedly, the bone being used as a lever. The weapon is a puzzle, too. It's just a sharp, short steel instrument, pointed at the top and rounded towards the hilt. Its handle is missing. It was broken right off at the shaft, presumably as it broke on a bone after piercing the heart, and it's hard to see just what it was or how it was thrust into the body. We've hunted everywhere for the handle and the case and can find no traces at all. It didn't take a straight line. It almost seemed to me as if she might have fallen on to it by some accident and smashed her head at the same time, but the police surgeon doesn't agree. They'll keep photographs of that, of course. And if it was some such accident, why should anyone conceal the body? The only fact we have to go on is that it wasn't presumably any common thief who did for her.

All her odds and ends of jewellery were on her, and a notecase containing fifty pound notes. They may, of course, have been left as a blind. She may have been wearing the famous jewel and that may have been the motive for the robbery. Only one other thing we know. Her clothes were identified by Effie as those she had laid out for her journey the night before, and the shoes, though dusty and mouldy of course, were unscratched and free from mud. She must have been carried from the place of her death to the shed. We can assume, therefore, that she was murdered either by one powerful man or by two confederates: no ordinary woman could have done it alone."

"But do you think yourself she left the train at Carstairs?" I asked.

"That's one of the main problems of the case," said Bob slowly. "We have no proof as to whether she took her ticket that morning or the day before. All we do know is that it had not been clipped. The guard may, of course, have missed her in the corridor when he looked at the tickets between Edinburgh and Carstairs, but it's curious, very curious. Another strange thing is this. We told the reporters that the ticket and pound notes were found on her person. So they were in a sense, and I thought that safe old phrase was enough for them, and Ard agreed with me. But as a matter of fact—forgive me for these details, Mrs. Morrison—they were in a pocket of her cape which was folded beneath her. When once she had been well—placed in the shed, no one could have got at them without moving the corpse. To my mind that puts it out of the question once and for all that it was done by some casual tramp on the road, or by anyone who had broken into the house at Warrielaw."

"What's the theory of the tramp?" asked John, puzzled.

"Well, Ard is considering alternative possibilities about the case which might possibly incriminate some well-known bad characters in the neighbourhood. He considers it possible that she was lured from the train at Carstairs by some pretext (Heaven knows what!) and was killed somewhere on that lonely high road and brought back and hidden in the tool-shed. Or he suggests that she left the train on some impulse, took a slow train back to Edinburgh, walked to Warrielaw and found someone making off with the valuables in the house. It's true, as he points out, that local gossip would make it known that the house was empty on that day. But all the evidence we have is against either hypothesis. Suppose this unknown and resourceful criminal persuaded Miss Jessica to leave the train and travel home in some van or motor of which he'd possessed himself, he would certainly have seen to it that she brought her suitcase, which would very probably contain any valuables she would have in the world."

"And why should he motor her corpse back to Warrielaw?" broke in Dennis.

"A corpse is a difficult thing to get rid of, Mr. Dennis," said Bob. "He couldn't leave it on the road or risk carrying it down to the river by Symington. If he knew something of Warrielaw he might well hope that she would not be discovered for some time on the premises. And the very fact of her being found there would increase the puzzle about her movements. It certainly does, you see! On the other hand no ordinary thief, out for what he could get, would fail to search the poor lady's pockets before he put her away. And above all Miss Jessica's character seems to me to make either theory untenable. She's not the sort of lady to be persuaded to leave the train to London, and her suit-case with it, by any story from some chance acquaintance in an odd encounter at Carstairs, and accept a lift home in a stranger's vehicle. Ard admits himself that is a bit farfetched. I'll allow that she may have let the London train go off without her by accident, when she was seen standing on Carstairs Station. No doubt she was absent-minded enough or little enough of a traveller for that. But even if she made up her mind then that there was nothing for it but to go home and start again by the morning train next day, she'd have had three-quarters of an hour to cool her heels at Carstairs. The express arrives there at 10.40 and there isn't a slow train back till 11.33. You don't tell me that she wouldn't have realised the suit-case was missing then, and bothered the whole staff of the station about it. There was a crowd of tourists going off on the same line to Midcalder by a slow excursion, the station-master told me when I was making enquiries last month—some Irish Catholic pilgrimage for Good Friday, you see. But after they were away the station was almost empty: there were only three tickets taken for the 11 33 to Edinburgh she'd have had to travel by. And the one fact I did get clear in my previous enquiries was that there had been no correspondence of any sort about the suit-case when we found it at Euston."

"Still the fact remains," said John, "that in some way or another she was got from Carstairs to Warrielaw on April 13th, alive or dead."

"That's true," said Bob gravely. "But I think we may put all these chance encounters out of the way once and for all if we're to get at the truth, though it's all to the good that Ard should be making public enquiries about tramps. As I see it, Miss Jessica must have been murdered by someone who knew she was travelling with this famous jewel, and was planning to get hold of it. That person must have known that Warrielaw was deserted that day, and I don't admit that even the gossips of a Scottish village would be likely to know beforehand all the several reasons for that coincidence: and the coincidence narrows itself down remarkably. The 11.33 gets back to Edinburgh at 12.31. Unless she took a cab, which was unlikely and would have been seen at the back of the house, she had to journey home by tram and then walk five miles. She couldn't have been back till two, and no local person could expect her then.

"The murderer must have known a great deal. He must have known, I consider, that in Miss Warrielaw's absence no one was likely to go near the tool-sheds. And the fact that the ticket and notes were left on the corpse makes it pretty evident that money was no object for one thing, and for another that whoever did it counted on getting back to cover the traces of the crime a little more effectively. No one could do that but some person whose presence at Warrielaw would arouse no comment of any kind, we can be sure of that. As a matter of fact, owing to Miss Mary's illness and to John's orders about the lodge, no one had the chance. The old woman of the lodge got her daughter in and her daughter brought a pack of children who are always in the drive, I'm told. No one would have dared to get round to the stables lest they'd be noticed, except indeed one of the women about the place. And not one of them could have moved the body alone."

"What you're implying", said John slowly, "is that it was someone very nearly connected with the family who was responsible?"

"It might be," said Bob equably. "Anyhow let's go through our papers here and mark off the people who can't be suspected. You see, in my earlier investigations I got hold of a good few facts about the 13th of April. First of all there's Miss Mary and Miss Macpherson. They certainly did walk seven miles to Erleigh, lunch there at one o'clock and walk home. I got that as precisely as you could wish from General Wise, who is a methodical gentleman, and agreed with me that you can't trust a lady's memory for dates. He had wished to send Miss Mary home in the carriage, but the vet. was over, looking at one of the horses, so he couldn't. I checked that up from the vet's ledger."

"And Effie and the other girl, Annie?" asked John.

"Yes. The district nurse vouched for Effie's presence at the confinement all the night of the 12th April and all morning on the 13th. Mr. Hay's master was going into Edinburgh about two o'clock, and she couldn't have got to Warrielaw by tram and then taken a five miles' walk afterwards to Warrielaw before 4.30, as he only dropped her at the West End at three o'clock. Annie has an even better alibi. She made the breakfast and took the children to school in Bathgate. She waited about for them there till 12, but when she went to meet them there was a difficulty. She seemed so odd in her ways that their teacher kept her waiting while she went to find out about the girl. The headmistress remembers because, when she was free, she vouched for Annie, as a note from the nurse had explained that Mrs. Hay was laid up. They remembered all the more clearly because Annie was very angry at being kept waiting for over half an hour, and all the teachers agreed they would never trust the girl in the house with a new baby. No, the other movements I have still to discover on that day are Mr. Logan's. It may be very difficult for him and for us to account for them."

"But his car's an Argyle," I broke in, "and it was a Lanchester I saw!"

"Betty!" said my husband, "it's a mistake to provide excuses when there has been no accusation!"

"And besides that," continued Bob imperturbably, "I want to hear a little more of Mrs. Murray's movements. You haven't been quite explicit about them, you know, Mrs. Morrison!"

I glanced appealingly at John, but he shook his head.

"That was my own impression, too, Betty. You'd better tell us the whole story from the beginning."

There was no help for it and I pulled myself together.

"First of all," I said, "it's perfectly true that Cora said she had come to get hold of Annie. As a matter of fact, John, your mother happened to tell me next day that Cora had been sending one of her maids away at a moment's notice. She's a byword for quarrelling with her servants in Edinburgh. And I wasn't in the least surprised at her wanting to get Annie because, you know, she always wants to know what is going on at Warrielaw. I admit that she seemed dreadfully upset, but I thought that was because she realised Miss Warrielaw had really gone to London with the jewel."

"But why", asked Bob, glancing at his notes, "should she have taken at least a quarter of an hour, and possibly three-quarters of an hour, to look for a servant who obviously wasn't there?"

"She did something else. That was what she came to tell me to-day. She went there to look for some correspondence of her own which had fallen into Miss Jessica's hands. I don't want to tell you what it's about, but I do assure you it had nothing to do with the jewel, or Miss Jessica herself."

"I expect I can guess what it was," said John. "I know something about Cora's correspondence from Miss Jessica herself. But what had it to do with you?"

"She must have realised that I noticed she came out of the house with her little red handbag simply bursting with papers or something! I think I did comment on it, and I know when the search for the jewel began I did wonder about it a little, John, and wonder, too, if I should tell you. But I couldn't believe she'd really stolen it, and I couldn't bear to let you in for the scandal in Edinburgh if you felt you must charge her with the theft and it was all my imagination. I made up my mind I'd wait till she came back from Cannes and charge her with it myself if the jewel hadn't turned up. I knew, you see, that anyhow it was safe with her. She was almost the only one of the family who could be trusted not to sell it or lose it."

"I say, John," broke in Dennis boyishly, "you haven't got Betty very well in hand yet! Of course she should have told you!"

I could see by John's expression that I should hear the same opinion from him later on, but Bob's manner was unchanged as I turned to him.

"Anyhow," I said, "I'm quite clear of one thing. She couldn't possibly have been into the stables or near them while she was at Warrielaw. You see, that path through the rhododendrons from the formal garden comes out by the stable gates and no one passed through them while I was sheltering at the lodge.

I was sitting near the window all the time, for it was so dreadfully stuffy, and I couldn't have helped seeing her. And when I got to her car it was all in perfect order inside. It's absurd to think it could possibly have been used to bring—to bring a corpse in! Why, there was a cream rug on the seat which was so fresh and immaculate that I noticed when her red bag left a mark on it. It was wet and some of the pink dye came off, I remember, and it looked so queer because the wrap was so tidy and perfect."

"Why was her bag wet?" asked Bob.

"I suppose she'd been in the gardens in the rain looking for Effie or Annie. How could Cora possibly be suspected of having done the sort of thing that happened, for a moment? Why, she's so slight and delicate, and Miss Warrielaw ..."

"That's all very well, but there's always the possibility of collusion," was Bob's comment. "When can we get at Mrs. Murray, John?" John went to the telephone and came back shrugging his shoulders. Mrs. Murray was out in her car for the day.

"All for the best really, however," he said. "We'll go round when Charles has come back from his office this evening. He's the only person to get any sense out of her."

"The police will be here to take their evidence this afternoon," said Bob. "I'll be here then, but I'd like to come with you to your office now and see how affairs stand with regard to the Warrielaw estate. I should like to know exactly who will benefit by Miss Jessica's death and to what extent. I must get down there again and look round tomorrow, but there are a good many jobs here today. It's a tiresome enough place to get to, I must confess."

"Look here, Sir," said Dennis, jumping up, "I want to ask you. Will you let me be your chauffeur and run you about? I've always been specially interested in your kind of work—and—and I'm specially interested in the whole of this story, you know."

Bob accepted willingly. He had not yet had time to purchase a car or learn to drive since he came into his money, and Dennis looked as if he had been appointed General of some military staff. John also applauded the scheme.

"And take Betty with you as much as possible wherever you go. Every gossip in Edinburgh will come to see her or ring her up in the next few days. Oh yes, Betty, I know you'd mean to be discreet, but you'd be no match for their ingenuity and experience in ferreting out a scandal. Go out with the car as much as you can, and if Dennis's Renault falls to pieces he can use our Albion."

It is curious to discover how the things one dreads in anticipation pass by easily, and the unexpected can prove so overwhelming. I was terrified by the prospect of giving my deposition to the police, and Dennis was not much better, but in the end it resolved itself into telling my oft-told tale to two pleasant, sensible men with notebooks, who made little or no comment save the inevitable Hmhm. We had only to give the facts and pursue their implications no further. But what was worse, far worse than I expected, was the sight of Charles Murray's face when he appeared unexpectedly just after dinner. From his worn looks and dragging step I could only realise, as John took him to the library, that the Warrielaws' tragedies were not yet over.

John's face confirmed the view when he joined us. We had persuaded Bob to dine with us, and Dennis and I sat on over the dessert plates and glasses, waiting interminably for news from the other room. That it was as bad as possible was clear when at last the front door slammed behind Charles and John joined us. Cora was ill, dangerously ill. That at least was the report to be spread in Edinburgh. She had spent the day driving out alone, no one knew whither, and returned at five o'clock. On her way upstairs she met the housemaid, Annie, who was just starting out in her best clothes for her afternoon out. Suddenly and inexplicably she lost her temper utterly with the girl. The other maids heard her voice raised in passion, and the butler was called upon to produce Annie's wages, with which she was turned out of the house at once by Cora herself. Then Cora had locked herself into her room, and Charles had got back from the office to find his household debating whether they should break in her door and try to stop her terrible moans and cries. Charles made his entry and sent for the doctor: the doctor rang up Lisle, the famous nerve specialist, at once, and now Cora was lying in charge of two nurses, shut off from all communication with the outside world, by Mr. Lisle's most stringent orders.

"And of course Charles is knocked out by this," added John. "She's been in this man's charge before, you see. She went absolutely out of her mind both before and after she had her one child, which was born dead. They've always warned Charles that he must guard her from any shock. As he says, it's the devil's own luck that she should just have got back here when this discovery was made. She wouldn't have felt it so much if she'd been at a distance."

"Then the police can't get at her for her evidence?"

John shook his head.

"Charles brought me a certificate from Lisle that she could only be approached at the gravest risk to her reason, if not to her life, for the present. Poor old Miss Jessica would boast that there really was something in the curse of the fairy jewel as far as you are concerned, Bob. You can't get hold of Miss Mary or of Mrs. Murray for the moment!"

"I must get hold of this queer maid of theirs some time," said Bob thoughtfully. "We must get her address at Warrielaw to-morrow. But her alibi on the 13th is too sound for us to expect anything much from that. Well, well, something may turn up at Warrielaw to-morrow and Ard may lay his hands on a suitable burglar after all. That scare of a burglary in February seems more significant to him than it does to me at present, but I may be in the wrong."

Dennis was so far recovered from the first shock of the discovery that he spent the rest of the evening in searching the history of our favourite detective hero, to discover if he had ever made a similar admission.

CHAPTER VIII
A BOX OF CHOCOLATES

IT WAS BY Bob's urgent request that I shut my eyes as we approached Warrielaw next morning, and turned my thoughts resolutely from any agonising comparison between the beauty of the beech trees in their early radiance, or the smiling serenity of the old house in the spring sunshine, and the ghastly circumstances of Miss Jessica's death. Bob was insistent that I must live over again the thoughts and events of the 13th of April, in the hope that some forgotten detail might come back to my mind. But I fear that all his good advice was forgotten as we drew up to the house, for at the open door stood Effie, engaged in conversation with Rhoda Macpherson.

I had not seen Rhoda since the news of the tragedy, and I was shocked though hardly surprised to realise that it had not changed her appearance in the least. She was prim and neat and composed as usual, but from the glare of those Warrielaw eyes set so strangely in her commonplace, pale little face, she was evidently very angry.

"Mr. Stuart!" she said abruptly, with sublime indifference to the terms on which they had parted, "I'm glad to see you. I really think you, as John's representative, should put Effie in her proper place. She not only refuses to let me go up to see my aunt or even consult with the nurses. She has the impertinence to refuse to admit me to my own grandfather's house."

"That's no fair, Miss Rhoda!" Poor Effie did not share the Warrielaw heartlessness. Her face was drawn in sharp, new lines, her colour faded, and every word and movement showed her age for the first time. "I'd no let you up to your Auntie for the doctors and nurses said she mustn't be disturbed, and she's been so worried of late when she heard you below at all. But I've let Miss Alison upstairs to see the nurses for you; she's aye so douce and soft-spoken that she can do no harm. And I'm no denying you the house, but the police themselves was saying last night that no one was to go into Miss Jessica's room for the present. They'd have locked it if there had been a key and they're sending a man to sort it this morning."

"That would be the regular procedure," said Bob, regarding Rhoda regretfully. "Though there'd be no harm, of course, if you cared to come up with me and just let me make a note of anything you wish to take away with you."

Rhoda stood considering the question for a minute. "No," she said without a word of thanks. "I don't want to take anything, you see. I only wish to see that nothing is taken and everything is put away in order. If the police are to lock up the room it can be left as it is for the moment, I suppose."

There was a step on the stair and Alison descended it, looking, as Dennis said afterwards, like a fairy who had been badly caught in a storm. She was pale and her eyes were still full of terror, but they brightened when she saw Dennis.

"The nurses have no better news than Effie," she said to her sister. "But the day nurse does agree with the doctor that as she's comparatively young and has such a wonderful constitution, she may pull through in the end."

"Did you go and see her?" Rhoda's voice was sharp.

"No, no, they wouldn't let me in her room, Rhoda. You knew they wouldn't let me. It wasn't my fault."

"I see." Rhoda accepted the defeat with an effort at composure. "Well, I must go. Alison, why don't you leave your bicycle here and let Dennis motor you home if Mrs. Morrison doesn't mind? You look so tired and I must hurry because I've got to see the lawyers!"

"And that's a good riddance," grumbled Effie as she led Bob and myself up to Miss Jessica's room. "Suspect here and suspect there! It's those who aren't to be trusted who's always suspecting others, I say!"

"Miss Rhoda does her best to help her aunt though," said Bob casually. He was at the writing-table in the window, looking absently through the drawers, his attention, apparently, far from the large, sombre room.

"That one!" said Effie contemptuously. "It's little help she gives but ordering and managing the nose off a body's face. But she's not been into Miss Mary's room alone since first Miss Mary took to her bed the night Miss Jessica—Miss Jessica went away. It wasn't likely I'd let her when there wasn't a thing safe from her and her mean ways."

I sighed a little impatiently, but in a mirror I caught Bob's warning glance. If Effie wished to talk now he was more than willing to hear her, I gathered, however little to the point her revelations might be.

"She'd an eye for her aunts' jewels and bits of ornaments then?" asked Bob. He was gazing now at the safe in the wall.

"Ma certie, yes, and anything else she could pick up as well. Why, there wasn't a pair of old gloves but she'd find some use for it! The very last present Miss Jessica ever made me she carried off with her. She'd given it to poor Annie, she told me, but it was for a poor woman Miss Jessica meant it, I told her, and that was myself. Every year when Miss Jessica got a new costume and took to her best for everyday she'd hand on her last year's second-best costume to me, and that was how I could put by a bit wages for my old age, and help my niece Ellen now and again, and her all cluttered up with her weans. But that didna matter to Miss Rhoda; she didna heed that. She carried off the hat and coat Miss Jessica had laid out for me without a word good or bad for me."

Bob was at the dressing-table now, looking through the small drawers, but he turned and put Effie through a long and, I felt, pointless catechism about the habits of the two sisters. Every spring, it appeared, the sisters went to their little dressmaker in Edinburgh and bought themselves new costumes. In solemn state Jessica would order a black skirt, blouse, coat, Inverness cloak and hat, while Mary bought herself the same articles in those unhappy shades of beige and grey which made the worst of her complexion. These were the state and Sunday garments of the ladies for the coming year, and they had only been purchased a week before the accident. On their arrival the best skirts and jumpers of last year were solemnly degraded to everyday wear, and the everyday clothes of the year before were passed on, by Jessica to Effie, by Mary to some poor retainer of Rhoda's. In Jessica's case they were a handsome gift, since for gardening she kept also a wonderful assortment of antique tweeds of every colour, and as nearly every day was devoted to her garden, her black second-bests were in excellent repair. Jessica had packed her braw new things, said Effie: she had travelled in her everyday outfit and left out the black hat and cloak she was discarding for Effie. And by the time Effie went to look for them, early on April 14th, when she had time to remember them, the day after the upset, Rhoda had spirited them away. "'There's many needing them more than you, Effie,' says she to me, and I was fair put to it not to let her know what I thought of her."

"Did she take off Miss Mary's old clothes too?" asked Bob.

"No fears! Ever since Miss Mary was took ill she'd told the nurse she wouldn't have Miss Rhoda interfering with her room or hunting among her things. Miss Rhoda was always saying she must sort her cupboards and put her things in order, but then Nurse, who's an awfu' genteel sort of body, would just put her off and persuade her out of the room. Miss Rhoda's so tidy and neat, you see, and Miss Mary keeps her things in a dreadful state, and Miss Rhoda's always been at her about it. Dear, how she's managed the poor lady since she was a bairn of seven! But she couldn't get past Miss Jessica!"

"No, Miss Rhoda does not seem a lovable character," said Bob absently. "What is it, Mrs. Morrison?"

I must have started violently, for, as I stood looking down on the drive, a sudden breeze blew my handkerchief out of the front of the car, where it lay forgotten, into the long grass and wild hemlock which grew, untouched by scythe or roller, up to the very edge of the gravel.

"Mr. Stuart!" I cried breathlessly. "I've just remembered something—something which might be really important!"

It was only at this moment that I recalled the scrap of paper which had blown from the car in the back drive on April 13th. Bob said afterwards that it must have been the first moment at which I had really set myself conscientiously to reconstruct the past, but I fear it was the accident to my handkerchief rather than deliberate concentration which suggested the incident to me. He listened to my story in silence and together we left Effie and hurried into the drive.

"It's not likely that the paper's still there, and it may be of no importance, remember," said Bob.

But his eyes were keen and his step quick as we went round to the stable-yard. A policeman was called from the back gates to serve as witness if we found anything, but Bob's warning had discouraged me so thoroughly that I felt it out of the question that the paper should still be there. Then, as Bob pushed back the broken lattice, and we saw a dusty envelope within, I imagined with a leaping heart that the Warrielaw mystery was solved outright. My hands trembled as Bob took up the paper carefully with gloved hands and we all peered over his shoulder. On the envelope was scrawled, in an uneducated hand, the words:

Miss McGully,
        Rose Cottage,
                by Harburn.

"Ever heard of that name?" Bob asked the policeman.

The man shook his head. He went off to the lodge to make enquiries if any tradesmen of the name were known there, and Bob went in at the kitchen door to ask Effie. We had no particular hope of any information, and Alison, whom Dennis had fetched from the gardens, had no suggestion to offer.

"Let's all go and find Rose Cottage at once!" my brother cried joyfully. "We'll get a spot of lunch on the way and have a day's outing. Come on, Betty! Come on, Alison!"

A glance at Bob Stuart convinced me that he did not altogether favour the suggestion.

"Rather a large party," he said drily. "However, if you and Miss Alison would like the drive, you could take a little walk on the hills when we find the place. Perhaps Mrs. Morrison will come and make the visit with me?"

Dennis the lover and Dennis the detective were evidently torn in two, but the lover triumphed. "Splendid!" he said. "And you can tell us about it afterwards!"

It was a long and cold drive south towards the Pentland Hills, and I grew sleepy after lunch in a wayside inn, but Bob's attention never wandered as we drew near the moors which lie on the high land by Harburn Station.

"I've seen it," he said quietly, "a wee way back. Mrs. Morrison, will you come with me? Mr. Dennis and Miss Alison, you should walk away up over yon hill. It's a fine view."

Bob and I walked back slowly along the road which stretches on one side of the wide rolling moors. The sun was shining, the air cold and fresh as the song of the larks rising from the tough tussocks of grass, and I asked him how he had noticed the cottage when none of the rest of us had even begun to look for it, a whole mile from Harburn.

"It was that 'by'," said he. "That showed me it was outside the place one side of the village or the other."

"But why expect it on the main road?"

"But of course it would be," said Bob in surprise. "And then I noticed two or three big bushes of briar roses by the wall, and there was a bairn in the porch with her foot up. So I was just expecting to read 'Rose Cottage' on the gate."

The shoots of the briar roses were fresh and green, and bees were humming in the wallflowers outside the little white cottage with its prim slate roof. In the porch, as Bob had observed, a child sat with her knitting, her foot up on the opposite bench. As Bob clicked the gate, a dog barked, and a broad, pleasant woman came to the door, wiping her hands and turning down the sleeves of her dress.

"And hoo's the wean?" asked Bob pleasantly. "She's been in the trouble on the road I jalouse?"

"Were ye enquiring about her accident?" asked Mrs. McGully suspiciously.

"Not so much that as about a driver who's been making a nuisance of himself the last month," said Bob. "There's a lad with a motor lorry ..."

"Ah weel, that's no affair of mine," said Mrs. McGully triumphantly. "It's eight weeks come Thursday since my Jeanie hurt her foot. And the gentleman driving the car was no lad but a real gentleman, aye he was that. For after a' it was the lassie's ain fault and she's had her lesson."

"Was she playing in the road then?" asked Bob. "She was that indeed. There she was jerking up and down with her rope never heeding the car and the gentleman hooting like one dementit. I ca'd to her, 'Get back, Jeanie,' I called, but she just ran this way and that like a silly hen, and just as the gentleman stopped dead, down she fell into the ditch, screetching; she'd twisted her ankle right over and broken it with an awfu' knock on a stone too, ye see, but, mercy me, it was a fair wonder she'd escaped alive. The car hadna touched her, but with the fricht and the pain she lay as if she were gone, and the gentleman jumps out and picks her up while I just stood staring, and he carried her ben the hoose as if she were a princess. Her father had come across frae the field by this time and he said straight out it was the bairn to blame, but not a bit of it, says the gentleman, and out he takes two five-pound notes. 'I'm sair driven,' says he, 'for I'm hurrying to Carstairs, and dinna want to stop for any formalities, if ye'll accept this as compensation. And I'll ring up the doctor frae the station,' says he, and he made me write down the address. And he didna forget the doctor for he was round within the half-hour, and sorted the bairn's foot, and a week later what comes but a box of chocolates as big as that kist for the wean? Aye, and the postman was fair amused, for the gentleman hadna made much of my writing. 'Mrs. McCully, Home Cottage', he'd written on the wrapper and there it is yet on the shelf, for my wee Jeanie was quite taken up with it all."

"Ah, the man I'd got my knife into was a dark little fellow with an Irish way of speaking, no what you'd call a gentleman," said Bob, as Mrs. McGully hunted in a blue vase from Dundee on the dresser, to find the sacred relic among nails and pencils and bits of string.

"Ma certie, no. He was tall and broad and verra elegantly dressed, fair too, with a mincing English way of speaking. Noo where's yon bit of paper gone? We've had it here for weeks, for as luck would have it the sweeties came on April 16th and that was her birthday. Aye, it was three days before that that she took her bad ankle."

"Ye'll be more careful anither evening, Jeanie," said Bob genially, turning to the child.

"Na, na, it was the forenoon. The ither weans were awa' to school, and it wis but half-past ten or a little past by the time the doctor came and wee Jeanie was to bed."

"And he drove carefully enough on his way home past this house, I'm thinking, Mrs. McGully, after that fright in the morning?" said Bob.

"That I can't tell, Sir, for we none of us saw him. He may have passed the cottage when we was to dinner, for before that the boys were wild to see his car—or when I took a wee rest wi' Jeanie afterwards when the bairns were awa' again. Aye, here we are! I knew it was some place!"

Bob took the paper wrapper and handed it to me. I gazed at it mechanically, for by this time I knew only too well what to expect. The address, with those errors which occurred so inevitably since the paper was blown out of the car and had lain useless in Warrielaw stable-yard, was written in the bold artistic hand of Neil Logan.

"Better say nothing about this to the others," said Bob when he followed me into the road. I had stumbled out, leaving a shilling in Jeanie's hot little hand, with a sense of utter bewilderment and despair. "I've got the bit of paper. Heaven forgive me for making the excuse that I'd send the lassie another box, but I had to have it."

"You can send her a box though," I said stupidly.

"Of course I will, but it's hard to take advantage of a man's kind action like this."

"It wasn't Neil's car," I repeated. "His is an Argyle. It can't have been Neil on the road to Carstairs on the morning of April 13th. I can't believe—Oh Bob, I can't believe all it might mean."

"We can tell nothing till I've been to the garage. Anyhow don't speak of it yet to the others, or anyone but your husband, Mrs. Morrison."

"How did you guess about the accident and all that?" I asked, to regain some composure as Dennis approached us.

"It would likely be something like that to make a man stop to take such an address in a car of that kind," said Bob. "That was why I knew it would be on the main road too."

Alison and Dennis came back in high spirits. The fresh keen air of the hills seemed to have swept away the horrors of the last few days for the moment, and Bob parried their questions wonderfully well. He left us at the West End, while Dennis and I took Alison home. Dennis insisted on going indoors with her and was punished for it. For Rhoda was sitting at her ugly desk in her dark corner in the very darkest of tempers.

"I've been writing to your husband," she said to me. "I shall have to come and see him again about the terms of this preposterous will."

Only the evening before, in absolute privacy, poor Jessica's remains had been laid in the family vault; only Charles Murray, John and Effie had stood beside the grave with the old minister, for Rhoda had absented herself. It seemed hardly gracious to learn that she had already discovered the terms of the will, or already found an occasion for a fresh dispute. Still it was clear, I must admit, that Jessica had not left affairs in such a state as to endear her to her sister or to her niece. It was twenty years before this date that old Mrs. Warrielaw died, leaving the house and estate so vaguely to Jessica and to her sister Mary after her. The husband who predeceased her had left the estate encumbered with some mortgages through sheer careless extravagance, but there had never been, as John told me on my visit to Warrielaw, any reason for that grinding economy which Jessica had exercised. The net result was that out of an income of £4,000 a year, she had saved in twenty years no less than £30,000: to that, by the sale of historic jewels and pictures and furniture, she had added some £20,000. And all this £50,000 was left to Neil unconditionally. I was sitting well back in my chair so that I trusted Rhoda did not see the shock this news gave me. It seemed as if the opportunity and motive alike for the murder of his aunt had been made clear this afternoon.

Rhoda's anger did not rest here. Over the estate, of course, Jessica had no control. That passed in trust to Mary, but Rhoda had never apparently recognised that Mary was powerless, save for any savings she might now make in her lifetime out of the estate, as Jessica had done. The family had repeated among themselves so often that the entail was broken, that its younger members, like Rhoda, failed to recognise that the trust was equally binding. When Mary died, and no one could imagine that her life would be prolonged indefinitely, the whole estate of Warrielaw would pass to the four surviving heirs of the whole family of the late Warrielaw sisters, to Cora, Neil, Rhoda and Alison. Miserable as I was I could not conceal a smile at the thought of those four settling down all together at Warrielaw for life. The place would have to be sold unless, indeed, Cora bought out the other three and settled in the family property: she was the only one who could afford it. And meanwhile the legal firm newly appointed by Mary and Rhoda herself, finding that Mary's income justified some of the extensive repairs needed on the tumble-down estate, were about to send down plumbers and gardeners, bricklayers and painters to set to work on any portion of the house which did not disturb Miss Mary. Every joint needed pointing, every inch needed weeding, every pipe needed mending, so their task would not be difficult. And poor Rhoda would have to watch Mary's income dissipated before her eyes, to improve a place she could never hope to inherit, passionate as was her love for the family home. She did not admit so much to me openly, but I am convinced that she really had imagined always that Mary would be free to make her her heir if only she succeeded to Warrielaw.

I looked away from Rhoda's staring, angry eyes round the room. Edinburgh is one of the few places which can invest the shabby genteel with a certain charm. Socially speaking, Comely Bank Acre was outside the pale, but the little, low stone houses were well built, and the mouldings of the ceiling, the old mantelpiece and high bow grate gave the room a dignified air. It showed equal and distinctive traces of Rhoda and Alison. To the elder sister it owed the cheap furniture, the ugly, serviceable carpet and oppressive neatness: to the younger the inexpensive, pretty cretonnes and bowls of tulips and wallflowers. From such rooms in that demure neighbourhood generations of decayed gentle people had looked out, from behind their window-curtains, on a world which had passed them by. To Rhoda with her love for Warrielaw on one hand,

and her longings for a new life in New York on the other, it could only seem mean and uninteresting. For the first time I felt a little sorry for her, ungracious and vindictive as she was.

"Where have you been?" she asked suddenly. "I expected Alison long ago."

"We went for a long drive in the country," I replied evasively. Alison looked uncomfortable, for Bob had suggested that she should mention the events of the day to no one, not even her sister.

I very much doubted if the warning would have any effect.

"Well, I hope this Mr. Stuart was doing some work while you were having your joy-ride," said Rhoda, and I noted her assumption with relief. "Surely the person they should get at is Cora, as I hear that she was at Warrielaw on April 13th. I expect this illness of hers is all a blind. It's so easy to produce a nervous breakdown with an unsuspecting husband like Charles!"

"Mr. Lisle would hardly be taken in," I said.

"And what's all this I hear about her dismissing Annie?" Rhoda had evidently made herself thoroughly at home in the affairs of the Murrays. "The butler told me when I went to enquire that she simply turned the poor girl out into the streets. There must be something behind her extraordinary behaviour in engaging her as she did and getting rid of her like this. Cora is almost mad, that's quite clear. She really is an impossible woman."

"All Warrielaws are impossible," was the phrase that crossed my mind, but I captured Dennis and left the house without disgracing myself. I could really hardly spare a thought for Rhoda till I knew what had happened about Neil.

By that evening we knew that the very worst had happened. Bob had found from the books of the garage that Neil's Argyle was undergoing repairs from April 10th to April 17th. On April 13th he had hired a Lanchester car and left the garage in it at about nine o'clock, returning it at eight o'clock that evening. All that could be said in his favour was that the garage reported that the car was, as far as they remembered, quite unstained and in good condition. Bob went on, however, inevitably to report his discoveries to the police, and the Chief Constable took so serious a view of the affair that they sent men with a warrant to open and search Neil's studio. At the back of a shelf in a wall cupboard, stuffed into an old tin of tobacco, they found a small parcel wrapped in tissue paper. It was the fairy jewel.

The police wired at once to headquarters in Paris. Neil's address was unknown to us, but he was traced easily through the Salon where he was exhibiting a picture. A telegram came through that he was apparently preparing to return home and would be carefully watched. That was on Monday afternoon, June 4th. On Tuesday evening he crossed from Calais, and Scotland Yard officials shadowed him on his way to London. A message reported from the Grosvenor Hotel that his luggage had been labelled for Edinburgh by night express of the North British Railway, and that he would be watched on his journey on the night of Wednesday, the 6th of June. The Edinburgh police were instructed to await him at his studio on his arrival on Thursday morning to ask for a statement as to his doings on April 13th. If he refused this, the authorities had decided that there was sufficient evidence against him to justify them in issuing a warrant for his arrest for theft and for the murder of Jessica Warrielaw.

CHAPTER IX
THE ARREST OF NEIL LOGAN

THE TELEPHONE bell rang persistently on Saturday morning, as we sat at breakfast.

We had been up very late the night before, for John, three days previously, had been rushed off to a client in London and had heard little of our news. Bob had outlined the case against

Neil with such terrible accuracy and precision that his guilt seemed assured to me. And then, directly afterwards, he astounded us by remarking that he thought the authorities were acting with undue precipitancy if they arrested Neil.

"I don't like the fellow," said John slowly. "I never did, though I'd have found it hard to believe he would really murder the old woman. He made no secret of disliking her, and that will be against him, of course. Really, Bob, I can't see that we can refuse to accept facts, and every one of them points to the conclusion that he did it."

"Oh no," said Bob, "there are some very loose ends. We can't apparently doubt that he was motoring to meet her by the London train at Carstairs, but we haven't a shadow of evidence to show that he brought her back alive, or dead. If he killed her on the road and put the corpse in the car he was a very neat-handed murderer. I've hunted every inch of the Lanchester and there isn't a trace of a stain. If he persuaded her to return and murdered her at home, he's responsible for as cunning a crime as one could devise. Only why ruin it all by advertising himself to the McGullys, and hiring a car so as to give the impression that he was trying to disguise himself? He didn't use his name, of course, but I traced him with the utmost ease at Mackie's in Princes Street. The young lady remembered the incidents, and remembered the gentleman perfectly, and another young lady had mentioned he was the artist Mr. Logan. Anyone who'd lived in Edinburgh all his life and dressed so conspicuously, must have known that would happen. And if it was the jewel he was after, why on earth didn't he take it to Paris with him and dispose of the diamonds there? It's unreasonable for a person to murder his aunt for the sake of a jewel, and then leave it lying about in an old tobacco-tin!"

"But I don't imagine it was for the jewel he murdered her," said John. "Much more likely they got in a fury with each other, and he pushed her over violently and finished her off afterwards. That's the sort of thing that might happen to any two Warrielaws left alone together."

"That's possible, of course. You mean he only made use of circumstances as he found them? And that they happened to be as extraordinarily convenient for him as they were? But for Mrs. Morrison's glimpse of the car and that tell-tale bit of paper, of course we might never have got on his tracks after such a long interval of time. But he couldn't have been sure he would have seven weeks to the good! She might have been found next day and then the fact of his driving out to Carstairs might easily have leaked out."

"Certainly he was never anxious to have her looked for," said Dennis.

"No. Only Rhoda insisted on that. But it was Neil who had everything to gain when her death was proved."

"He could wait for some months," said Bob. "The longer the better for his own safety. He knew that the cabman would prove she had really left home on the 13th."

So we had sat up, puzzling over the affair, and I had prolonged matters by returning again to Cora's bag. I had wronged her by suspecting that she had got hold of the jewel, but was her story about the letters true, or had the bag contained some clue which might have helped us? It was obviously essential that Cora's deposition should be made as soon as the doctors would allow; it, certainly before any news of the arrest reached her. That there might be collusion between Neil and Gora was probable, and Cora's doings must be submitted to a far closer scrutiny.

Dennis introduced the question of the weapon, which had by this time an unholy fascination for him. Already the puzzle was beginning to make the horror fade for him. But over the weapon Bob was not encouraging. Warrielaw had been searched again and again, save indeed for Mary's room into which entrance was forbidden, and nothing in Neil's studio had been found remotely resembling the handle of that sharp short point. We went to bed at an impossibly late hour, and when the telephone bell sounded in the room our nerves were so badly on edge that I ran to answer it as if the police were coming to arrest us all at once.

I took the receiver off sharply, listened for a minute and then turned sharply, my hand over the mouthpiece.

"Doesn't Alison know anything about this?" I asked.

"No, how should she?" said Dennis, springing up.

"The longer Rhoda's out of it the better," added John.

"Well, Alison is asking you and me, Dennis, if we'll come round at once to Neil's studio. She got a wire from him last night asking her to go and get breakfast ready for him because he's coming back this morning, and she's there now, wondering why he hasn't turned up. What are we to do?"

"Go!" said John briefly. "He'll be stopped by the police at the North British Station and never get there. Join her and tell her about it somehow, poor child. Of course, if he's a story to tell that will clear him completely, he'll get back in the end, but—" John's pause showed that he hardly felt it worth while to contemplate that possibility.

"Be as quick as you can, in case his old woman has some suspicions, for they've posted a policeman in the square to watch."

So we raced off to St. Mark's Square in anxiety too acute for words. Not even Dennis's skill could suggest the way in which we should try to break the truth to poor Alison.

But that task we were spared. When we reached the studio there was no answer to the bell. In the sleepy square with its silent, decayed houses and prim circular garden, we saw a little group of people and in the midst of them Neil's housekeeper. How much she knew, and how much she suspected, we could not tell, but the frequent visits of the force to the house in the last few days, and the breathless interest aroused by the case in Edinburgh, were enough to make her put two and two together, prematurely but accurately. Only after endless agonised tugs at the bell from Dennis did we hear slow steps on the stairs within, and Alison stood before us with tear-drowned eyes and white face, crying uncontrollably as she saw us:

"Oh Dennis, Dennis! And I do love him so!"

On the low divan to which Alison returned lay a pathetic little heap of paper parcels, from the baker and dairy, and on the table stood a bottle of milk. Alison must have been greeted just after her message by the housekeeper with her suspicions, and had had the heart to do no more. I was pouring some milk out desolately into a cup, trying to persuade Alison to drink some and then come away with us, when a step sounded below. I glanced at the clock. It was ten o'clock, and Neil must have been in the hands of the police since his arrival at 7.30. John, I imagined, must be coming to our rescue, when Alison lifted up her head suddenly as she heard the footsteps and cried:

"It's Neil! It's Neil!"

And a minute later, debonair and casual, Neil walked into his studio.

All his life Neil loved a theatrical effect, and certainly he had one now. For Alison ran into his arms, Dennis sprang up gasping, and I stood as if stunned. Neil gazed at us with a faint frown of surprise, over Alison's shining hair. His ridiculous cape was thrown aside, his hair and dress were as immaculate, his hat and cane and gloves as exquisite as ever. His eyes questioned us whimsically, but his lips smiled unconcernedly.

"But what a welcome!" he said. "There is nothing wanting, except indeed, my dear Alison, some less rudimentary suggestions of a meal! Still I have had tea. I am sorry, by the way, if it is my late arrival which causes this rather excessive display of emotion and surprise. Gentian Borrodaile was on the train—(what a patron flower for a hoyden)—and persuaded me to slip out with her at Berwick, where she had left her car on the way South, and motor home. Her theory was that we should beat the train, but by the time we had roused the garage and stopped every mile to powder Gentian's nose, it proved fallacious. But now will you please explain why I seem to cause you all so much interest? Is it my absence that wins me this unexpected and gratifying display? I must hide myself oftener!"

"Haven't you seen the papers?" asked Dennis bluntly.

"The papers? I never look at the Continental *Mail* or at the London evening rags. Gentian and I have that point in common. We contented ourselves with her comic papers from Germany: they are dull, but more amusing than *The Times*. Why, what has been happening in this hub of the universe?"

"It's Aunt Jessica!" cried Alison distractedly. "She was found dead at Warrielaw on Monday, dead and hidden in a shed seven weeks ago! They found her there, after seven weeks."

The Northern summer light shone down upon the studio and upon Neil who stood inscrutable, in absolute silence for one long minute.

"Do you mean she was murdered?" he asked at last in his slow, drawling voice. "Murdered. But how and when?"

"On her journey to Warrielaw, or at home, on the very day she went South," babbled Alison, silencing us. "Neil! Neil! You'd nothing to do with it?"

Neil did not answer her. He was silent again and then he suddenly turned on me.

"Is Cora's name mixed up in this?" he demanded.

"No—Yes—Well, yes," I stammered. "She's too ill now for anyone to find out what—Oh, it's such a long story and—"

"Well, well, let us have breakfast," said Neil, with a careful assumption of carelessness. "In the midst of death we are at breakfast time. Let us send Mrs. May out for some sausages—plenty of sausages, for I fancy two more guests are arriving—"

It was too late to say any more, too late to try to explain, too late to do anything. The door opened and an inspector, followed by a constable, walked into the room. He looked from one to the other of us and then faced Neil squarely.

"I have to ask you", he said, "to explain to us certain facts in connection with your actions on Friday, April 13th, of this year, and the subsequent disappearance of your aunt, Miss Jessica Warrielaw."

"I am so sorry to be disobliging!" I saw a sudden movement in the hand Neil rested on the table, but to all other appearances he remained unmoved. "But I make it a rule never to tell anecdotes about myself before breakfast."

"Oh Neil!" cried Alison, springing forward, but the constable waved her back. I helped her back to the sofa, and bent over her, while Neil and the police exchanged a few words which escaped me. It was clear that Neil's manner and voice could only exasperate them and I was not surprised when the inspector produced a warrant, and said firmly:

"Then, Sir, I have no choice but to arrest you on the charges of the murder of Jessica Warrielaw and of theft, and I warn you—"

"That we may take for granted," said Neil. "I dislike these legal phrases. I may not wait for a little breakfast? No? Doubtless the State will provide me with that. Must I accompany you? I will put no difficulties in your way. Till we meet again, Alison and Betty! Dennis, so long!"

"Nothing in his life became him like the leaving of it!" The ominous words flashed through my mind as Neil was led away, pale but smiling. Then I had to dismiss all thoughts but those of Alison. The poor child rushed screaming to the door as Neil disappeared with his escort, and ran up and down the studio when the door was shut, like one demented. She had never, I suppose, recovered from the shock of that day at Warrielaw, and now she had lost every semblance of self-control. She turned shuddering from Dennis, and repulsed me fiercely, and implored to be allowed to go home alone. At last, when she collapsed into low, shuddering sobs, she let me lead her away and let Dennis drive us to Comely Bank. Rhoda was out and I insisted on taking her to her room, for the poor child was not fit to be left alone. She passed from one fit of hysterical crying to another, and when I left her to try to warm some soup for her in the little kitchen, she fainted away altogether. When I brought her round she clung to me and implored me not to leave her alone, and then feverishly she began to discuss the whole dreadful question, listening to no word I said, protesting only her belief in Neil. It was seven o'clock before Rhoda returned, and by that time Alison was so near the sleep of exhaustion that I did not mind leaving her in Rhoda's bracing charge. Rhoda herself knew our news by this time though she made no comment on it. All Edinburgh knew it, and the streets, as I dragged myself home, were full of paper-boys, and excited groups discussing the latest develop-ments of the mystery. They meant nothing to me. All I wanted to do was to get home, get John to myself, and talk about anything and everything in the world but the Warrielaws till bedtime. It seemed to me that I must insist on getting away at all costs for some hours from the dreadful story.

But my hopes were futile. During dinner, in Christina's watchful presence, we did indeed keep up some semblance of conversation on other topics, but as soon as we reached the library I realised that yet another sensation had occurred. Bob Stuart was announced as coffee came in, and I was informed that already, that afternoon, Neil had sent for John as his solic-itor, and put the case unreservedly into his hands.

John had done his best to get out of it. He had gone up to Neil, when the police telephoned Neil's summons, deter-mined to make him employ other legal aid. The Morrisons' firm had been almost exclusively devoted to Scottish family interests till John came into it and tried to enlarge its sphere. He had undertaken already a fair amount of Criminal Court work, so that could not be his excuse, but he had had till lately too many Warrielaw interests in his guardianship to wish to undertake this. It was, moreover, his private impression that Neil was guilty, and that he would prefer to keep his hands clean of the affair. A most cogent and obvious reason for his refusal lay also in the fact that Dennis and I would both be called upon as witnesses for the prosecution. Dennis was one of the last people to see Jessica alive: it was through me that the police had discovered proof of Neil's probable guilt.

But Neil, smiling urbanely, would take no excuse. His own story, he said, would dispose of any need of Dennis's evidence or mine. When John had heard it, he could make up his mind what to do. But from John he was determined to hear the whole story of events as they were known to the force at present. Only John could tell him that, he gathered, and he must know what was being said before he appeared in the Sheriff Court next day. All the facts John offered to give at once to any other legal firm Neil liked to name. But at Neil's final plea that family affairs made it essential he should deal with someone who knew all the wretched Warrielaw intrigues and quarrels already, John gave way and undertook the case. I imagine that Neil's charm had already begun to work on my sober husband.

Neil withheld his tale till John had given him every detail of my story of that April afternoon. He had considered it carefully and asked many searching questions—("All that pose of his is only surface, Betty," said John: "he's a very good Scot mind under that silly Bohemian manner.") Then he told his tale, prefacing it with the remark that it was one which could only set a noose round his neck—"if, indeed, nooses are still worn".

Jessica had remained behind us in the studio on the evening of April 12th. She had been even more overbearing, fussy and mysterious than ever. She had raked over all his drawers, she had sent him out to buy newspaper with which to line them. Finally she told him she had chosen him to do an important errand for her. He was to take his car and motor to Carstairs next morning in time to meet the London train, and there she would entrust him with some very confidential and serious negotiations for her. Neil was bored and impatient, but the old lady had just given him a handsome cheque and he was, he

said cynically, inspired by that spurious affection we feel for relations who are about to relieve us of their presence for some
weeks. He promised his attendance and next morning he went
to the garage, found that his car was still undergoing repairs,
and hired a Lanchester instead. He was late already and he
was delayed further by the accident at Rose Cottage and his
promise to telephone for the doctor. When he reached Carstairs the London train had gone. He motored on to Lockerbie, looked up and down the train and saw no signs of Jessica.
He motored back, in a bad temper, at top speed to Warrielaw,
imagining that Jessica must have put off her journey after all.
He approached Warrielaw by the back entrance, as he did not
wish to be run in for repairs to the tyres of the hired car by
the insufferable surface of the front avenue. He rang at the bell,
walked round to the front, looked into the hall and called out,
to get no reply. He went to Jessica's room, which was empty,
and then out into the garden. After searching there in vain he
made up his mind to go, and he finally left in disgust at about
3.30. It was, as he pointed out, quite obvious that his story was
too thin to be believed, but such as it was, it was the truth.

"Well, anyhow, the story about Lockerbie could be ver-
ified!" cried Dennis. "If he really went on there, he'd never
have had time to get back to Warrielaw and do the trick and
get off by 3.30!"

"Seventy-five miles and she'd have got off the train at
12.21," said John, looking at the Murray time table. "He could
have got back with her by three o'clock, I'm afraid."

"What was he wearing?" asked Bob. "A hat and cape?"

"No, just tweeds. I asked him. And he didn't lunch at
Lockerbie or speak to anyone, not even a porter."

"And even if anybody could identify him as a tall, fair gentleman he spoke to some two months ago, it wouldn't clear
him, it appears," said Bob, making a note. "We'll have a look at
Lockerbie though. But it's not much of a story, even if it's true,
and that's a fact."

"Did you think it true, John?" asked Dennis. "He's such a poseur and liar that I imagine—"

"He wasn't posing at all, and I believed him at the time," admitted John, "but I must admit I didn't feel he was being absolutely candid with me about that afternoon. He'd nothing to say about Warrielaw or leaving the house."

"Did you not say Mrs. Murray told you she had some trouble with her car at the lodge gates of the North Avenue, Mrs. Morrison?" asked Bob slowly.

We all stared at each other, as a new light dawned on us.

"Yes," I said, "yes, she did. You mean he may have seen her there? But that was before she went to the house."

"Yes, but if he saw her and passed her, perhaps without a word to her, perhaps just mentioning that no one was at home, and then heard later that she was on the premises that day, mightn't he assume that she'd gone down and found the jewel and walked off with it?"

"But then how did it get into his room?" asked Dennis.

"Well, remember, he knew nothing, according to his own story, of how the jewel got there at all. All he knows is that it was found in a cupboard of his, stuck away in a tobacco-tin. For all we know Mrs. Murray may have been to his studio when Jessica was safely out of the way. He may well think that she stuffed it into one of his drawers, fearing that she'd be found with it on her, and not liking to take it abroad with her."

"But then, surely she'd have told him!"

"She may have. That may be what he wishes to conceal. How does he account for its presence, John?"

"He says he imagines Jessica must have stuffed it into his drawers when she was poking into them. No, by the way, it was I who suggested that. He wouldn't offer any opinion."

"I must get hold of that tin and have a look for finger-prints," said Bob, feeling for his notebook again. "But it's not likely we'll get much out of that. And of course we've no way of getting hold of Miss Warrielaw's."

It was remarks like that which brought the horrible story, in its full ghastliness, back to us again, and we were all reduced to silence.

"What looks worse in the case, of course," said Bob at last, "is that he kept quiet about the jewel when there was all that hue and cry after it."

"But he didn't know he'd got it," I cried.

"If his story is true," repeated Bob.

"You must remember, though," urged John, "that if it's true he's fighting absolutely in the dark. He hasn't seen this thing develop as we have. He comes back to find Jessica murdered and the jewel in his keeping, to hear that Mrs. Murray was seen leaving the house in what to him must seem most suspicious circumstances, to hear that she's too ill for any message to reach her, so that any question of collusion now would be impossible even if he hadn't been arrested. 'It seems to me that Agag must be my model,' he said to me, and I could get no more out of him."

"Well, anyhow, I'm clear of the case now," said Bob, rising. "I've no official status any longer."

"Not at all," replied John. "I said I must employ a detective on his behalf at once, and he declared that he would have no one but you. His point is that you know all that is to be known, and a new man would merely begin to stir the dust up again. 'You can use your influence with him if I have any instructions to give later,' he said. I fancy he thinks that I could persuade you to keep quiet about Mrs. Murray if she becomes involved in any way."

"He's wrong there," said Bob grimly.

"Well, right or wrong, I'm to employ you. When that was fixed he asked how long it would be before the Crown officials would have prepared the indictment. Naturally I said that I couldn't tell him. It seems to me that though the police have suspicion enough to warrant his arrest they can't produce a really convincing case. It depends of course on what sort of evidence, if any, they collect in the next week or so. He is resigned to the fact that they'll bring the indictment, and that he'll have to reserve his defence and appear in the High Court. He is quite willing that I shall retain the best possible counsel for his defence when that happens. I suggested Askew Firle— he's far the most outstanding man—and Neil murmured that any economy in this particular business would be misplaced. He is brave, you know, and one can't help liking him. And he insists that the case must be hurried forward, and that the defence is not to create any delay by prolonging the search for evidence. I urged him then to admit that he was trying to shield someone whom he had reason to suspect, but he merely laughed and told me that heroism was not in his line, but that he wished to be able to smoke again as soon as possible. That will be permitted to me as a free man or a convicted murderer,' he said, 'and till then my life will be hell.'"

Far away in the street below I heard the newsboys shout out: "Late Special Edition!" and shivered to think of the story the papers had to tell.

"Well, I'll do my best for the case," said Bob. "The trouble is that there's so little to work upon. I can't imagine that the police will make anything of the place where the jewel was found. I had a look myself to-day. It's just the sort of cupboard where a man with a huge, untidy studio might overlook a thing for months, or equally well, hide a thing in the hope of concealing it for ever, because the place was so little used and inconspicuous. I shall have to pool my information with the police, you know, if I'm to get anything from them in return. They've let me in to everything so far. But it's hard to see what more direct evidence we can get till we can interview Miss Mary."

John shook his head.

"Physically she's much better, the doctor says. She has re-gained movement in her arm and leg in a way which surprises him. But she hasn't spoken yet."

"When you next go down," said Bob, "you might find out if she could at least be moved from her room soon. I've never had a look round it yet and though it's not a promising spot, should like to cast a glance over it. But of course the really important witness is Mrs. Murray. How is she?"

"She's better. The fever is leaving her, Charles says. But I imagine Lisle will shield her from any questions for as long as possible. At the moment I imagine the police are occupied with the case against Neil."

"Hmhm," said Bob. "Well, as soon as I can make time I must see if I can get anything out of this queer maid of hers, Annie Hope, at Carglin. At least she hasn't taken to her bed yet!"

CHAPTER X
THE WITNESS OF A HALF-WIT

NEIL WAS brought before the Sheriff Court next morning, Friday, June 8th. He refused to make any statement and was remanded in custody. Early that morning Bob ran down to Lockerbie and hunted in vain for any station official or local gossip who could remember any particulars about the London train on the morning of April 13th. The police reported to him that there were no results from the most careful scrutiny of the tobacco-tin. Just after lunch Bob appeared to request Dennis to take him out to Carglin in search of Annie. If, as he said, there seemed little hope of finding out any information of importance there was nothing else at the moment for him to do in Edinburgh. By John's instructions I was to accompany them.

We spread out a map and then for the first time I realised how curiously varied is the country to the south-west of Edinburgh. From the Caledonian Station a branch of the Caledonian Railway and a main road lead through suburbs, under winding hills, to the village of Balerno, ten miles away. There the Pentland Hills rise like a miniature mountain range with lonely crags and valleys, lochs and burns. A mile or so to the north of the village the Erleighs looked from their terraces, across a valley, to moors untenanted save by sheep and curlews. To the west of that country the road, and the main Caledonian line to the South, strike through a country fringed by industry until at Midcalder, seventeen miles from the city, they plunge into a patch of the black shale country, from it they emerge to strike triumphantly southward to the Lanark Moors and the upper waters of the Clyde, by Carstairs to Lockerbie. West of that line country roads from Edinburgh wind out to country places like Warrielaw which lie beneath the menace of the smoke and dirt of industry. And west again the North British line plunges from Edinburgh into the heart of the mining districts which lead to Glasgow, and here in the shadow of the shale pits lies Bathgate, with the little village of Carglin two miles to the north. From Warrielaw, it may be seen, one could walk some seven miles eastwards into the heart of the hills or some ten miles westwards into the dark satanic land of oil and coal on the North British line. Few countries can show a swifter transition.

"I've looked at that map often enough," said Bob, staring over my shoulder. "I can't get over one feature of it, that here on the radius of a rough semi-circle lie Erleigh, Warrielaw, Carstairs and Bathgate with no means of communication between them except by car, unless you get back to Edinburgh first. It worries me badly, that map of the district!"

The road to Bathgate was grim and dull enough, but I was thankful to be out of Edinburgh, and safe from the unceasing telephone and door bells of my house in those dreadful days. From Bathgate we struck northwards and found a little oasis from the shale heaps in a lane overtopped by hawthorn trees. Their scent in the sun obscured every other, and made me realise with a sudden pang that for Neil there were no white highways nor flowering hedges. Behind us lay rows of ugly slate-roofed miners' cottages, but before us a low, white-washed cottage on the edge, evidently, of a private estate.

Larches rose in radiant green behind the house and a garden crowded with polyanthus and tulips in front. Beyond it a long, straight open road led to a little village centred round a square, dull country church. The place seemed asleep in the sunshine, but even as we drew up, and Dennis remarked he must have a good look at his sparking-plugs, a woman came swiftly out of the house. Her hair and eyes were dark, her figure and bearing majestic, and her voice the slow sing-song of the Highlander who learnt English as a foreign tongue. Nothing in Annie's shapeless figure, greasy hair and wide, fat face had ever reminded me of her tinker father. But Ellen Hay, her married sister, proclaimed her descent, and proclaimed also the kinship between the tinkers' clan to which she belonged and the true gipsy race. And all the gipsy's distrust of law and order woke in her glance as Bob said he had come for a few words with Annie Hope.

"She and Jock have never done any harm to anyone," she said passionately, holding open the cottage door to let me through.

I heard Bob reassuring her on the threshold as I went inside. The low room was untidy and crowded enough, but the window was open and every corner was filled with glass jars full of kingcups and cuckoo-pint. Annie knelt by a wooden cradle on the floor, and for a moment, as she gazed absorbed at the baby, I saw in her eyes a devotion as unexpected, and as oddly contrasted with her clumsy personality, as were the wild flowers with the confusion of the cottage. Then she saw me and her face changed altogether. It was not to-day disfigured with tears or grease, and yet I recognised at once that Annie herself had changed for the worse. In February she had resembled a miserable overgrown child: beneath her misery one could discern, however, a simple, willing nature, capable of hard work and tolerable cheerfulness under proper control. We had not in those days taken the problem of such characters into proper consideration, yet it did cross my mind that her bewildering experiences at Warrielaw, and at the Murrays', might have had a bad influence in Annie's life. Her face was set in a sulky frown, her eyes lowered, and her voice was loud and defiant as she rose and said to me:

"If it's about me and my cousin Jock you've come, we've done no harm to nobody."

"Whist Annie!" Mrs. Hay came to her sister's side swiftly. "It's about Mrs. Murray and her putting you away like that the lady and gentleman have come!"

A look of such obvious relief crossed Annie's face that Bob glanced at her meditatively.

"No," he said, repeating the phrase both women had used, "I haven't come about you and your cousin Jock."

"Jock's a real good boy," said Mrs. Hay nervously. She glanced at us in turn as if to discover whether Annie had protested unwisely. "He's been at work on the railway two years now, and he's my own husband's brother. The station-master will answer for him any day, Sir. What was it you wished to ask about Mrs. Murray? Annie was treated very badly there, Sir, very badly indeed. Tell the gentleman about it, Annie."

But Annie grew red and turned to the window stubbornly, and Mrs. Hay told the story in her pleasant, monotonous voice.

She had been against Annie's taking Mrs. Murray's situation from the first, for she'd been in service herself, and who ever heard of a lady motoring up like that in the gloaming and carrying a girl off without a reference and driving her into Edinburgh at such a rate that Annie was terrified, or engaging her for just a week, and then promising her a month's holiday on board wages? Once Mrs. Murray swerved so violently at the sight of a car that she ran right on to the pavement and, altogether, Annie was so upset that when she got to that grand house and the smart Englishfied servants she was terribly put about. The head housemaid set on her at once, and told her to go up and sort Mrs. Murray's room before she dressed for dinner. Annie was but just setting a match to the fire when Mrs.

Murray came in, and stormed at her because it wasn't burning properly. When Annie came up again, after Mrs. Murray was down the stairs to dinner, she found it near out with a pile of papers Mrs. Murray had been burning on it. And on the top of the smoking coals was a wee red bag, blackened and spoilt, but a pretty thing still. And in the waste-paper basket was a little red hat, all crushed up to be thrown away. Annie took the two of them and why not? Who ever heard of a lady wanting her things again when she'd thrown them away or behind the fire? Annie just put them by in her drawer because the poor fushionless lassie aye liked a bit of gay colour. They were no good to her, for the hat was too small, and the bag was locked and the wee key missing, and Annie wouldn't tear it open for fear of hurting it.

It was hard not to betray my interest in this story too clearly, but Bob's face was as impassive as ever.

"We might have had a look at that bag," he suggested.

"But it's no here," said Mrs. Hay. "I've never even set eyes on it. Annie didna bring it back when she came home a week later on board wages, the house being shut and Mr. Murray at his father's. She just left it there with her uniform until she went back there at the end of May. She'd been boasting about it, though, and I told her to cut a slit in the wee hat and wear it, and dangle the bag on her arm for show, even if she couldna open it or use it. Well, back she went, and then Mrs. Murray came home, and the very day after that was poor Annie's night out. She'd dressed herself up in the red hat and was carrying the red bag when she went downstairs at five o'clock. And on the staircase Mrs. Murray met her, and gave her an awful look, and miscalled her and said she was a thief. She dragged the hat off Annie's head, and she dragged the bag from her hands, and called the butler to pay Annie her wages and board wages and put her out of the house. Annie wouldn't even have had a hat if the housemaid hadn't handed her an old straw sailor hat at the area door! They sent on her clothes the next day, but either

Mrs. Murray or the maids had kept the hat and bag, for they weren't in her box. And that's the simple truth, Sir," concluded Mrs. Hay dramatically.

"Why didn't you search the house?" I asked breathlessly, as, after a little inconclusive chat, Bob said good-bye and returned to the car.

"I'd have to get a warrant for that. I'll do so if there's no news of the bag at Moray Place, of course. But I'm inclined to say that they were telling the simple truth."

"Do you think so? I was sure they had something to hide! Didn't you see how relieved they both were when they found we had come about Mrs. Murray, and not about something in which her cousin Jock was concerned?"

"Yes, I noticed that," said Bob. "I'm going to ask Mr. Dennis to stop at the station, and have a word with the station-master about this boy's character and what he was doing in April. But that had nothing to do with the story of Mrs. Murray and the bag. They were unreserved enough about that. Besides, look at Mrs. Murray's behaviour! Their story of that tallied in every detail with Mr. Murray's about the way Annie was dismissed. It's not likely since Mrs. Murray attached such importance to the bag that she'd let Annie go off with it. She wasn't too violent to lose her senses then. She got Annie paid off and saw her out, and she would have seen she got hold of the bag herself. Wait here for me, will you?"

Bob disappeared into the station, and emerged some minutes later with the stout, superior station-master. A dark boy in porter's uniform followed them out of the office, and Dennis and I were agreeing wisely that, though he looked pleasant enough, he had shifty eyes, when Bob climbed into the seat.

But Bob was not interested in eyes. The station-master had given Jock an excellent character, and proved beyond a doubt, with the corroboration of the signalman, that Jock had been about the station all day on the 13th of April. It was impossible to connect him with the murder at Warrielaw. He and Annie had excellent and independent alibis.

"I'm thinking it was that affair in February which was worrying them," said Bob. "In any case, we'll leave them alone till we've found out what we can about the bag from Mrs. Murray."

If Dennis and I felt impatient, and indulged in gloomy anticipations that Jock and Annie would be occupied that evening in destroying the last traces of the scarlet bag, we had to admit we were wrong. Bob got out at Moray Place to interview the butler and rejoined us almost at once.

"The man remembers the incident perfectly," he said shortly. "Mrs. Murray took the bag from the girl and was clutching it when she walked upstairs. I'm going to wait here till Mr. Murray gets in and see if he can get hold of it quickly and will bring it round. Would you mind ringing up your husband, Mrs. Morrison, and asking him to get home as soon as he can."

Dennis had intended to run down and see Alison, but it was out of the question now. Like myself he could only sit in the library, waiting while the clock ticked loudly and slowly. It was a relief to hear John's latch-key, and to tell him the events of the day, but it was impossible for any of us to look forward to the next development in the case. If the contents of the bag threw any light on the problem, it was hard to see how they could exonerate Neil without incriminating Cora, and to all of us was present the haunting fear that the proof which was to confront us, if there were any, would bring two Warrielaws as accessories in crime to their trial.

And then at last the door-bell rang, and Charles Murray and Bob were shown into the library. As we all rose to greet them our eyes were all fixed upon a little parcel in Bob's hands.

"I hope you don't mind my coming," said Charles heavily. "I must know the worst before this gets into the hands of the police."

"It must do that, I fear," said John, glancing at Bob.

"That's unavoidable." Bob stood at the table unwrapping the parcel slowly. "Whether it tells against our client or against Mrs. Murray, we can't keep this dark. Apart from anything else, Mrs. Murray's servants would be talking."

There was something at once trivial and terrible about the little bag as it lay on the table. It had been so gay and useless and pretty when Cora swung it lightly on her wrist in shops and drawing-rooms. It was so blackened and spoilt now; the edges were torn and scratched and there were queer little dents upon it everywhere.

"Her maid tells me that she found it by my wife's bed on the night she was taken ill," said Charles tonelessly. "It looks as if she or Annie had done their best to tear it open and it's strange that they failed. I suppose we can do it now?"

"We shouldn't," said John. "After all, the police …"

"I've got some little keys of that kind," I said, moving to my desk. "I'd so many bags of that sort for wedding-presents and I put the keys away on a ring."

"If only Cora had been so business-like," groaned Charles suddenly. He sat down heavily and shaded his face in his hands.

The lock turned easily enough, and we all stood staring in silence as Bob extracted the contents. Out of the inmost pocket he drew a bit of singed linen. It was wrapped round something and Bob unrolled it with meticulous care. Before us lay a little narrow handle of ivory, some six inches long. At one end it was rounded neatly: at the other was a broken, jagged steel edge.

"So that's the handle of the weapon," said Bob thoughtfully.

"Whatever is it?" asked John.

"It's a handle from a work-case," I said. "It's one of those little instruments you use to pierce holes in the material for *broderie anglaise*. But is that …?"

"Yes, that's what did the murder right enough," said Bob.

"Cora never did any embroidery in her life," said Charles Murray suddenly, after a long pause.

"They did—both the Miss Warrielaws did," I volunteered.

"Yes. Clearly the weapon was snatched up from a basket or bag in the room," said Bob absently. He had taken up the little piece of singed wrapping now and was straightening it out with careful fingers. And as he did so we all saw that the crumpled linen had a hemstitched edging and in the corner were embroidered initials. It was as though all the horror of the last few weeks culminated in that one moment when we made out the twisted monogram of N.L.

Charles was the first to speak. In his voice was nothing but almost unbearable relief.

"So that was it," he said. "She was trying to save him. As you say, Stuart, certainly this must go to the police."

"It must, I agree," said Bob, with, as I thought, a strange absent-mindedness in his voice. "But I'm afraid it means that Mrs. Murray will have to face an interview with the Fiscal as soon as possible. It clears her in a sense of course, but it's possible that, as things stand, she might be arrested as accessory to the crime."

Charles' face, beneath the low light, grew strange and stricken. He seemed to struggle for speech in vain and looked hopelessly at John. But John had little comfort to give him.

"She's better, isn't she, Charles?" he said insistently. "You told me that there really is a marked improvement. I should go to consult Lisle at once, and see if he can manage to consent to her making a statement. It seems to me it's the only chance of saving an arrest. We can hold this up to-night, can't we, Bob? Official hours are over at the Courts, and I think we're justified in leaving it till to-morrow morning. I'll go to see the authorities myself and make it all as easy for you and her as I possibly can."

There are certain undoubted advantages in living in a small and friendly city. Charles, John, the Procurator Fiscal and Mr. Lisle had known each other all their lives, and were each of them willing to be of as much assistance to the other as their duty to their offices allowed. Dennis and I left the house next morning before any definite arrangements were made. We had promised to take Alison down to North Berwick for the day, and though I was too wretched and unsettled to wish to make the expedition, anything was better than to sit at home and think of Charles and Neil and Cora, and wait interminably for news. When we returned that evening, after dropping Alison at her flat, the interview with Cora was over, and Bob and John were sitting together in the library over a pile of notes. They had been putting together the points which would appear in the indictment against Neil in the Sheriff Court, and they were glad, I think, to leave that most depressing task and tell us their story.

It was one to which we could only listen in horror. Bob sat silent, lost in his meditations, but each word John spoke seemed to incriminate Neil beyond hope of redemption.

John and the Procurator Fiscal, to whom Cora was to tell her story, were led up to her room, and there Charles stood on one side of her, and the nurse and doctor on the other. Cora was lying, propped up by the pillows, on the great gilded Florentine bed. She was utterly worn and emaciated and her face was dead white, but the nurse evidently by her orders, had put a gash of red lipstick across her lips and a bright red shawl round her shoulders; on her bedside table was a bowl of red Canna lilies, as if even now she insisted on a last gesture of coquetry to her visitors; but her voice was strained and harsh, and her eyes wandering. All this John saw as Charles introduced the Fiscal. He had naturally to wait outside for his interview and the questions for the defence he had to raise.

Cora was composed enough. She promised indifferently to tell the truth, and the doctor urged them to let her talk without interruptions. She had, she said, gone to Warrielaw on April 13th because she had heard, through Effie, that the house would be empty, and she hoped, she admitted openly, that she might find and take possession of the fairy jewel. She motored down, being delayed at the lodge gates by some trouble with the handle of her car, after stopping the engine by accident, near the lodge. She was in a hurry, therefore, on her arrival and she went straight to the library, where she hoped to find a few old family papers which Jessica had refused to give to her, though she considered she had a right to them. (Charles repeated this later to my husband with no trace of suspicion.) It was just beginning to rain so she went to close the window. Her eye was caught by something white under a rhododendron bush opposite the windows. She picked it up and found it was a handkerchief wrapped round the little ivory handle. Both were stained with blood.

"I can't bear to touch blood," she went on, her face livid but for that scarlet gash across her lips. "Charles knows I never can. So I stuffed them into my bag, though the handkerchief was dripping wet with rain. I was so terrified that I nearly ran out to the car, but by that time the rain had really begun. I got frantic, I think. I thought there must be some dreadful thing somewhere in the house, and I ran all over the place, hunting and crying. And then in Jessica's room I thought of the—the papers, and I found them, in an old despatch-box. I stuffed them into my bag too and ran down and found Mrs. Morrison in my car. I suppose she told you I seemed rather queer. All I wanted to do was to get home and burn everything. But I made up that story about Annie on the spur of the moment as a blind to Betty, and then, as I drove away, I began to think sensibly again—I'd only been in a panic till then—and I saw that I might find out from that stupid girl something about what happened at Warrielaw—and it was quite true, too, that I was shorthanded and had meant to ring up a registry. So I went to Carglin and got Annie, and I suppose she told you the rest. I mean that she hadn't lit my fire properly. Charles tells me that was how you found out about the bag. (No, Nurse, I don't want that medicine. I feel perfectly all right. I'm not tired.) Well, the flames were burning brightly enough to catch the

—the papers as I stuffed them into the fire. I suppose I locked the bag before I threw it in after them, just because I had been feeling all day that it was so important to keep it locked. I don't know what I did with the key, because when I came up again after dinner the fire was burning beautifully and I thought the bag and everything in it was destroyed for ever."

The Fiscal left and John was admitted. He was warned to be as brief as he could. "On June 1st, you got back and found Annie with the bag?" he asked.

"Yes, you know about that! I needn't tell you, need I? I took it from her and tore at it and bit at it to get it open, and then I suppose I dropped it when I fainted, and my maid found it and put it away. I know you've got it now."

"There's just one question I must ask you!" John had received such urgent instructions from Bob to question Cora about one point in my story, and one point in Annie's, that not even that desperate cry could harden him. "We have reason to think you saw Neil's car that afternoon and again that evening. Was that the case?"

"Why do you ask, if you know?" Cora turned and flashed the question at him from her embroidered pillows. "Yes, I saw him pass the front lodge gates on my way to Warrielaw where my car was stuck, and I saw him again that evening on my way home, in George Street. Charles, send them away, please, Charles!"

And with that note of agony ringing in their ears the two men went away.

"And so you see the case for the prosecution is complete now," said John bitterly. "The indictment will damn Neil completely. The case will come before the Sheriff Court almost immediately now, and I've got to go to Askew Firle with this story. It almost justifies him in refusing to undertake the defence. No one could get Neil off now."

"Hmhm," said Bob. It was the longest and loudest he had pronounced in my presence, and the prelude was justified by his next remark.

"It's a queer thing, John, how you lawyers make your living. Here you are condemning Mr. Logan to the gallows when we've just got almost convincing proof of his innocence."

"Proof?" said John sharply. "Of his innocence? What d'ye mean?"

"One point you noticed, I'm glad to see, is Mrs. Murray's story that the handkerchief was dripping wet with rain when she put it into the bag. And it was dripping wet, too, Mrs. Murray said, when she picked it up from the bushes. I looked up the weather reports for April 13th when I first undertook the case, as you never can tell what won't be useful. It rained heavily all the night of the 12th, leaving off at about 12 o'clock next forenoon. From that time onwards there was only that one sharp shower of rain which drove Mrs. Morrison from the stable to the lodge, and kept Mrs. Murray from exploring the garden. By her account that handkerchief was wet before ever the shower began."

"You can't trust anything she says," objected John.

"Not if she's any reason to lie. But have you any reason to suppose that she saw any importance in what she was saying?"

"Not in the least. I don't see any myself."

"Well I do," burst out Dennis triumphantly. "You mean that the handkerchief couldn't have got wet through if it had been thrown out of the window by Neil? Because all the time it was raining he was miles away at Harburn."

"He might have tried to wash the stains off," I suggested.

"In the kitchen?" asked Dennis. "And then brought it back to the library and put the handle in it, and thrown it out of the window? I used to think him a fool, but not such a fool as that."

"But I don't understand," I said. "You say the handkerchief must have been there all night. But Jessica was alive and well next morning!"

"So the handkerchief's no bearing on the case?" said John. "And Cora was simply deceived by the fact that it was lying near the handle? The two things aren't connected with each other? Well, that might be so, but I don't see how that clears Neil. It was his handkerchief after all!"

"It doesn't incriminate him, anyhow," said Bob, his brow wrinkled almost into a horseshoe. "A handkerchief's a very easily movable article, either by accident or by someone who's making a cross trail. There's a lot in this I don't understand. I've got to get hold of all this from the other end. No. I won't talk it over any more, Mr. Howard. I want to keep a clear mind. But what is absolutely essential is this, John. I've got to get down to Warrielaw and hunt every corner again, including Miss Mary's room. You've got to get her out of it and you've got to get me in. I must see that room and I must get into the library with Mrs. Morrison as well, in case any other memory comes back to her."

"It's all right about the room," said John. "I rang up the doctor when you first suggested that, and found a controversy had been raging about it. The nurses wouldn't let Effie give it a thorough clean, and Effie holds that dirt never did a body any good yet, 'stroke or no stroke, and the room hasn't been sorted properly since Miss Mary was ill'. Yesterday the tide was turned, because Miss Mary suddenly moved herself in bed and began to speak. The doctors are amazed, but Hewetson always said she was tough enough to make a sudden recovery and amaze them all. You shall get into the room in three or four days now, though I can't imagine you'll find anything of interest."

"Not if it's been thorough-cleaned first!" agreed Bob. "Make it clear to Effie that I can't find any sign of the devil about after it's been swept and garnished."

CHAPTER XI
EFFIE TELLS HER STORY

IT WAS FROM this moment that Bob Stuart began to work alone in the Warrielaw affair.

Up till now he had shared all his news with us, and until this moment the police had also been entirely in his confidence and handed on to him any information which might help him. Their case was complete now. They could prove motive, opportunity and Neil's presence at the scene of the crime. And they could assume theft, for there, somewhere, in a dark safe in the keeping of His Majesty, lay the jewel brought to middle-earth five hundred years ago, from the palaces of fairyland, to be the ill-luck of the Warrielaws. Cora's evidence was, in their opinion, and in John's also, all that was needed to convict him. Askew Firle, however, accepted the case, and refused to share John's depression. He reiterated to John the axiom that no jury will hang a man on circumstantial evidence unless it fits like a jig-saw puzzle. That much we knew, but naturally we were not allowed to know the result of his professional consultations with my husband. It was Bob's suggestion, we were to learn afterwards, which found most favour in Mr. Firle's sight. The evidence given to them by Cora, which seemed so fatal to Dennis, John and myself, suggested to him the line of defence. From the first he had wondered whether there were any possibilities of proving suicide or accident: the medical evidence depended on the reports of the police surgeon and specialist alone, supplemented by the photographs taken of the corpse. It had seemed incredible that any woman should stab herself to death, even if the blows on the skull had been caused, as was arguable, by a sudden fall. But the discovery of the handle of the embroidery instrument threw a new light on the case. It was apparently the habit of both sisters to pick up their needlework at any moment and work at it standing. Would it not be possible for any woman, and especially an elderly woman, to stumble forwards at a sudden fright, fall upon the point of the instrument she held and, as she fell, knock her head violently upon the fender? As Jessica's head banged upon the fender, her heavy body would strike the ground with such force that the instrument would be driven right home to her heart.

Two doctors were willing to admit the possibility of such an accident, and from this Mr. Firle reconstructed his story. Neil, he would explain, in terms calculated to throw suspicion on all other members of the family, was the only human being trusted by his aunt. She had herself concealed the jewel in his studio, meaning to tell him of her deed when he met her at Carstairs, and to instruct him how to dispose of it. Proofs of her eccentricity were not wanting, nor of her suspicions of her relations. When Jessica failed to find her nephew at Carstairs, she left the train, unnoticed in the holiday crowd, caught the 11.33 to Edinburgh and then took a tram and walked home. She could easily have reached Warrielaw by two o'clock, and from that moment onwards she was alone and unprotected in that vast, solitary house, the prey of any passing tramp or bad character. Witnesses might be called, including Rhoda herself, to show that some such were always in the neighbourhood, though after the lapse of so many weeks the police could find no reliable evidence. As Jessica stood alone at her work in the library she either saw or heard something which alarmed her. She stumbled as she moved hastily (and all of us who knew the library could bear witness that it was easier to stumble over the superabundant furniture than not). At this point Mr. Firle would reconstruct the manner of the fall, and make some scathing remarks on the blindness and haste of the prosecution in making the arrest and bringing the case forward so prematurely. They had assumed murder where no murder could be proved, in his contention. Supposing, therefore, that his theory was correct, Mr. Firle would ask the jury to consider the position of the hypothetical tramp who looked into the library just before or just after the fatal fall. He might have been seen in the vicinity: he would be identified at once if the body were discovered that day. He had done his best, it would appear, to extract the weapon and staunch the wound. The handle had broken in his hand; the lady was obviously past hope. His one idea would be to conceal her till any memory of his own appearance in the neighbourhood of the place had died away. It was absurd to say that the reputation of Warrielaw and the talk about the owners was only known in a small area: for years their odd ways had been the gossip of the countryside. He could surmise from their appearance alone that the stables were an ideal hiding-place, and thither he had conveyed the corpse. How could he, however, under the circumstances, be expected to come forward and clear the accused? It would be only too obvious to him that his own neck would be in danger. No chivalry could be expected from a tramp, but Neil's chivalry, the chivalry of an ancient family well known in Scottish history, was to be displayed by the great advocate in an heroic light. To Mr. Firle, Cora's statement was a godsend. He would make the most of the fact that Neil had seen Cora Murray's car at the gates, that he had suspected her of the theft of the jewel, which was now, all unknown, in his own possession, in the studio where Jessica had left it hidden. For Cora's sake, rightly or wrongly, Neil had kept silence. He was absent when the body of the deceased was discovered: he was unjustly and over-hastily accused of the crime with no certain knowledge of his cousin's position in regard to it. She, on her side, was driven to silence by the memory of seeing his car on that April day. There had been no collusion between them. One word between them, indeed, would have sufficed to enable either of them to clear the other. But circumstances had forbidden it, and Neil was standing on his trial to save his cousin's fair name.

Such was Mr. Firle's case. He accepted Bob's argument about the condition of the handkerchief, but he had no wish to bring it forward till it was forced upon him. The initials on the handkerchief would prejudice the jury against Neil so strongly that he would leave it to the Crown to mention the subject, in the hope that it might not assume much prominence. Dennis and I found the defence unconvincing, and we were not in the least cheered a few days later by the news that Mary would be moved into another room at Warrielaw that afternoon and that Bob could prosecute his search. I was only more depressed than ever when John told me that Mary had expressed a wish to see me and thank me for all my kind attentions. She was physically so much better, though mentally still so inert, that the doctors approved of her wish to see a new face. But I had no wish to go to the hateful house, and I accepted Bob's invitation to go down in his cab rather gloomily. It was from breakfast that I was called to this message on the telephone, and it did not cheer me any more to find Dennis in the hall preparing to fetch his car and go down to persuade Alison to go out with him for the day. I should have been glad to go with them, away from Edinburgh and its busy tongues, away from Midlothian, or indeed Scotland, altogether, but I had to refuse. I must spend the afternoon at Warrielaw and devote the morning to all those household and social duties which continue uninterruptedly even when the life and death of another is at stake.

So it was that I was sitting at my desk in the drawing-room when, to my speechless surprise, Christina opened the door and announced:

"Miss Rhoda Macpherson."

I had hardly seen Rhoda since our visit to her flat; nor had John heard more of her since, on the following day, he had assured her with great severity that she could trust her own legal advisers to protect her interests when the estate was divided at Miss Mary's death. When Rhoda had gone on to enquire about the fate of Jessica's legacy to Neil, he had snubbed her so severely that even she had gone away subdued. Dennis had reported, after his recent visits to Alison, that Rhoda's temper was worse than ever, and she would hardly speak to Alison for days on end. It was the one object of Nurse and Effie to keep her away from Mary at Warrielaw. Although it was her own fault, she struck me suddenly as rather a tragic and lonely person, as she walked into the room, trim and erect as ever.

"Please excuse me," she said abruptly, sitting very upright on a hard chair and placing her bag beside her. "I came to you because I really must know what is happening."

There was no answer to that question, I felt, but John's answer of silence.

"You won't tell me anything. But I must know, and even Dennis tells Alison nothing. We're Neil's cousins after all."

"Why not go to the lawyers?" I asked bluntly.

"Surely they'll find that some maniac did it?" she said, ignoring me. "In any case, John doesn't think there's evidence enough against Neil for a capital sentence, does he? Doesn't he think that the verdict will be Not Proven?"

"We don't have that in England," I said vaguely. "Rhoda, I had no idea you were so fond of Neil."

"I'm not," said Rhoda, her voice growing cold and hard. "He and Cora have always had everything they wanted all their lives and made a mess of everything. I'm not fond of them or even very sorry for them. I grow so intolerant of all the silly sympathy of the world for useless people. I'm not very sorry for anyone in this business. I don't walk about hoping Aunt Mary will get better. Why should I? Her death would clear up ever so many complications and we should all know where we were."

"And if Cora dies too and Neil is hanged," I said rather brutally, "you and Alison would inherit Warrielaw, I suppose, and know just where you were?"

"I don't want it," said Rhoda decidedly. "I only want money enough to get away from this dreary old place and our old family, and sick people and old people and half-witted people, to somewhere new and efficient and progressive—like America. I suppose you're sorry for that wretched Annie? I went to see her sister the other day, and Annie was so offensive and violent that I suggested she should be investigated and sent off to an asylum. But of course Mrs. Hay was scandalised, and so are you! It seems to me there are hardly any people who can see things clearly and sensibly without wrapping them up in a veil of sentiment!"

"When do you mean to go to America?" I asked. I felt at the moment that Scotland could well spare Rhoda to the New World.

"I can't go till Aunt Mary dies and the estate is divided," said Rhoda impatiently. "I wanted to get away before this dreadful trial, but she seems to be getting better."

"I don't think," I said, outraged, looking straight into Rhoda's eyes, "that I ever met anyone as heartless as you in my life."

"Oh no, I'm not," said Rhoda, her eyes softening. "I love Alison in a way you'll never love anyone all your life. I love her enough to want her to have her own life without me. It's because of her that I'm so worried about Neil really. If he's hanged it will brand Alison for life. You wouldn't like your brother to marry the cousin of a murderer, I suppose?"

There and then I saw for life the horrible dangers of boy-and-girl friendships. Rhoda's question was absurd, of course. Dennis was only nineteen and Alison a year younger: their marriage was out of the question for years to come. And yet, of course, there they were, as devoted, as exclusive a couple as you could imagine. If they were four or five years older, the whole Edinburgh world would have been standing round expecting the news of their engagement every day. Had not Rhoda some right, in spite of their youth, to assume that a friendship like theirs was likely to lead to something more?

"But they're mere children!" I answered Rhoda with as good an imitation of my mother's manner as I could achieve.

"Dennis has some money, I imagine? Boy-and-girl marriages are almost as common as boy-and-girl friendships nowadays."

"But he's going to Oxford next autumn. It will be years before he can dream of marriage!"

"I don't object to long engagements," said Rhoda. "I think a long attachment helps to keep a boy straight."

"Still, if you take Alison away to America, I imagine—"

"I shan't take her to America. I want her to live her own life, not cling on to mine. I shall leave her behind with someone, some friends, I suppose. Don't be prejudiced against her, Betty! She's not in the least like me in any way!"

It was the first time Rhoda had used my name and in her voice I caught, for once, something of her family's charm. But the cold cruelty of her attitude to life sickened me and made the prospect of my visit to Warrielaw, that home of hate, even more distasteful than usual. To be free from this entanglement of horror seemed far more desirable than the discovery of any clue when Bob came for me after lunch. I hated the whole affair, I hated the drive down and I hated the place. It seemed to me as if the dull grey clouds which hung over Warrielaw that afternoon had spread themselves all over my early married happiness, as if that gaunt Palladian front were a barrier shutting me away from the outer world. Nor did I hope for one minute that Bob's visit to the house would do any more good than my visit to Mary. Death and decay seemed in the air we breathed as we drove past the nettles in the drive to the weary old house. Jessica lay dead, Neil was awaiting death. A doom lay upon the place and I could do nothing to avert it or escape from it into my old life.

"Even the workmen seem to have deserted the house now," I said drearily to Bob. For the first time for the last few weeks no ladders were in evidence, and no men were working on the roof or at the windows of Warrielaw.

"Your husband told me that the noise disturbed Miss Mary," said Bob, "and the agents have ordered all the men round to work in the stable-yard. They're carrying the drainage system from the house to the stable lodge and on to the back gate, and a fine mess they're making of it."

The doom lay upon Miss Mary, too, as I left Bob with Effie and was led into a bedroom beside the top of the big staircase, some three doors from Mary's room. The nurses had wheeled her on a small bed to the window, they had cleaned and polished, but made no efforts to brighten the room. Like Jessica's it was furnished with heavy Victorian furniture, uncared for and marked with the damp of winter rain and frost. Gloomy prints hung round the walls and the long mirrors were tarnished and spotted. The chintz curtains and bed-hangings of dingy green were frayed and tattered, and the fire was smoky. Miss Mary lay in the midst of this desolation, as worn and battered and bereft as her home. She was propped up on her pillows, and the sunlight reflected from the trees outside shone on her white tired face and yellow-grey hair, and on her freckles round the little mole on her sunken forehead. She greeted me pleasantly enough, but her eyes were wandering, her mind preoccupied.

"Did you bring anyone with you?" she asked.

"Just a friend of John's," I replied evasively. No one knew, so far, how much Mary remembered, or realised, of her sister's tragedy, and I had been warned not to refer to it.

"Did she come upstairs?" asked Mary suspiciously.

"I'll go and see," I answered with some embarrassment.

"You're sure it wasn't my niece, Rhoda?"

"No, indeed not," I replied.

"Don't think me very tiresome, my dear, but would you just go and make sure? I don't want Rhoda: she worries me and she will try to come. Just wait outside till you are sure she is nowhere about."

"I will," I said. "You're not really well enough for visitors, Miss Mary, are you?"

"Perhaps not, my dear, but I shall be soon. But if you don't mind we'll say good-bye now. Only don't go till you've made sure Rhoda is out of the way."

I was glad to escape from the dismal scene, and I tiptoed anxiously to Mary's former room. Bob must be warned not to let Mary hear any sound from him or have any reason to guess he was upstairs. I hoped his task was nearly over, but I had not reckoned with Effie. The strain of the last few weeks had told on the poor old woman, and Bob had been constrained to listen to her confused complaints over the mess in the stable-yard, "and indeed a body's no safe going to look for an egg with all the holes they've dug and the walls they've pulled down," with a dirge over the tragedy of her beloved and ill-fated family. After distrusting and snubbing every policeman or official who came near the place for weeks, she had realised apparently that Bob was responsible for Neil's defence, and was pouring out her heart to him. "As if that lad would ever take and kill his auntie," she was saying tearfully as I entered the doors.

The desolation of Miss Mary's bedroom struck me even more painfully than that of her sister's. Not only was it dingy and sad and filled with the appliances of a sick-room. The bed lay vacant and unmade as if a coffin had been carried from it, and from the mantelpiece an old enlarged photograph of the five Warrielaw sisters with tightly curled fringes and staring eyes looked down, as if in triumph that yet another of the group had rejoined them. But Bob was occupied in no such morbid thoughts. As Effie talked on ceaselessly he was hunting through drawers and wardrobes with method and precision.

"That's the costume she was wearing that day," the old woman volunteered, "and that's her bag and gloves and veil. Miss Rhoda was at her bag, and hunting through it before her aunt came to her senses again, but I made sure she'd got her hands on nothing in it, and she never laid hands on these either."

"Did she have a try?" asked Bob, shaking out the skirt and feeling at the pockets carefully.

"Aye, and that she did. She was at us again and again, but I wasna having any of it. I thought it might be yon jewel she was after, but, there, it wasna there!"

Effie sighed heavily at her memories and then looked with surprise at Bob. He was searching in the sleeves of the blouse and produced a handkerchief.

"And how did you know", I said, voicing her thoughts, "that women keep their handkerchiefs stuffed into their sleeves sometimes?"

"It's common to both sexes after all," smiled Bob. "My sister's always losing handkerchiefs—"

His voice died away: his eyes had become narrow and bright. One corner of the handkerchief was knotted, and as he untied it, there was a slight rustle of paper. I ran to his side, my heart beating high, though what I expected it would have been hard to tell. Bob's face expressed no sort of emotion as he smoothed out the thin slip, and I stared at the talisman to find it nothing but a cloakroom ticket. My mind flew to the suit-case, but no, the suit-case had been found in London, and Jessica had never reached London.

"It's nothing of any importance probably," said Bob. "It's only a cloakroom ticket. Or part of a ticket I should say, for the top's torn off and therefore it's impossible to tell the place which issued it or the date. It's not likely to be of any use to us though. It's a North British ticket, not a Caledonian."

"Shall I go and ask Miss Mary if she remembers anything about it?" I asked, but Bob frowned at me.

"No need to worry her. This had better not go beyond the three of us, by the way. You'll remember, Effie?"

"Why would I be chattering about yon?" asked Effie contemptuously. "It'll likely be some parcel of plants from a nursery-man or such that Miss Mary was to call for on her way home that day, and she just took and forgot."

"There's just one other thing," said Bob. "Mrs. Morrison, now we're standing here, I wonder if you can reconstruct the scene a little. You were here with Miss Mary, and Miss Macpherson came back saying the jewel was gone. Had she got any keys in her hand?"

"Oh dear!" I said helplessly. "I don't remember. She'd gone to look for brandy, she said, and when she came back she hadn't the brandy, but she had the empty case in one hand and—yes—let me think—something was hanging down from her hands too. Yes, it was a bit of black ribbon with some keys on it—I'm nearly sure it was."

"It would be that," said Effie. "Miss Jessica had the key of the medicine cupboard, the key of the safe in the pantry and the key of the wee safe in her room where yon jewel was, on a bit of ribbon."

"Then I presume she always wore them?" asked Bob.

"Yes, I've hardly ever seen them off her. She'd just tuck them into her blouse when she was out working in the garden."

"And yet she left them behind in her room when she went to London," said Bob slowly. "They must have been lying loose, too, on the dressing-table or table where Miss Macpherson would catch sight of them at once. Doesn't that surprise you, Effie?"

Effie stared at him, her mouth wide open.

"Aye, that's a gey queer thing," she said. "I've never known Miss Jessica forget to put them on before. She must have been that flurried getting off that morning and I not there to help her. She was in a hurry or one of them was, I know that, for there was but two cups and dishes for two used in the kitchen where I'd left their breakfast laid out."

"Or she might have left them," I said impulsively, "if they weren't important any more, if she really had given the jewel to Neil the day before!"

"What was that, Ma'am?" Effie, as usual, had failed to understand my English accent and Bob was frowning at me. I turned hastily to a chair and pointed to an object which had attracted my notice.

"So Miss Mary did finish her bedspread?"

"Aye, she did, just the night before she was taken ill, and I had it washed for her but she's never seemed to care to have it out yet, so I just put it away and thought I'd try it again now to see if it pleased her."

Effie led the way down to the library at Bob's request, and as she did so another memory stirred in my mind.

"Did Miss Jessica finish hers?" I asked breathlessly.

"No? Mr. Stuart, I believe we have got hold of something important to-day. Look!"

I dragged open the wide drawer at the bottom of Jessica's work-table. There lay three or four handkerchiefs embroidered with the initials N.L. and another little pile with the initials stencilled but unstitched. Bob's eyes narrowed as he took them and counted them.

"Eleven!" he said. "So the other makes the dozen. That'll be a fine point for Mr. Firle to surprise the Crown with. The handkerchiefs were just lying here for anyone in the world to pick up! The one found with the handle had no connection necessarily with Mr. Logan. That's what reconstructing the scene does for the memory, Mrs. Morrison!"

Bob's commendation urged me to further efforts.

"There's her bedcover," I said, pulling it out of the drawer. It was nearly finished, too, and a needle and thread still hung from one of the holes. Bob was examining the work-tables thoughtfully.

"Did the ladies borrow each other's needles or scissors and such-like?" he asked Effie.

"There was trouble if they did," said Effie emphatically. "Even whiles they'd walk about the room embroidering neither would ever venture to pick up as much as a needle of the other's."

I saw the point of his question. Miss Jessica's little embroidery stiletto with its mother-of-pearl handle still lay in its drawer. I preferred not to think of Mary's, but clearly this piece of information made Mr. Firle's reconstruction of the scene unlikely.

"There's points we needn't trouble Mr. Firle with," said Bob with meaning. "Well, well, there's a lot there I don't quite understand, and the less said about to-day the better."

Effie detained me at the door with a worried face.

"There's something troubling me sorely, Ma'am, and I'll make bold to ask you if you'll say a word to Mr. John. Miss Rhoda's been making trouble again. She's been through to Carglin and she took upon herself to say that my poor wee Annie should be put away to an asylum. Ellen stood up to her and said it was no business of hers, but Annie took such a fright that she's made off. She's away with the tinkers, Ellen says, and she doesn't know how she'll get her back."

"But she's got to appear as a witness at the trial, surely?" I appealed to Bob, who was listening to us.

"Ellen understood that," said Effie. "She doesn't doubt that Annie will come home if she's ordered to by the Law, for she's a fair horror of going against the police. Will they send a note to the girl soon, Ma'am?"

Bob reassured Effie on the point, but his eyes were more absent than ever as we drove home.

"We'll have to trace her down, and see that she's back in time, yes!" he said in answer to my questions. "But why does Miss Macpherson want her out of the way, and is there anything else Annie is afraid of? There are several things yet I don't understand."

He said no more till we reached Moray Place, and there all the events of the afternoon were driven out of my mind for the

moment by John's news. The Criminal Courts had a light cal-
endar at this time and Neil's case was to be taken on July 15th.

CHAPTER XII
THE KNIFE IN THE CHURCHYARD

THERE WERE TO be for me, as for all my generation in days
to come, months and weeks and even hours that were to drag
interminably into preposterous lengths. And yet I think that
never in the Great War did I realise the meaning of that phrase
as clearly as in the week before the trial. For after all, in the
War, those who were temporarily widowed fell to working
violently. My children were small then, but I left them to my
nurse when John was in France, and worked daily at a hospital
where time sped by because one was busy, and the nights were
short because sleep was so precious. But there was nothing
to do in the weeks before the Warrielaw trial. I could go nowhere and see no one lest I should be tempted to indiscre-
tion. Alison spent most of her time with us, so crushed and
pitiful that it seemed heartless even to take refuge in a book,
and when she was not there, Dennis poured out to me all his
boyish misery because she was so wrapped up in Neil that he
would never have a chance. It was useless in that crisis to de-
mand what chance he would ever have: the last few weeks had
aged Dennis, and his chivalrous pity and care for Alison were
those of a man rather than a boy. John was very busy at the office and we hardly saw Bob Stuart. He was often at Warrielaw:
he and Dennis took long drives, in vain, in search of the other
half of the cloakroom ticket found in Mary's room. He had
some occupation in keeping track of the movements of the
tinkers whom Annie had joined. No class of the community
has changed its habits more completely than these casual wan-
derers since the Great War, and in those days, when commu-
nications with the Highlands depended only on rail or boat, it
would have been easy for Annie to evade justice for a fortnight

or more if the caravans made for the wilder parts of the north-west coast. But news came of her regularly enough from the south-west borders. There were no signs that she was trying to evade the ordeal of the witness-box. Later on Bob owned to us that he would have been almost glad if she had tried to disappear. Then his vague suspicions that some mystery about her was escaping him would have crystallised, and at least he could have gone South to seek her out. As it was, his task grew daily more disheartening. No new facts transpired about that day three months ago, and where memory failed the people whom he questioned, in the environments of Warrielaw, imagination was called in to supply the deficiency. He achieved an interview with Miss Mary and the poor lady assured him that, though she could remember little of the events of the 13th of April, because her memory had failed her since her illness, she did remember noticing an unknown, and therefore suspect, cart on the road near Warrielaw. She could, however, supply no details, and Rhoda made no definite statement to verify her incoherent suggestion. When Bob made casual enquiries about the cloakroom ticket the poor invalid grew vaguer than ever, and only replied that she and her sister so frequently called for parcels of cuttings and plants at both stations in Edinburgh that this particular one had quite escaped her memory. Bob found out later that this statement was true enough. Miss Jessica had impressed every garden of the neighbourhood for gifts, and indulged to the full the passion of every Scottish gardener for getting something for nothing. Those were certainly bad days for him, and all the worse because he could produce no reason for delaying the trial. The Crown was prepared, and Neil never wavered from his wish to get the whole affair over as quickly as possible. John reported that Mr. Firle was still confident of a verdict of Not Proven, but I could see he did not share the Counsel's faith.

It was on the 14th of July, the day before the trial, a day of lowering clouds and that dull, oppressive heat which the east coast experiences so seldom, that Bob suddenly appeared and asked Dennis if his Renault was available.

"I'm going to Carglin," he said. "Mrs. Hay sends word that Annie Hope is back again. I want to go and have a look round once more."

"Any luck about the ticket?" asked Dennis, rising at once. Alison was with us for the day, poor child, but she had refused to leave the house for the afternoon. It was my lot clearly to stay, and look after her. Rhoda for weeks had been absorbed in her shop, and had let no sign of her feelings escape her.

"None. If I had my way the trial would be postponed till we've traced it. We've been through every record in every station within a thirty-mile radius of Edinburgh, and can find no trace of any unclaimed parcel which could conceivably be the one we want. It seems to me that there's something behind its disappearance we don't understand. It's too curious to be a mere chance. However, Mr. Firle differs from me, so there it is. I'm going to Carglin."

I have heard the details of that afternoon so often that now, as I grow older, I almost forget I was not present when Dennis drove his car out of Bathgate and took the narrow road to Carglin.

The dark clouds, darker still in that smoky countryside, hung over the white, dusty road and the dull, grimy bushes and long grass of the hedges. No birds were singing, and the world seemed asleep in its blackened cloak beneath the grey dome of the sultry skies, when they turned the corner and saw before them the Hays' cottage and the long narrow road to the village and the church. And then Dennis slowed down and ran his car up into an open gateway, for advancing towards them was a funeral hearse. The black plumes, the dark horses, the bedecked undertakers and the carriage or two which followed passed him by very slowly, the white dust enveloping the car, the creaking of the wheels resounding like a grim funeral march. Some dweller in the neighbourhood had evidently been laid to rest in his native village of Carglin, beneath the shadow of the ugly little kirk. Dennis jumped down to start up the car again, when, with a glance up the road, he dropped the handle, and stood aghast with staring eyes.

Bob jumped out and came to his side. Down the road acquaintances and spectators were strolling homewards, in little groups, their faces full of the ghoulish appreciation of their class for the last rites of death. But it was a solitary figure, with its back towards the car, which had arrested Dennis's attention and kept him still staring up the road.

"Lord!" he said. "I thought for a moment that was Miss Jessica herself!"

The big woman in the black hat and long, black cape stood still as he spoke, her rough, ungloved hand playing absently with the long grasses by the road. Then Bob pulled Dennis back into the shelter of the hedge by the gateway, for she turned abruptly and began to walk towards the Hays' cottage.

"It's just poor Annie Hope," said Bob drily. "It's only Miss Jessica's hat and cloak that have come back to haunt you. They'll be the clothes Miss Macpherson gave her which should have gone to Effie. No, don't start your car yet."

For a few minutes Bob stood lost in thought, and Dennis realised suddenly that the episode seemed to his companion to have an unexpected significance.

"Would you mind moving the car straight back from here," said Bob, "and studying the beauties of Bathgate till I join you? It's most important that I shouldn't startle that poor lass more than I can help, and I'd prefer to drop in on Mrs. Hay informally."

Dennis nodded with some disappointment, and Bob turned and made his way to the cottage alone.

The room was dark and oppressively hot with its open fire as Bob obeyed a summons to enter. Mrs. Hay was seated beside the fire, nursing her baby. Through an open door Bob could see Annie bending down among the pots and pans in the little scullery to admire herself, at a mirror, in her funeral outfit.

"Mrs. Hay," said Bob clearly and firmly, as he took out his pocket-book, "I've come to ask the meaning of this. Now don't attempt to contradict me. You and your sister have seen this cloakroom ticket before?"

"There, Miss Rhoda's told on the poor girl after all," cried Mrs. Hay in despair, as she held out a trembling hand for the piece of paper. There was a noisy gasp from the scullery, followed by a clatter of cutlery as a drawer was pulled out hastily. Next moment Annie, her cheeks red and her eyes blazing, erect in her black hat and cloak, swept past Bob and her sister and ran out of the kitchen door.

"Oh, what's the girl after?" cried Mrs. Hay distractedly. "Oh Sir, Sir, we must get hold of her, but have a care to yourself."

Bob was out of the house before she had finished speaking and looked up the road. It was empty now, for the last mourners had drifted back to the village, but through the hedge Bob saw Annie moving towards the church. She was crossing a ploughed field, and her breath came in heavy gasps between her sobs. The sweat was running down her cheeks as she laboured on in the heat, in her heavy clothes, but Bob had to hurry his steps to keep parallel with her along the lane.

The churchyard wall was surrounded with thick stunted yew trees, and, as he shut the gate cautiously, Bob concealed himself behind one. The burying-ground was silent and deserted now, and the church door locked. The little square building, with its windows of plain green glass, looked down reprovingly from its long record of uneventful sabbaths and silent week-days, as Annie scrambled over the wall and alighted heavily on a grave.

Bob stood motionless. The black cloak had revealed, when the girl jumped, that in her hand was a long sharp knife. For a moment he thought of rushing at her, in the fear that she might be about to injure herself, but he changed his mind as she looked cunningly about her from side to side. She was here evidently with some definite purpose and at all costs he must find out what it could be.

She was clearly afraid of onlookers. One glance around her was not enough and she vanished round the far side of the church. Bob emerged from his shelter and followed her cautiously as she hurried round the building, staring anxiously from side to side. Then, feeling herself secure at last, she crept up to a grave by the side of the church wall which abutted on the road. Bob, taking cover behind a pretentious tomb crowned by a marble angel, stood watching her, lost in amazement. With one more anxious glance around her she knelt down and raised her knife. Then, very busily, she began scratching with it at the inscription on a tombstone.

"In affectionate remembrance", read Bob, "of William Carruthers Reid, Farmer, of Stobo, Lower Carglin, of this parish. He deceased April 10th, 1906, and was interred in this grave with his wife Isabella Rose Reid on the first anniversary of her death.

"They were lovely and pleasant in their lives and in their death they were not divided."

It was not, however, upon these words that Annie was making her impassioned attack. Above the inscription was an earlier one to Isabella Rose Reid, and out of the memorial composed for her by her surviving husband it was one detail only to which Annie apparently took exception. She was scraping vigorously with the knife, but the date stood out clearly before Bob's eyes. It was the date we knew so well—April 13th.

The churchyard gate clicked suddenly as Bob stood transfixed in thought. Annie rose with a cry as Mrs. Hay ran towards her up the path, white and distracted. Bob sprang forward as he caught the wild glare of the hunted animal in Annie's eyes, and was just in time to seize her arm as she raised her knife, as if to run upon him and her sister.

"Oh Annie, Annie! What's to do now!" moaned Mrs. Hay, rocking herself to and fro.

"Come awa' there's but one thing for it. You must just come away home and confess to the gentleman just what you and Jock have done between you!"

It was an hour or more before Bob rejoined Dennis at the station, and then it was only to disappear into the station-master's office. It was true that he offered to find his own way home and leave Dennis free, but by that time Dennis was too curious to leave his companion. When Bob emerged from the station he asked Dennis to drive him to the local doctor's, and then at last, after a lengthy visit, owned that his business was finished now.

"But if you'll believe me," said Dennis indignantly, "he never said a word to me all the way home. He just gave me this note for you, John, and then walked straight off. Do open it at once, for he's got hold of something—there's no doubt of that."

But there was nothing to satisfy Dennis in the pencil note, scrawled in the car as Bob neared Moray Place.

"I have a new and puzzling clue," read John, "but I must get away to think it over by myself. There may be unexpected developments to-morrow, but I must see my way clearly as to how to deal with them before I speak to anyone. Ask my pardon of Mr. Dennis. Don't count too much on this. B.S."

"Oh, there is some hope after all!" I cried, but John refused to take comfort.

"No, I can't think so. He can't find out anything at Carglin that can materially affect the case, it seems to me. If it were anything of importance he would be asking me to make arrangements to postpone the trial. My God, if only it were all over!"

"How is Neil?" I ventured at last to ask the question which had been on my lips all day.

"Very brave. It doesn't bear thinking about," said John briefly.

"The doctor rang up before tea to say Mary is much better. They're even getting her down to the library now," I said to change the subject. "She's been asking all sorts of questions. She knows about Neil now: she got it out of Effie."

"Poor old soul! Well, it's something she's better. Cora Murray is worse, they say. No one's seen Charles for the last day or two. You know Betty, you're not to be called on for your evidence to-morrow morning, that's certain. It's strange to think you were the only witness at first! But it's a queer case. The prosecution and the defence are both addressing the Court first, by Firle's special request, though it's a most unusual procedure."

"Then I can go there with Alison? She's been begging me to."

"Oh yes, that's all right. You and Dennis can go to look after her and Rhoda if you want to. It'll be a pretty hateful show for you, but it's a good thing for you to get accustomed to the atmosphere of it in case you're ever called in the future. I'm glad they have decided that. Small's cabman and Peter Carruthers are all that's necessary, and as Neil's own story admits that he was at Carstairs and Warrielaw, even your evidence about his car won't be wanted. As I say, it's a strange affair. It was only through you that Neil was suspected at first. If it hadn't been for you he'd hardly have been arrested, Betty!"

"Oh John, did he do it?" I cried involuntarily.

"We'll know by the end of this week, I hope," was all the comfort John could give. We sat up till far into the night reading, for what was the use of taking our bodies to bed while our two minds were imprisoned with Neil Logan in his cell, awaiting the morrow.

STOP

THIS IS A CHALLENGE TO YOU. At this point all the characters and clues have been presented. It should now be possible for you to solve the mystery.

CAN YOU DO IT? Here's your chance to do a little detective work on your own—a chance to test your powers of deduction. Review the mystery and see if you can solve it *at this point.*

Remember! THIS IS A SPORTING PROPOSITION, made in an effort to make the reading of mystery stories more interesting to you. So—don't read any further. Reach your solution *now.* Then proceed.

CHAPTER XIII
THE TRIAL OF NEIL LOGAN

THERE ARE NOT many hot days in an Edinburgh summer. It seemed a hideous irony that on one when the sun was shining in shimmering heat on the rocks of Arthur's Seat, on the gay window-boxes of Princes Street and the distant waters of the shining North Sea, we should only see it beat inexorably through beams of glancing dust on to the panelled walls and wooden compartments of a stuffy Court Room in Parliament House. In that light the clothes of the prisoner and the witnesses, the robes of the judges and the lawyers and the uniforms of the officials were toned into one drabness, and every line on every face stood out mercilessly clear. I felt as I stared before me, at everyone but the prisoner, that for the rest of my life I should remember every wrinkle on the macer's face, every hair of each wig, every turn and twist of each mouth. Only at Neil I dare not look lest I should lose my composure altogether.

It was all wrong and out of place, I felt confusedly. As we drove up through the streets of that old town which lie wholly outside the ordinary orbit of Edinburgh domestic and social life, between frowning stone houses three hundred years old, breaking, like cliffs, to reveal, through narrow closes, glimpses of the Forth and the far Highland hills, it was borne in upon me that the Warrielaws and their story did not belong to this world at all. Their tale was a ballad tale of internecine strife and sorrow. It was in a lonely burn beside a rowan tree that Jessica's dead body should have been found, and high upon a gallows tree that her retainers should have strung up her murderers, while in a plaintive refrain the Fairy Jewel told the story of the Curse of the Little People upon the House. Somewhere in my mind echoed the memory of a Chief of the Forty-Five, who, led to execution on Tower Hill, stared round the crowding London houses and complained that the faces fixed upon his were like a pack of rotten oranges. Upon these Warrielaws, strayed from the Border minstrelsy, such rotten oranges were gazing now. On their wild feuds the reason and justice of a new strange world sat in condemnation. It was all wrong and out of focus, I felt, just as this narrow, stuffy place with its commonplace officials refused to fit into my imagination of a vast hall of judgment where remote judges sat enthroned. Nothing seemed real to me, and yet I knew that all the ultimate reality of Neil's life depended on the words and thoughts of those queer ordinary staring faces on the bench and in the jury and in the seats reserved for the witnesses.

Dennis sat on one side of me, and Alison, poor, pale fairy princess, strayed into a drab ugly world of reality, on the other. Rhoda was some way off: she had made it clear that she must be alone that day, though she sat cool and composed as ever. Bob Stewart was near me, and I took what comfort I could from John's bent head at his desk, and Askew Firle's inscrutable face with its air of bland assurance. But I hardly noticed the rustling around me as the proceedings began at last. Late the night before I had sat over an old murder trial in my husband's library, and the words of the old-fashioned indictment, now wholly disused, drifted through my mind, fitting themselves erratically to the present circumstances.

"Neil Warrielaw Logan, you are indicted and accused ... that albeit by the laws of this and of every other well-governed realm murder, as also theft, are crimes of a heinous nature; yet true it is and of verity that you the said Neil Warrielaw Logan are guilty of the said crime of murder, and of the said crime of theft in so far as (i) On the 13th day of April, 1909, in or near the house of Warrielaw of Midlothian, lately occupied by Jessica Warrielaw, spinster, deceased, of the aforesaid Warriclaw House, you did with a sharp instrument strike the said Jessica Warrielaw, piercing her heart, and also inflicted upon her skull blows … you ought to be punished with the pains of law, to deter others from committing the like crimes in all time coming."

I felt Alison's head on my shoulder and, as I fumbled for my smelling-salts, the dream voice faded from my bewildered mind and I awoke to the present. For the Judge was speaking, in so sharp and clear a voice that it seemed as if the sword of justice was proceeding in actual fact from his mouth.

"You have read the indictment charging you with the crime of murder and also of theft. Do you plead guilty to either of these crimes?"

Neil stood up, but again I did not dare to look at him. Only the odd, charming, affected drawl made the words sound like some casual epigram rather than a statement of fact as he replied: "Not guilty, my Lord."

Bob was at my side and took Alison's arm, and together we led her into the passage outside.

"You must get her round while the jury's being empanelled and sworn," he said. "Can't you persuade her sister to take her away? Miss Alison's not to be called, and she'll do no good here."

"I won't go," muttered Alison. "I must stand by Neil. I won't go."

Bob motioned to a policeman standing near.

"MacDougall," he said, "would you be so kind as to show this young lady a window where she can get some fresh air and recover herself? Mrs. Morrison, I want a word with you."

Bob's voice and manner were urgent, so urgent that I trembled a little. Queerly and irrationally, a text flashed across my mind, words that had taken my fancy in my schooldays: "And God hath sent his angel and stopped the mouth of the lions." It seemed to me that Bob was about to entrust me with a secret of real importance, a service of real moment at last. But his request seemed so small, so inconsequent, that as he made it I could only stare at him blankly:

"Mrs. Morrison, when Miss Warrielaw's pulled herself together, I want you to go back into Court. And when you're there I want you to look as hard as you can at Mr. Logan. I want you to look at him and then try to remember every detail you can of Miss Jessica Warrielaw as you saw her on the morning of April 13th, and of Miss Mary Warrielaw as you saw her yesterday. Will you do this for me during the speech for the prosecution? And then, if you've anything to tell me, beckon to me, and come and see me when you can slip out easily, before Mr. Firle begins? I can't speak more plainly because it's for you to remember all you can. Will you do your best, and look at him and remember both the old ladies as if you'd never seen them before?"

"Let's go back, Betty!" Alison was at my elbow, shuddering still but composed now, and we crept back to our seats. The speech for the prosecution had begun, and the cold clear voice of the Crown Counsel numbed for a little my bewilderment at Bob's request. My subconscious mind puzzled vacantly over Bob's words, while my conscious attention was riveted to the story unfolded for the Crown. He offered no dramatic story, he made no sort of appeal to the emotions. Only in the fewest possible words he sketched the story which we knew so well. He pictured the lonely lives of the two Misses Warrielaw in their old country house: he told of Jessica's love for her nephew and how that love had been requited by indifference and dislike. He told of the sacrifices and economies made by Jessica for Neil and of the legacy he would inherit on her death. He told of the discord in the family over the famous heirloom which Jessica proposed to sell. The case looked black enough to me before he began to recount the incidents of that 13th of April: as he went through the story he did not fail to point out at every turn how Neil, and probably Neil Logan alone, had reason to know that the house would be empty in the middle of the day. It was useless for the defence to attach the crime to some unknown thief who passed by. What passer-by could know of the different domestic reasons which had left the house unguarded? What tramp would dare to assume that he could commit murder with impunity and conceal a corpse in a house like Warrielaw? As the remorseless story went on, to the discovery of Jessica's body and the subsequent discovery of the jewel in the studio, my heart sank lower and lower. Up till now I had at least believed in Neil, and trusted in John and Mr. Firle for his salvation. Now it seemed to me that there could be no doubt that there before me sat Neil Logan, a murderer and a thief.

And at that conclusion Bob's words suddenly came back to me and I steeled my heart; for the first time looked straight before me and fixed my eyes on Neil.

The light fell full upon his face, and I saw at once that his chalky pink colour had faded, and that new lines of misery and anxiety marked his brow: that he was much thinner and his hair was more closely cut. But none of those details affected me so much as the sudden knowledge that here before me sat an imprisoned man, that here was a fellow animal in a trap. As I gazed, my predominant feeling was one which distinguishes above all, I believe, the man in the street who watches a trial or reads of a murder case. He does not remember the crime which preceded the imprisonment: he does not consider the rights or wrongs of the case. If the verdict is given for the prisoner he cheers: if against him he signs endless petitions in his favour. Only the few of judicial and legal habit of mind, only the jury strung up by their consciences to view the affair impartially with due concern for the ultimate welfare of society, can escape the universal instinct to loose the trap and let the prisoned animal free. That was, as I first gazed at Neil, my predominant instinct. Never, I realised, could I bear to do or say anything which might ensnare another human being into captivity.

And then that first passionate instinct of revolt against the orderly working of justice faded, and I stared at Neil, not as a prisoner, but as a Warrielaw. Still my mind refused to see any point in Bob's request, but now as Neil moved a little and let his head sink forward, I saw beneath his carefully assumed pose of nonchalance a weary patience that recalled Miss Mary's face as she lay helpless on her bed. And then as a ray of sun fell from the high window I saw his eyes with their large yellow-green irises and narrowed pupils, and I saw something else. It was not only his weary air of discouragement which made me see Miss Jessica's face as she sat, half-averted from me, in the railway carriage at Princes Street Station on the morning of April 13th. The light fell direct on a small golden mole surrounded by freckles. I had noticed a similar one on Jessica's forehead then. How strangely persistent these family peculiarities could be! And how prominent the mole on Mary's forehead had seemed the other day, as she lay in the bedroom. ...

And then some half-forgotten words of long ago woke in my memory, and I suddenly clutched Alison's hand.

"Alison," I whispered fiercely, "was it Jessica or Mary who had a little mole on her forehead?"

"Why, Mary," replied Alison, her eyes fixed on Askew Firle.

For the great lawyer had just arisen and his cool critical voice was falling upon the Court like ice after the long slow stream of the speech for the Crown. "My position to-day is", he said, "in my experience at least unique, for I rise to refute a charge of murder when not the faintest shred of evidence exists to show that any murder has been committed." The words, I believe, were to become a catchword, but I could pay no attention to them. Somehow or other I stumbled out of the Court to the passage where Bob stood awaiting me anxiously.

"Oh Bob, Bob!" I cried incoherently. "What has happened? What shall I do?"

Bob grasped my arm and gazed at me with keen eyes in his queer sunken face.

"What is it?" he asked. "What is it?"

"Why, just this," I said. "It wasn't Jessica I saw at the station. She hadn't a mole on her forehead: Alison says it's Mary who has a mole. It was Mary I saw at Princes Street, and Mary looked just like Neil now. Oh, what does it mean? What does it mean?"

"You're sure of this for yourself? You'll swear to this?" Bob's voice was like a rapier.

"Yes! Yes! I saw the mole. Did you know that Jessica had none and Mary had one?"

"I found that out from Effie long ago. But, you see, Effie was not at the station. I had no means of knowing who it was you all saw at the station."

"But it must have been Jessica!" I cried, bursting into tears as if I were a child. "How could it be Mary? What does it all mean? Why do you look as if you expected this?"

"Never mind now. We've got to act. We've got to get down to Warrielaw at once at all costs, and we've got to get Miss Mary to give us her evidence or sign this deposition I've got here. You must come too. You must be ready to swear to what you've said after you've seen her again. I'll just scribble a message to give some warning to John. Firle must go on till lunch. He can put the medical evidence through. That may still be of use."

"But why? How? To whom?" I cried.

"We can't talk now. Look here, I'll go and get hold of the man we want. We must have a Notary Public and he'll take a policeman, too, I expect. I'll tell you what I can on the way. Stand you here and keep your eye on Miss Macpherson if you can. If she gets wind of this she'll try to get down to Warrielaw before us, and we must prevent that at all costs."

"But what are you going to do there?" I was still too much upset to see any light in the tangle of events.

But Bob vanished, and I stood there, still as stone. It must have been at that moment, unnoticed by any of us, that yet another witness slipped out of the Court. That I did not notice, but I realised that Dennis was by my side and Alison behind him, leaning against the wall, and I pushed my smelling-salts towards her frantically.

"Are you ill, Betty?" he asked. "Why did you go? I had to get Alison out. The woman next me said I must or she'd faint. Firle is marvellous! What on earth's the matter? Have you seen a ghost?"

I shook my head, though I was not sure that Dennis's surmise was far from the truth. You see a ghost, I imagine, mainly because you expect to see one. Small's cabman had seen Jessica, I had seen Jessica at Princes Street, Dennis had seen her at Carstairs, simply because we expected to see her in those circumstances, and we were accustomed to see her in that outfit. We had none of us seen through the simplest of all possible disguises: we had none of us questioned ourselves as to whether Jessica looked the same as usual or not. We had simply expected to see Jessica, and so we were ready to swear to having seen her. A man's life had depended on our observation, and not one of us had questioned who it was we had seen. Because I believed in the evidence of my imagination rather than my eyes I had nearly helped to condemn an innocent man to death. That truth was so overwhelming that I could hardly find words for Dennis. And when I stammered out my discovery he stood stricken.

"But what does it all mean?" he stammered as I had myself.

"Well, for one thing I suppose it means that Jessica may have been murdered at any time after that evening in Neil's studio!"

"Then why was Mary at the station?" asked Dennis. "Why did she dress herself up like Jessica?"

A thousand suggestions and implications began to stir in my returning reason, but there was no time for discussion. And Dennis made no reply, but turned round with a start. Alison's colour had returned, and she stood behind us unnoticed. She had heard every word of our conversation, and now too she chimed in like a ghostly echo—"Oh, what does it mean?"

We all stood in silence staring at each other till Alison turned.

"Rhoda must know about this!" she said.

"Hush, Alison!" I said. "You can't go in again. People can't run in and out like that! You and I are supposed to have felt faint, I imagine, but now we're out we must stay out, till you can creep in behind a policeman."

Alison turned with a hunted look and began to scribble suddenly in a little notebook. I paid no attention, for at this moment Bob appeared in the doorway.

"Come on," he said to me briefly. "Mr. Howard, you must stay and look after Miss Macpherson."

As we turned I saw Alison give a note to a policeman and the man disappeared into Court. I had no time to think over this move, for Bob was hurrying me on, and my heart was set on doing what I could to atone for my fault. A tall slim man with an impassive face was waiting for us, and behind him was a short, fidgety policeman. I remember reflecting vaguely that the two should, by rights, exchange roles, when I found myself in the car, introduced to Mr. Mair, and the policeman was taking his place on the box.

"I'll have to call round by my office to say I'll be away," said Mr. Mair, and as he spoke I grasped Bob's arm.

"Look!" I said. "There's Rhoda."

Rhoda's back was towards us. She was pulling out her bicycle feverishly and mounted even as I spoke.

It was our car in which we sat. John had borrowed his father's chauffeur for the day, and Bob turned to Mr. Mair.

"We've got to be at Warrielaw before that lady," he said briefly. "It's essential. Could you leave someone to ring up a message?"

But Mr. Mair was not to be hurried. There was no risk that a bicycle would get ahead of our car, he pointed out, and he vanished into his chambers. Bob sat immovable as the clock slowly ticked out the minutes, and the tension in the car as the five minutes wore on to ten, and ten to fifteen, and fifteen to twenty, was almost unbearable. Nothing could have enabled me to speak politely to Mr. Mair when at last he emerged and got into the car beside me, but as, at our directions, the car started swiftly westwards down Princes Street, Bob's composure was unruffled and his eyes shone alert and resolute in his kind, delightful, ugly face.

"D'you know the details of this case, Sir?" he asked.

"Who doesn't in Edinburgh? But what's the new evidence you've got hold of? Why wasn't the trial held up?"

"Because it was only at six o'clock this morning that I made out the truth," replied Bob. "I went to bed late last night without seeing any way out of the puzzle, and it was only when I woke up that I saw the solution, what is the true solution, I believe. It was only Mrs. Morrison here who finally convinced me just now."

"But what does it all mean?" I repeated yet again. "It means that Miss Warrielaw never started for London at all. Miss Mary impersonated her at Princes Street and took her place in the train. And the reason she did it was because Jessica Warrielaw already lay dead, hidden away in an outhouse by her own stables."

"That's a startling theory," said Mr. Mair, roused out of his usual calm. "How do you get at that?"

We were safely past the tram terminus and sweeping down the country roads by now. At every corner Bob leaned forward to see if he could catch a glimpse of Rhoda's bicycle, and his voice was almost uninterested as he replied:

"My disadvantage throughout in this case has been that I never saw Miss Jessica—at least I never saw her alive. No one has ever happened to convey the impression to me that one sister was so like another as to make such an impersonation possible. Nor had such an idea occurred to me even remotely till your brother, Mrs. Morrison, started at the sight of Annie Hope in Miss Jessica's clothes, as if he had seen a ghost. There was no likeness at all between maid and mistress, but the idea that one sister could easily pass for the other if their clothes were exchanged crossed my mind for the first time. After all, I remembered too, none of the witnesses who saw Miss Jessica on the 13th knew her well or exchanged any words with her. Naturally it took some time to adjust my ideas. I always felt there was something suggestive about the relative positions of Erleigh, Warrielaw and Bathgate, just as I knew there was some mysterious link between Miss Macpherson and Annie Hope, but it was only yesterday at Bathgate that I found out what it was."

"Then Rhoda's mixed up in it?" I queried confusedly.

"Up to the hilt. It was all her scheme, no doubt of that. I mean it was her scheme to make everyone think Miss Jessica had really gone off to London, by persuading Miss Mary to dress up in her clothes, go off in her cab and travel in her train as far as Carstairs."

"But Mary!" I cried. "But Rhoda! You don't mean it was they who … ?"

I could not bring myself to finish the sentence, and Bob only shook his head.

"We don't know who did the crime," he said soberly. "Remember, at the moment Mr. Firle is protesting that there was no crime, only an accident. But there's no doubt that it was Miss Mary and Miss Rhoda who concealed it between them."

"My God!" said Mr. Mair suddenly and explosively. "That girl! That young woman! What about a warrant?"

"No question of that yet. What we're going to do now is to try to take a deposition from Miss Mary Warrielaw. It may kill her, but we've got to try."

"She'd best die that way perhaps," said Mr. Mair grimly.

"We'll never get the whole story out of her, ill as she is. I suppose it's in order if I ask her leading questions and she answers 'Yes' and 'No' in your presence—assuming of course she's been warned in the ordinary way?"

"That's all right, if you can get the truth from her. But she'll never own to being guilty."

"We needn't go into that too far. (I say, this man's an abominably careful driver!) What we've got to do is to get her witness that Jessica was dead and hidden away before ever Mary left Warrielaw in Jessica's dress on the morning of April 13th. That'll clear Mr. Logan straight off with no more fuss, and that's what we've got to do for the moment. There's a chance we'll get at a confession by shock tactics, and it's worth trying. What's that, Grier?"

The policeman had turned and was beckoning to us. We had turned off the high road now down the road to the front avenue of Warrielaw. Just by the gate a laundry van was turning heavily down the lane to the village and before it was a figure on a bicycle.

"She'll be taking the lane and in at the back avenue," muttered Bob, as we bumped down the familiar ruts of the drive. "If she'd been wise she'd have got a hurl in that laundry van from Edinburgh! Well, Mrs. Morrison, get you hold of Effie and keep Miss Macpherson out of the light any way you can. Grier will help you."

"But why must you keep them apart?" I asked. "Because there's no hope of getting at the truth if they're together. You can't look at Miss Macpherson without seeing that she'd use all her influence to make Miss Mary give herself away and let her get clear out of it all. I expect she primed her up with some tale in case they were suspected long ago, and bullied the poor old lady so terribly that she's been glad of nurses and doctors to keep her niece at a distance ever since!"

"Can we get at Miss Mary without the doctor's authority?" asked Mr. Mair.

"I've 'phoned him. That's his car before the front steps, I expect."

CHAPTER XIV
MARY WARRIELAW SPEAKS

I HAD NEVER seen Warrielaw in midsummer sunshine before. Through the glimmering branches of the beech trees the plaster shone a mellow apricot, and a warm, sunny peace brooded over the long grass of the park and the glittering shrubs. But the windows were all blank and shuttered now by order of the nurses, the great door under the portico was closed, and one lonely spaniel lay pathetically before it. As the engine of the car stopped we could hear the bees in the clover and the coo of the wood-pigeons in the plantations, but to me even these murmurs of the summer seemed like the distant chanting of a funeral hymn. Not even sunshine nor July could lift the curse that lay upon the lonely ruined house.

It was just as Effie's step shuffled from within the hall towards us, as we stood waiting before the great door under the portico, that we heard the sound of a car hooting at the locked gates of the back drive.

"Remember you and Effie have got to keep her off somehow," reiterated Bob, as Effie flung open the doors, and we saw the cool, silent hall, and the doctor's anxious face looking at us through the swing door.

"Where is Miss Warrielaw?" asked Bob.

"In the library. She is very much better to-day, but not in a state, I must warn you, to sustain any sort of shock if it can possibly be avoided."

"It can't," said Bob briefly. "Mr. Mair will explain to you."

"There is no doubt at this juncture that we must hear what Miss Warrielaw has to tell us," said Mr. Mair seriously. "She is, I imagine from what I have heard, quite collected, in full possession of her senses?"

"Oh yes, entirely so, but—"

The nurse came cautiously out of the library, closing the door behind her. Effie and I were standing at the swing door in the big hall, staring down the long passage of the old house to the library as the conversation took place. It seemed to me as if in that wide, sun-lit background we were waiting in a lighted theatre, looking at a long, narrow stage, still in the darkness, where the scene-shifters were busy at their work. Nowhere had time stood still more definitely at Warrielaw than in this corridor. Heaven and some early-Victorian Warrielaw only knew when last painter or paperer had been near it. The dull, drab, faded flock-paper was covered with endless dark prints framed in satinwood: spiders nestled uninterrupted in the dark corners, and mice had made their exits and entrances in the skirting-boards for years: the worn carpet was stained to a uniform dull purple. A door on the right led to the kitchen quarters: the only door on the left was that of the library. The passage ended in a rounded window on the glass of which some Victorian lady had achieved transfers of the family coat of arms and of a ruined abbey: they were faded and cracked, and beyond them the green shrubbery enclosing the semi-circular garden looked no less faded and unreal through the grimy glass. Against that background the four men, my two tall, alert companions, the stout little doctor, the jerky, embarrassed constable, and the slim, genteel nurse, moved and spoke in lowered tones which added to the sense of unreality. So I remembered watchers had waited outside a closed door in a scene from a play of Maeterlinck's. With all my heart I longed for this drama, this fantastic, sinister drama of real life, to come to its conclusion.

"She's getting worried, Sir," said the nurse in a polite whisper. "I think you should come in as soon as possible to set her mind at rest."

No one but myself seemed to notice the irony of the phrase. Bob stopped to direct the policeman to wait at the library door, and with a nod of consent from the doctor, he left it open. Miss Mary must not be alarmed by the sight of more visitors than were absolutely necessary.

"Good morning, Miss Warrielaw." Bob's voice reached me, low and serious, but with no sort of menace. "I'm afraid we've come on an unpleasant mission."

"Oh dear!" Mary's reply came weak and fluttering. "Nurse, I'm hardly well enough to see these gentlemen!"

"I fear you must, Miss Warrielaw." Mr. Mair was speaking now with that queer, kind detachment which seemed to characterise him. "I think you know that your nephew stands on trial for his life to-day, and information has just come to light which seems to prove him innocent. We want you to give us your help. We want you to save him and make your own peace with Heaven at the same time. Remember this, that the truth or most of the truth is clear now."

There was no answer from Miss Mary but a long, choking sigh, and then I heard the murmurs of the nurse and doctor. Effie, who had been standing beside me till now, mute with bewilderment, started forward suddenly, but I seized her hand and held her back.

"She's got to go through with it, Effie," I muttered, "if Mr. Neil isn't to hang."

"Eh, Sirs, what a work!" Effie muttered, and then leant back against the wall in resignation and the silence of despair. From the library came the sound of clinking glass, as, I imagine, some restorative was given to the patient, and then Mary's voice reached us, thin and dignified.

"No, Nurse, I must manage this somehow. Doctor, tell me, I couldn't live if they tried to arrest me or take me to prison, could I?"

I did not hear the answer, for Effie suddenly seized my arm. Up above us, in the wide passage at the top of the great flight of stairs, we heard footsteps, light steps moving rapidly in the direction of Mary's room.

"Who'll be there?" whispered Effie. "That's no the girls up there."

"It's Miss Macpherson," I said. "She must have got in at the back door. She's not to get to Miss Mary now, you understand, Effie."

"She can't forbye she gets past us," said Effie grimly. "But what'll she be at, up there?"

I shook my head, but I knew well enough. Even at this eleventh hour Rhoda was seeking wildly, hopelessly and in vain for the other half of that cloakroom ticket. If she could find that she could still hope, I imagine, that any case against her, at least, could not be complete.

At least she was safely out of the way for the moment, I thought, and I crept a little way down the passage, to tell the policeman to be ready to guard the room in case of need, as the intruder we must repel was already in the house. And even while I spoke to him the library door swung open a little wider and I could see into the room.

The big couch which had guarded one wall had been drawn into the centre of the room, and Mary lay upon it facing the window. The round ottoman which had marked out each sister's territory was pushed aside, and the rearrangement seemed to make the room look more crowded than ever. But it was only one room now. Jessica's corner stood empty and intact. The endless mirrors and dark pictures and china cupboards and chairs and desks, the whole jetsam of the Warrielaw past, crowded round Miss Mary alone. The garden, too, showed Jessica's absence. The gardeners employed by Mary's agents had cut the grass edges and cleared away the bulbs, but they had not bedded out any substitutes, so that the empty, formal beds lay in vacant mounds like newly-dug graves.

I must have made some slight movement, for Miss Mary raised her head a little.

"Is that John's wife outside there?" she asked. "I should like her to come and sit beside me!"

In after days I wondered if that request meant that the poor old lady was rallying every possible defence to her side against the danger she dreaded.

I went up to the big couch, took the chair to which she beckoned me on her right. On her left sat Bob and Mr. Mair, his pen ready in his hand. Behind them on the wall hung a great Victorian mirror framed with silly smiling cupids and garlands in tarnished gilt. In it, from the angle at which I sat, I could see the reflection of Miss Jessica's desk and work-table and arm-chair by the other French window, orderly and un-disturbed now for ever. Beyond, the mirror reflected a narrow strip of the rhododendrons which circled round the formal garden. The flowers were overblown now and falling: and the big purple blossoms lay on the vacant mounds like funeral offerings falling to decay.

It was easier to look out of the window than to face Miss Mary. She was swathed in Shetland and cashmere shawls, from which she looked out with flushed cheeks but vacant eyes. Her hair was brushed back tightly, and the yellow mole I had observed so clearly at the station, whose significance had so entirely escaped me till this morning, stood out more clearly than ever. ... Yet the chief impression I had of her was how small and how shrunken she seemed. I could feel nothing but pity for her, and no effort of my imagination could make me believe that the story which Bob was to tell was true, nor that down the pathway she and Rhoda had somehow between them, in an agony of fear and shame, carried Jessica to her last hiding-place.

"I'll put what we have to say to you in the form of questions," said Bob. "That will save you as much as we can. But they're not simple questions, Miss Warrielaw. There comes a point where we have to learn from you whether the responsibility of this crime rests with you or your niece. Or again, it may be that your sister met with her death by an accident, and that the crime of which we must accuse you and Miss Macpherson is the far lesser crime of concealing all traces of her death. But remember before you tell us that you must first take your oath to tell us the truth and nothing but the truth."

The Notary was leaning forward now, and I could see his clear-cut profile. His slow vigorous voice contrasted strangely with Mary's mask-like face and lowered eyes as she listened to his formula. Upstairs, Rhoda was apparently growing desperate. I heard drawers open and shut noisily and a door banging in the wind, so that only a few phrases reached my mind—"freely and voluntarily ... of sound and sober mind ... emit this declaration ... and warn you ..."

The voice died away, and Bob spoke in his cold matter-of-fact voice.

"Did you", he said "on the afternoon of April 12th await here with your niece, Rhoda Macpherson, the return of Miss Jessica Warrielaw from Edinburgh? Did you both at some subsequent hour that evening enter into a serious quarrel with her over the steps she proposed to take in disposing of a certain jewel belonging to the family?"

A low murmur of assent came from Mary, and Bob went on.

"Did Miss Jessica at some hour of that night meet with her death? I will question you more fully on that subject later. Most of all we wish to make sure of your subsequent movements, that your nephew may be acquitted before matters proceed further.

"Did you therefore agree with your niece, Rhoda Macpherson, to remove the corpse of your sister to the stables? Did you seek to extract from her body the embroidery dagger which had, by design or accident, pierced her heart, and in so doing, from violent contact with the breast-bone of deceased, break it at the hilt? Did you then carry the body away, returning when it was so late and dark that you omitted to find the handle of the weapon and the handkerchief in which you had wrapped it, and were further prevented in your search by the heavy rain which fell that night?"

Again I hardly noticed the answer, for the door of Mary's bedroom banged above us, and I heard Rhoda's light foot in the corridor upstairs. Effie told me afterwards that she had seen her at the head of the stairs. From her words I gathered how Rhoda's eyes were blazing in her face: how it was again a trapped animal who stood there, the fierce Warrielaw at bay; how the trim business woman had disappeared and it was the wild Border lady who glared down on the old maid. She made a step forward as if to rush down the stairs past Effie. Next moment she must have seen the constable and changed her mind. She turned, and I heard the swing door opposite the head of the staircase creak loudly. Evidently she was making her way down the back stairs, but whither I could not imagine. She must have lost by now all hopes of reaching the sitting-room door.

"Did you," went on Bob's voice remorselessly, "after consultation with Miss Rhoda Macpherson, agree to disguise the disappearance of your sister by taking her place next day, assuming the black coat and hat left on her bed? Did you take the train as far as Carstairs, get out there unnoticed in the holiday crowd and return thence by the slow train to Midcalder Station? Did you at some point on your way thither discard the black coat and hat, and replace them by those of your own which you carried in a parcel for that purpose? Did you or Miss Macpherson then parcel them up, and did she then bicycle with them to Bathgate, leaving them in charge of a porter, Jock Hay, in the cloakroom because she failed to meet Annie Hay for whom she destined them? Did she then join you at Erleigh, where you took your lunch? Did you then return here, hoping to find and take possession of the family jewel, and did the shock of its loss and your subsequent illness lead you to conceal thenceforward what you had done?"

"That is all true!" I could see Mary's face in the mirror. It was flushed still and her lips were purple, but her eyes were clear and her voice firm. And then, even as I looked at her, a strange horror shook her as I could see her shawls quivering and her hands spread themselves nervously. The nurse and doctor bent over her. Bob and Mr. Mair on her other side, with their backs to the window, saw nothing but her natural shame and misery. But I could see something else. Reflected in the mirror was a dark form on the path among the laurels, pressed back among the branches, and through the leaves stood out a pale face lit up with anger. In the mirror Mary could see, as I could see, Rhoda gazing straight at her with fierce, compelling eyes.

"Shall I sign your form?" Mary's voice came with obvious difficulty now. "I have told the truth."

"There is one thing more we must ask you," said Mr. Mair in a low solemn voice. "You have been very ill, Miss Warrielaw: even now you are not far from the presence of your Maker. On this paper I hold is this confession that you, Mary Warrielaw, did stab your sister to death. On this other paper is your confession that it was your niece, Rhoda Macpherson, who gave the fatal blow. And here again is a paper on which it is stated that by one unintentional push your sister fell before you, striking herself with such violence that her head struck the fender and the point of the instrument which she held pierced into her heart. Only you and one other person know which of these statements describes what really happened. Before you sign it, I ask you to remember that here, before God, you are pledged to tell the truth." Mary's eyes were fixed upon the mirror, and my eyes too were hypnotised by that pale terrible face staring from the shadowed shrubbery. Surely one of them must see Rhoda, I thought desperately. Was it my duty to interpose and point to her? What was the message she was trying to give but an urgent command to her aunt to incriminate herself? It was my duty to interfere, I knew it was, and yet I stood silent and motionless. It was of no use. I had seen one trapped animal in the Courts that morning, and now he would be set free. I could bear no more. I would take no part in this ghastly business. I must leave Mary alone to play out the hideous drama to its bitter end.

And then Mary spoke, her eyes still fixed on the shrubbery.

"Give me that last paper," she muttered. "It was an accident, all an accident! I—we—were going to speak if Neil were convicted. I would have spoken long ago, but I was ill and—and—I was not allowed to—"

There was a long pause while the Notary produced a pen and Mary wielded it in her powerless, swollen fingers. It was difficult to believe they would ever have the strength to trace laboriously that ill-omened Border name, but the sound of the slow scratching of the pen stopped at last. The Notary took the paper and, as he and the other two men bent over it to sign their names as witnesses, I turned to Miss Mary, longing to express some of the pity in my heart. But at one glimpse at her face I drew back in horror. On that grey, lined countenance was no misery nor shame: her eyes were still fixed on the mirror, and in them was a queer ugly glance of triumph.

My eyes followed hers to the mirror, and as they did so I started and tried to cry out a warning, but in my terror my voice failed me. For a moment I saw Rhoda's pale face in the bushes, convulsed with sudden fear and horror. She was struggling to turn; her arms were raised as if to free herself from some unseen force that was pinioning her from behind. The bushes rustled, branches snapped, and next moment Rhoda's form disappeared, and I saw another figure, tall and ungainly, pushing her into the depth of the shrubbery towards the stable wall. No one noticed my effort to speak or my movement of horror, for Miss Mary was speaking again.

"Annie!" she muttered, raising herself upright from her pillows, "Annie! At last Rhoda's gone! At last!"

The doctor and nurse sprang to her side as Mary fell backwards with staring eyes and convulsive breath. She was dying, I told myself, she was dying, and yet through my mind passed the incongruous thought that even at such a moment, as all her life through, she was taking a second place in the thoughts of those around her. Before the doctor could speak I dragged Bob somehow to the French window.

"Something queer is going on there," I panted inarticulately. "Something I don't understand. I saw Rhoda in the bushes! Then I saw Annie! She—she's trying to hurt her! Someone must go and see!"

Upon our ears fell suddenly an appeal more urgent than mine. From the distant bushes came a sudden cry of terror and the sound of a heavy thud. Next moment Effie darted in from the passage and ran past us to the French window.

"There'll have been an accident in the yard!" she cried. "The workmen warned us we were no to go that way to the yard. They'n been digging holes by the gate right under the yard! Someone will have taken a fall! Eh, Sirs! Eh, Sirs!"

Even as she spoke the bushes parted and Annie emerged, breathless and dishevelled, with a strange secret smile in her vacant eyes.

"Miss Rhoda's awa'," she said shrilly. "She's awa' down one of yon holes, and she looks awfu' bad!"

"Whist, lassie, whist!" cried poor old Effie, running to her side, as we paused in sudden horror. "Now don't you be saying any more. Come you ben with me—"

But Annie was past commands or persuasion now.

"I pit her doun there!" she said in the same high voice. "I threw her doun! She'll no' go trying to get me taken awa' in the yellow van any more! Yon was a bad yin!"

At that cursory epitaph Bob started forward and motioned to the constable. The girl made no effort to move as he took her arm, and Mr. Mair turned back to the library and summoned the doctor to the garden hastily.

"Miss Warrielaw's still breathing," said the doctor, as he realised the urgency of the new task before him. "Would you sit beside her, Mrs. Morrison, and let Nurse come with me? We may need help, and there's nothing to be done for our patient there, nothing. It's only a question of hours or even minutes now."

I have no coherent memories of those long minutes during which I sat by Miss Mary's side, listening dully to her fitful breathing, and hearing now and again men's voices raised in orders or suggestions from the yard. The events of the morning had left me incapable of thought. While one part of my mind grappled vainly with the hideous knowledge that Annie had tried to drive Rhoda to her death, I could visualise nothing clearly but queer pitiful visions of three children playing hide-and-seek in and out of the rhododendron bushes with their purple blossoms. Before my eyes ran visions of a tall, fair, laughing boy pursued endlessly by a dark, beautiful, tragic little girl, while from the bushes a sullen, jealous child with staring eyes watched them at their play. Neil, Cora, and Rhoda ran in and out of the shadows of glossy branches before me, as they had been running in and out of the shadows of death for the last few months. They were more real to me than the glimpse of a still, huddled figure, borne by Bob and the policeman on an improvised stretcher towards the kitchen door; their cries were clearer than the low moans which came from the stretcher. Then my dreams faded and I sat listening while upstairs and downstairs I heard doors opening and shutting and men's voices raised in consultation.

Mary was still breathing. Rhoda, I gathered from the sounds above, must still be alive, but to what purpose I wondered should either aunt or niece struggle their way back to life? Surely the ghosts of the black Borderers who still lingered round their home must rejoice over so wild a ballad of crime and madness as their house knew to-day.

Time seemed to have stood still for ever when the doctor joined me at last. Bob and Mr. Mair had to return at once, to place the astounding *dénouement* of the case before the Courts during the lunch interval. He asked me to remain with Miss Mary till someone could be spared from Rhoda's side.

"Yes, she may live," he said soberly, in answer to my hushed question. "But her head's badly damaged. It's doubtful if she can ever conceivably be herself again. Try not to think about her if you can. I am very sorry to leave you here, but if you could just sit here till the other nurse gets down? Or till Miss Alison comes? Someone must bring her at once, but she'll need a friend like you so badly when she gets here."

So I sat and waited while the shadows fell slowly, hour by hour, over the formal garden and the circling rhododendrons and the tall beech trees behind. Beyond and above them the sun was shining and the doves were murmuring, but I sat beside Mary, it seemed to me, in the cavern to which I had likened the room long ago, in the green depths where the ghosts of the dead and their doomed vessels floated restlessly for ever.

CHAPTER XV
MR. STUART EXPLAINS

THESE EVENTS, as I said, took place before the Great War. It was not till the August of 1914 that the story faded into insignificance. Even now, I believe, in the legal world, the tale of the trial ranks as unique, but the strain laid on the imaginations and memories of our generation by the years 1914-1918 makes it possible to-day to mention the name of Warrielaw without arousing a storm of comment and controversy. All that day while I sat in the library at Warrielaw, trying in vain to understand the whole tangled story, the Edinburgh Law Courts were enjoying to the full the greatest sensation of the century.

The Court had adjourned for lunch when Bob hurried to John, and the two men at once sought out Askew Firle and his junior counsel. I should love to have been present at that conversation, especially as Mr. Firle was, according to John, rather disappointed than relieved by Bob's revelations. He had been delighted with his theory of the fatal accident, and he had looked forward keenly to his cross-questioning of the Crown witnesses. Still he allowed himself to relent in the end and spare a thought of congratulation for Neil. After all, as he handsomely admitted, it is probably more pleasant to escape outright than to listen to the most brilliant advocacy of your cause when your life is at stake, and you are aware that a verdict of Not Proven is the best you can hope!

The lunch interval was almost over when the defence approached the Lord Advocate, and there was barely time to acquaint the Judge with the change in affairs before the Court sat once more. Neil had been put out of his misery at once by a scribbled note from John, and appeared in Court so urbane and patronising that, said Dennis, any judge and jury would have sentenced him to death at once if they had had the chance. (This, I should add, was Dennis's later opinion. Bob told me that the boy was uproarious with relief when he first heard the news on the way to the Courts, and was only sobered a little when he heard more of the story, and realised what the effect of the news would be on poor little Alison.) The Court was crowded to overflowing, and stifling in the July sunshine, when the Lord Advocate arose to make his statement that important information had just been received which altered the nature of the case. Amid stupefied silence Mary's statement was read aloud. The Judge made a few almost commonplace remarks and urged the jury not to try at this moment to disentangle the whole extraordinary tale. The confession of the dying woman could not be used as evidence, yet the fact that the murder was committed at another time and in other circumstances, gave him no alternative but to discharge the prisoner on the major count. Further, the confession of Mary Warrielaw confirmed in every point Mr. Logan's story of his own doings. They must remember that the story of the theft remained as yet obscure, yet it might be natural to suppose that Mr. Logan had told the truth over the one affair as over the other. On the count of theft, however, they must give a separate verdict. The jury retired for exactly one minute and returned with a verdict of Not Guilty. In scenes of indescribable excitement and enthusiasm Neil left the court a free man only an hour or two after Bob's return from Warrielaw.

Of these events at the time I knew nothing. It was not till a nurse crept in to rouse Mary for some nourishment and bring me some food that I could realise anything but the tragedy of the house. It was only after three cups of strong tea that my curiosity woke to life again, and I was finding my solitary confinement unbearable when release came at last. It was granted to me by the one I least expected, for I could hardly believe my eyes when Neil himself came into the room.

"Don't bother, my dear!" Neil's composure was as perfect as ever. Nothing in his look or manner suggested the strain of this dreadful day or the last two months. "Just embrace me by way of congratulation!"—I was, I must confess, wringing his hands and crying—"and then make your escape from a family which can hardly, I fear, count among the pleasantest of your acquaintance."

"But Alison, poor little Alison! Is she here? I must stay and see if I can be of any use to her!"

"Betty, I have a curious message for you," said Neil. "I trust that its practical advantages for you will outweigh its rudeness. I brought Alison here, under protest, on the sole condition that I took you away and relieved her of your presence and mine.

She is the sanest of us all but like most women she is not legal-
ly-minded, and her strongest emotions at the moment are her
love and pity for Rhoda. Though it was to save my unworthy
neck, she insists that it is John, and to a lesser extent you and
Dennis, who have brought Rhoda to her doom (those are her
rather exaggerated words). She does not want to see you or
me or any of us. I have been talking to Dr. Hewetson and he
agrees that she should have her way. She and Effie are in each
other's arms already. Effie is finding consolation for Annie's
tragedy in having Alison to comfort, and Alison feels Effie a
rock beneath which she can shelter. The nurses are in charge
with one or two more to help them, too, and by nightfall
the Law will have decided how many policemen to add to
this curious house-party. The Procurator Fiscal is gloriously
intrigued, you see, about the position of the case. They ought
to arrest Mary and Rhoda for concealment of Jessica's death,
if not for suspicion of foul play, but they can't bring either of
them into the Sheriff Court; and even when an indictment
is made out, it can't be read until they are well enough to be
present. Mary will, I hope, be dead by then. If Rhoda has lost
her reason for good she can't be tried as she can't plead for
herself. As far as I can see, the house will remain a sort of place
of detention for days or weeks. However, that's not the immediate point. My only errand is to extract you and leave Alison
in charge by her own wishes."

Neil's glance strayed to Miss Mary as he spoke, but his eyes
were inscrutable.

"Not a lovable family," he murmured in his old manner.
"When one thinks of her and Rhoda, and of Cora still on the
brink of insanity, one might almost believe that the fairy jewel
kept up its old reputation after all. It's a sordid little fairing! If
it comes to me I shall send it to a Jumble Sale in aid of the
Feeble-Minded."

"Have you seen—her—Rhoda?" I asked falteringly as a
nurse came in and we left the room. "My dear Betty, I have

done my duty in every conceivable respect to-day," said Neil lightly, though a shadow passed over his face. "Don't think I shall indulge you in your morbid interest in horrors. She is said, in that idiotic phrase of the medical world, to be going on as well as can be expected. So far my day has been far more objectionable than if I had spent it quietly in the Courts being tried for my life. Now I propose to have some pleasure. I am going back to shave and bathe and join Firle and your husband for dinner in Firle's rooms. I must insist on the resurrection of my body!"

It was late that evening before John came home, but Bob and Dennis were waiting with me, and now at last we could all settle down to hear Bob's story complete. Up till now each of us had extracted one item or another and tried to set the pieces of the puzzle together as best we could. But the time had come for a full exposition, and John moved the whisky tray to Bob's elbow.

"For you've got a good long sermon before you," he said, "and a very good audience!"

"Please, I want to know," I said, "what would have happened if I hadn't realised this morning that it was Mary, not Jessica, whom I saw on the morning of April 13th?" That was the point which had been troubling me all day and I wanted first of all to have it settled.

"It would have delayed everything," said Bob, "delayed everything badly. You see, I'd got the whole thing clear in my mind by then, but the point was that I could hardly get all those admissions out of poor Miss Mary unless I was absolutely sure of my ground. If you'd stuck to it that it was Jessica you saw we'd have had to get at all the rest piece by piece. That meant the risk of Miss Macpherson's intervention, and we always recognised the danger to Miss Mary's health. I was haunted by the feeling that we might be too late to get her confession."

"Could you ever have got a solution without it?" asked John.

"That's the question I ask myself and I have hardly had time to make sure of the answer. You see, I've not much to congratulate myself on in the case. I suppose my excuse must be that my original task was to find Miss Jessica, and that all along I accepted the first story of her departure to London. Once in those early days when I was making out a description of her I asked Effie if I could use Miss Mary as a model. 'Oh no,' she said, 'they werna alike at all when you knew them.' Miss Warrielaw and Miss Mary would be about the same height, she added, but Miss Jessica was broader and a much more energetic, stirring sort of body. Then her hair was a good thought greyer and she hadn't the mole Miss Mary was always fingering on her forehead. Finally she showed me a photo of all the five sisters, and there was such a marked difference in the way of their hairdressing, and the shape of their heads, that I started on the second course of investigation with no idea that one sister would look very like the other in her outdoor costume. That has been a bad mark against me throughout, and I owe the final discovery as much to Mr. Dennis's exclamation at the sight of that poor girl Annie as to anything else. It's uncanny enough that it was the sight of a funeral which helped the case.

"But on the other hand I can honestly say this, that all along I felt some clue to the mystery must lie in the relations of Rhoda—I'll leave out all my 'Misses' if you please, Mrs. Morrison—and Annie. And I had come to the conclusion, too, that they centred round that cloakroom ticket, when there wasn't a trace of the duplicate half to be found anywhere in the south of Scotland. These things don't disappear in a well-ordered station, but the friendship between Annie and her Cousin Jock, the porter at Bathgate, suggested that there might be some collusion about the affair there. You see, in the story there was a missing parcel, the parcel Jessica was said to have taken to London, and a missing cloakroom ticket. I had made up my mind to see if the two were connected on the day we went to Bathgate—and that was only yesterday."

"But the parcel was said to be sandwiches!" I said.

"Yes, but I never believed that a cab-driver would have noticed a parcel small enough to hold the few sandwiches a lady would take with her in the train. And there was another parcel in the story, too, that black hat and cloak which Rhoda had spirited away before ever Effie got home on the 13th of April. Those three items were always at the back of my mind. They were bound up, too, with the mystery about that handkerchief. You and Mr. Firle let that drop, John, when once Mrs. Morrison had proved that half a dozen of Neil's handkerchiefs were lying about in Jessica's work-case, and that its presence did not incriminate him in any way. But I was never satisfied about it. I studied the weather reports of the day, and I studied the bushes where it lay with the handle. The soil is light and sandy and the shrubs grow very thickly. A mere shower wouldn't get through there in a way which would drench a handkerchief. Now from midnight on the 12th to noon on the 13th it rained heavily off and on. Any piece of linen would be soaked through, and any bloodstained rag would be wet, and there would drip from it just that pale-coloured stain which you, Mrs. Morrison, noticed, and assumed to be the dye from Mrs. Murray's bag. At twelve o'clock the wind got up and the sun came out. It must have shone directly on the shrubs opposite the window, and those wide leaves and that sandy soil would dry up in a few minutes. You thought me tiresome; you pointed out that anyhow it might still have been raining at noon, and the murderer would have had time to meet Jessica at 10.41 and get her down here and throw away the stiletto before the rain was off. But Neil, owing to his accident at Harburn, could not have got here before 12.30, even if his tale about Lockerbie was untrue. And all along I felt sure of this, that if we'd found the corpse and the handkerchief on the evening of the 13th, we should have agreed unanimously that the murderer must have left the rag and handle out all night as they were soaked through and through. Of course it made no sense while we believed Jessica to have been alive next morning. When once I guessed that Mary had impersonated her, that detail and every other fell into place."

"Well, begin at the beginning, please," said John.

"And how does Annie come into it all?" I asked, bewildered. "What had she or Jock to do with it? What did you find out at Bathgate?"

"I think I'd better tell you that as we go on along. Let's reconstruct the whole story. And first of all let me say that though both the motive for the crime and the manner of it, when the whole story seemed to depend on the possession of a car for the transport of the corpse, tended to incriminate Neil, there was another character in the story who had laid herself open to suspicion again and again."

"You mean Cora?"

"No, not seriously. I admit her behaviour with regard to the bag and to Annie Hope suggested some mysterious complicity in the crime, but one thing was certain, that Annie was at Bathgate from the night of the 12th to the evening of the 13th and that Cora couldn't have done the crime alone. There was the chance that she was in collusion with Neil, but all their actions tended to show that they were trying to shield each other while each was in the dark about the other's movements. He had seen her at the Lodge in the afternoon and later in George Street with Annie in the evening, and suppressed both facts. She had clearly suspected him and tried to clear away any evidence against him, but she also was evidently working on the vaguest suspicions without an idea of the real truth. Her one idea was to get hold of Annie to find out what had been happening at Warrielaw. If she knew all there was to know she would have certainly left Annie safely at Bathgate. No, the person who had obviously a good motive for the murder, and the coolness and audacity to carry it through, was Rhoda.

And yet the fact stared me in the face that when Jessica was murdered Rhoda was either on her way to lunch or lunching quietly at Erleigh."

"What motive?" asked Dennis.

"The outstanding point in the case was that it was Rhoda who was set upon getting hold of the jewel. Her behaviour at Warrielaw on the 13th, and to John and myself over the suitcase, betrayed that she had a touch of the family madness on that subject. That story of the mysterious burglary in February was so clearly, too, a premature effort on her part to get hold of it. You agreed with me over that, John?"

"I thought she'd seized an opportunity to have a try then, certainly," agreed my husband. "I imagine that she noticed the light in Jessica's room as she rode slowly or walked down the avenue that evening, and then, as she passed the front door, saw the kitchen in darkness, heard Effie and the dogs in the garden, and Annie busily tidying a deserted room which she had evidently been using as a shelter for some man friend of hers. Rhoda was quick-witted enough, too, to remember that there were tinkers about and that they would be suspected if anything in the house was missing. She must have run lightly upstairs, prepared to make herself pleasant to Jessica if she was in her room, and, when she found it empty, disarrange it in just the way which would throw suspicion on Annie, before she hunted for the jewel. I expect she hoped to find a duplicate key in the hoards of keys an old lady like Jessica usually keeps in her dressing-table—or she may merely have hoped that for once Jessica had left the real key lying there. It was what you told me of her conversation with Annie which suggested it, Betty. I am pretty sure she hoped to find that Annie was harbouring someone in the house that night to whom suspicion would attach. The fact that Jock had only made his appearance at the New Year, and couldn't have got down there from the hospital for a week at least, didn't suit her book. But she used it skilfully enough to establish such an ascendancy over

Annie that she extorted a half-confession from her that she'd disarranged the room. And she had got the threat of exposure about Jock's room to hang over Annie if she ever needed her services."

"That's so," agreed Bob, filling his pipe. "That story made me go into the case with a strong bias against Rhoda apart from her behaviour. It was clear, too, that she had a personality which dominated weaker natures entirely. She could clearly count on Mary and Annie as her tools."

"Now we come to the twelfth of April, and how far the true story of that night will ever be known depends, I suppose, on the next action of the Crown. They may accept Mary's statement that Jessica's death was an accident or they may not. If they refuse, and if either Mary or Rhoda are capable of standing on their trial, the police will have to reconsider the evidence they do possess about the actual course of events. One thing at least is established now. The accident or the murder, whichever it was, had taken place before nine o'clock that evening. There's no doubt of that, for the post goes out of the village then, and before it went, Rhoda posted a note to Annie which I found yesterday in that black cape of Miss Jessica's which the poor girl had been wearing for funerals. I've got a copy here," said Bob, searching in his pockets, "and it proves to me that Jessica was dead and Rhoda's plans laid by that time. 'I've a parcel for you', she wrote to Annie, 'of old clothes which Miss Jessica forgot to give to Effie, and I have persuaded her to let you have them instead. Don't mention this to Effie, or show the clothes to her or to anyone for the next few days, as Effie may think she should have them herself, but I want to make you this present as I know how much you have always wanted nice black things to wear at funerals. I can take a little run on my bicycle to Bathgate to-morrow, so be on the look-out at the station any time after 11 o'clock and I'll hand them over to you. Yours truly, R.M.' She did not date the letter, but the envelope is clearly marked April 12th. I am convinced that this sudden access of philanthropy on Rhoda's part was due to the fact that her really wonderful powers of improvisation were already at work. It was, you see, essential to her scheme that she should dispose safely of the black hat and cloak which Mary must wear when she was to impersonate Jessica next forenoon. She had schemed all that before even the post went out. She had indeed a rare gift for organisation."

"But what do you think really happened?" urged Dennis.

"What, indeed?" said John. "And you speak of Rhoda's improvisations. Was it improvisation or, if she were responsible for Jessica's death, was the whole thing part of a premeditated design? How do you reconstruct the scene?"

"First and foremost," said Bob, filling his pipe slowly, "I am quite convinced it wasn't an accident. I attach no importance to Mary's confession. I don't say we have proof enough to disprove it in law, but you've only to consider the characters of both aunt and niece to see that it's impossible. There's no doubt, I imagine, that there was a terrible scene in the library. No doubt Jessica turned upon Mary and Rhoda as they argued against the sale of the jewel, no doubt both old ladies were beside themselves with passion. But if Jessica really stumbled and fell, as the story goes, the fall would have sobered Mary. She is not an inhuman woman, she's not a member of the professional criminal class whose habit of mind leads them to think at once: 'The police'll get me!' Her one instinct would have been to summon assistance. It wouldn't even have occurred to her that any suspicion would attach to her. Rhoda, on the other hand, was inhuman enough, but Rhoda, as we know, is a clever woman. If she'd planned this affair beforehand we may be pretty sure she'd have stage-managed the scene as an accident. If the quarrel in the library hadn't suddenly had this fatal ending she would have seen for herself that they might present it as an accident. I haven't the least doubt that when Firle started his line of defence—and you may be sure she heard of it—she hasn't cursed herself a hundred times for not thinking of such an obvious way out for herself and her aunt, instead of her own tortuous schemes. No, to my mind it's certain that both women hastened at once to try to disguise the deed because they were so suddenly and awfully conscious of their crime."

"Then you think they were both involved?" asked John, shading his eyes.

"That's my theory, though it could never be proved. I imagine that in the height of the quarrel Mary hit her sister so violently that Jessica fell, knocking her head against the brass fender with such force that she was stunned. Then I fancy she may have run for help and Rhoda, left alone, bent over Jessica, rejoicing to think the enemy of herself and her family was dead. When she saw that Jessica still lived, I imagine that her eyes fell on Mary's stiletto, and—and she did the rest."

"Mary couldn't have done that, I feel sure," agreed John hoarsely.

"No, but I think we must believe that she some share in the first blow. Otherwise if Rhoda could have persuaded her to act the part she played next day. I feel convinced that only the consciousness that she herself was partially responsible could have made her submit to Rhoda's wishes after that. Rhoda, I suppose, called her back when all was over and brought home to her her share in the crime. And then I suppose the two women stood there in that dim room, Jessica's body lying by the firelight, in that vast lonely house, wondering what on earth to do next. I expect Rhoda left Mary to shudder and cry while she made her plans and wrote and posted her letter to Annie. There was enough for poor Mary to do after that."

"Of course, there's not a shadow of proof of all this," said John, as if refusing to be convinced.

"Only one bit of evidence, such as it is. We know that Jessica was engaged in working the initials on that handkerchief of Neil's which Rhoda snatched up when she threw it with the handle of the stiletto into the bushes. Mary or Rhoda must have flung them into the bushes when they were tidying up after the crime. Perhaps, as it wasn't done very efficiently, it was done by Mary. It seems strange that Rhoda did not notice them next morning, but then her work was cut out for her. She had to keep Mary up to her task, give her breakfast, disarrange Jessica's room as if she had slept in it and get off to Midcalder on her bicycle. Even she couldn't manage everything. But my point is now that Jessica was not doing her embroidery that evening. Even if she had been we know from Effie that an iron unwritten law existed between the two old ladies that neither must touch the worktable or the implements of the other. If it had been Jessica's stiletto we discovered, Jessica's stiletto which had pierced her heart, I might accept the accident theory. But it wasn't. Mary's stiletto was by her side; it was she who was working with it that evening. It cannot have been in Jessica's hand when she fell. So I feel assured from what I know of the sisters, but naturally it is not a point on which you could convince a jury!"

"Go on with the story, please," muttered Dennis.

"The next part must have been pretty horrible," said Bob, staring before him. "Somehow or other Rhoda had to persuade Mary to carry her sister's body with her to the shed. That I don't believe she could have done if she hadn't convinced Mary she was a partner in the crime. I expect it was the appalling nature of her job which led Rhoda then to make a bad mistake. She must have run upstairs to get the hat and cloak Jessica had laid out for the journey: she must have taken Jessica's handbag and put it in Mary's room assuming that her aunt's pound notes and ticket were within it. She may have felt the cloak—and Jessica's body—to assure herself that Jessica was neither carrying nor wearing the jewel. But she didn't notice the flat notecase, and when at last she'd forced Mary to her horrible task, and in the rain and darkness they'd carried the body to the tool-shed, they placed it in such a way that the pocket with the notes was beneath it. Rhoda, we must assume, forgot to take off Jessica's keys then as well. One can't wonder!

Picture the two women at work in the dark, for there were no signs of candle grease in the shed and the risk of being seen from the lodge would have been too great if they had brought a lantern! I expect Mary was in such a condition that Rhoda had not the time she wished to attend to details. After all, somehow or other she had to calm Mary enough to be ready for the part it was essential she should play on the next day. How difficult the job was we can gather from the fact that obviously Rhoda had no opportunity to retrieve the keys and make sure that the jewel was in her possession at last.

"You know what Mary's part was. Mary, in Jessica's hat, cloak and heavy veil got into the cab next morning, took the London train, alighted at Carstairs and took the slow train back to Midcalder. It was a fearful risk to run, a fantastic risk for any people better known than those two solitary old ladies were. As it was, luck, undeserved luck, attended that part of the scheme. No one who saw Mary had any suspicions; Neil, as we know, failed to arrive at Carstairs. They knew nothing of that possibility, of course, but if he had been up to time the whole plan must have miscarried. Mary passed unnoticed in the excursion, travelling by the slow train from Carstairs to Midcalder. I imagine it was according to plan that she left her suit-case in the train. It would add to the presumption, when it turned up, that Jessica had really travelled to London. The only thing which must have dismayed Mary was the discovery that neither the pound notes nor the tickets were in Jessica's handbag. She must have had enough with her to buy a single ticket to Carstairs and another to Midcalder.

"It was Rhoda's part of the scheme which miscarried. It was of course the part she had planned in the first panic of self-protection. She had been quick-witted enough to see at once that the difficulty would be to dispose of Jessica's black clothes after Mary had discarded them and put on her own fawn cloak and hat for lunch at Erleigh. She dare not carry a big parcel on her bicycle there, I suppose, and leave it on her bicycle while she was at lunch. She would picture it falling off, opened by an inquisitive maid or torn by a dog—"

"But why shouldn't she have a parcel of old black clothes?" I asked. "Why should anyone think that suspicious?"

"Why didn't she simply throw them away into a ditch?" added Dennis. "I don't see why she took so much trouble."

"You've got to place yourself in her position on the thirteenth, remember. We know now that whatever she'd done would have been overlooked or forgotten probably after the lapse of seven weeks. But she didn't know that she could count for certain on seven weeks or even seven days. The odds were that no one would go near the stables for months, but if by some accident the body had been found in a few days the investigations of the police would have been a very different affair. Presumably they would still have assumed that Jessica had travelled as far as Carstairs, that she had been lured from the train and brought home, alive or dead, in some vehicle. Or that she had changed her mind and returned, to be murdered by some passing ruffian. But if only a few days had elapsed the police could have gone through the evidence of every car and every person seen in the neighbourhood with a toothcomb. When nothing suspicious could be traced they would have extended their investigations. Effie knew every item of Jessica's wardrobe, and any hint of the contents of Rhoda's parcel at Erleigh might have attracted attention. Any passer-by who picked up a parcel of old black clothes, if she'd thrown them away, as Dennis suggests, might have reported the information to the police. She might have risked throwing them away, weighted, into some burn, but even so Effie would have demanded where the missing garments were. Annie was a fairly safe recipient. She was not bright enough to attach much importance to dates or times: she would not be considered a trustworthy witness in any case. If Rhoda could have managed, as she intended, to get rid of the things quietly to this half-witted girl, she would have a reply to Effie's questions which would rouse no suspicions. But unfortunately for her, her plans went wrong. Annie as we know wasn't at the station. Rhoda would have been wiser, as things turned out, to have gone back with her parcel and risked its exposure at Erleigh, but she hadn't the time to reconsider her scheme. Her work was cut out for her to get back to Erleigh in anything like time for lunch, and her mind was set on disposing of it. She took it to the cloakroom and left it with Jock, who, we may assume, was a stranger to her. It was, I expect, only as she bicycled furiously away that she realised that her appearance at Bathgate at 12.30 might seem suspicious if anyone got wind of the whole plan, as I did only yesterday."

"But, my dear Bob," interposed John, "women can be late for an appointment without one's suspecting that a murder delayed them!"

"Just so, but think of it again from Rhoda's point of view. We know that Mary's impersonation had succeeded, but all she knew was that Mary had owned to being seen at Princes Street by Miss Wise and Mrs. Morrison, and, for all we know, she may have seen Dennis at Carstairs. Rhoda cannot have assumed that they were deceived for certain. We can imagine that it was because she felt she had made a mistake that she handed the cloakroom ticket into Mary's keeping. That she felt might avert suspicions from herself. She had no possible reason to expect that the whole plan would miscarry on just that one trifle.

"And yet it was there that her troubles began. Annie, you see, got to the station at last, to hear that her precious black outfit was in a parcel in the cloakroom. She had set her heart on wearing the things at a funeral at Carglin that afternoon in spite of Rhoda's prohibitions, and she managed to wheedle the parcel out of Jock for just that occasion and then let him have it back in the cloakroom. Then Cora carried her off to Edinburgh, and while Annie was there I expect she bothered Rhoda unceasingly for the missing ticket. Rhoda must have become terribly harassed by the prominence which the parcel and the date were coming to have in Annie's mind, and as we know, she could not find the ticket at Warrielaw. At last apparently she told Annie that if she had any sense she'd just get Jock to give up the parcel and destroy the counterfoil. Jock did so when poor Annie came back in such distress from the Murray's, but then their troubles began. Rhoda came over and professed great horror at their misdemeanour. She told Annie and Jock, who seems to have picked up a tinker's horror of the law from Mrs. Hay, that if their doings ever became known Jock would be dismissed and probably put in gaol. She had already reminded Annie again and again that one word about her sheltering Jock at the New Year, or her behaviour in February, would mean lasting disgrace for her. In short, she gave them to understand that only the strictest secrecy about the parcel could save them if the police enquired about it. And there, like so many clever criminals, she overreached herself. It wasn't till I saw the poor creature Annie working to scratch out the date of April 13th on the grave that I realised there was some urgent reason for secrecy about the parcel; and only when I got the whole tale out of Jock that it was clear that Rhoda brought that parcel from Midcalder to Bathgate. Then I realised that it must be for one reason, and for one only, that she had impressed on Annie at all costs that she must hide the date when she received the parcel.

"Now we must go back to the 13th of April. Rhoda bicycled back at a tremendous rate—she may have got a lift, but I doubt if she'd risk it, and I did find out lately that the Wises were not punctual people, so that she may have been even a quarter of an hour behind time that day. How would his host remember that? I don't envy that lunch party or the walk home. For Mary must have reiterated that she had found herself at the Caledonian Station without the ticket or the pound notes and that she had been seen by two friends at least —and Rhoda must have told her that they must search the corpse again when they got home. Your presence, Mrs. Morrison, made that impossible. It must have been a terrible shock to them both to find you there, and Rhoda must have rushed straight round to the shed and secured the keys from the corpse, which was all she could manage alone. As we know she got the keys and unlocked the safe, only to find the jewel-case empty. After that Mary's illness, and the discovery that the jewel had gone, upset the whole scheme and made the whole business a ghastly failure from her point of view. She had to leave Warrielaw with you that evening, knowing that she could hardly get to the shed again, for there was the lodge occupied by Mrs. Lee's niece and her pack of bairns: there were doctors and nurses about and there was no one to help her to move the body, so that she could remove the notecase. She knew, too, from you, Mrs. Morrison, that the place had been open and deserted all day, so that the jewel might have been stolen in reality, just as she had planned might appear to have been the case in February. She must have fixed her hopes on having missed it in the suit-case after all, and nearly went out of her mind when that proved fallacious. She found out from Annie, I expect, that Cora had been enquiring about the happenings at Warrielaw on the 13th. She may have known that Cora was there alone. From the moment that she gave up hope of the jewel turning up in the suit-case, her one aim was to get the discovery of the corpse over and done with, in the hope that the enquiries about the murder or accident might lead to the discovery of the jewel. I fancy all her extraordinary behaviour in trying to get hold of money from the estate was a wild alternative plan to give up hope of the jewel and get away safely to America. By that time, you see, she must have found out, I fancy, that the handle and the handkerchief had been removed from the garden, and every now and then panic seized her."

"I can't feel sorry for her even now," I said, "when I think of her behaviour to Neil."

"I think", said John, shading his eyes, "that you might if you'd seen her to-day, Betty, when she was brought in."

"Remember, too," said Bob, "that she wasn't really quite sane about the jewel. She may have thought Neil really stole it that afternoon, as the case developed. She could not forgive him, too, for all he was to gain by Jessica's will. The jewel and Warrielaw itself and money were the only things she cared for, and Neil was to deprive her of them all."

"She dreaded his influence over Alison, too," said John. "I think she really loved that poor child."

"I still don't understand about Annie," said Dennis hastily. "What set her against Rhoda in that ghastly way, in the end?"

, "Well, Rhoda, you must remember, was growing wild with panic over our search for the missing counterfoil of the cloakroom ticket. From the moment we found Mary's half, and from the moment I went to Bathgate, her one idea was to get rid of Annie or to discredit her as a witness. She went over, ostensibly, I imagine, to ensure her silence, and found Annie recalcitrant because Jock was anxious to own what he'd done. He realised by then that though he would be rebuked severely for having handed over the parcel to Annie and destroyed the counterfoil, he was likely to get into far more serious trouble over suppressing the truth when the enquiry was made. Either deliberately or in a passion Rhoda told Mrs. Hay that Annie was not to be trusted and not in command of her wits, and that she would send the doctor to observe her and see that she was put away into a proper home. That was, of course, why Annie ran away: it was always the fear of her life that she'd be taken away in the yellow van, as these country people say. After the scene yesterday afternoon when she was as near as possible to threatening myself and her sister with her absurd knife, I got the doctor to look at her. Rhoda had evidently wanted to clear a witness out of the way by throwing doubts on Annie's sanity. I wanted to be assured of it. The doctor rang me up last night to say that he thought Annie should be kept under observation, but he saw no reason why she should be shut up as yet. He had mentioned to Mrs. Hay that the subject had been referred to him by a Miss Macpherson but he thought she was in the wrong. Annie heard that, and then and there, I suppose, made up her mind to be revenged."

"I suppose that poor girl will be shut up in an asylum?" asked Dennis as Bob stopped to fill his pipe.

"Yes, inevitably. I think that would have happened anyhow. She hasn't been responsible for her actions for a long time."

"She would read in a tragedy as an instrument of the Fates," said John abstractedly. "Well, Bob, you've done a fine piece of work to-day, and your reasoning about the whole affair is convincing enough but for just one thing. There's one personal aspect of the question which makes it difficult for me to accept your theory. I've known Mary all my life. She's essentially an honest woman, whatever Rhoda made her do, and she's at bottom a religious woman. I find it very hard to believe that in the presence of death she would have sworn to a lie. She knew she was going fast. All these last few weeks she's been dominated by her fear of Rhoda and her hatred of Rhoda. Would she have endangered her soul, as she'd have thought, to protect Rhoda in the end? I can't believe it."

I was sitting beside a table on which stood an electric lamp, and as John spoke I turned the lampshade a little so that its light no longer fell in my face. Bob's eyes were upon me, and as if in answer to that searching gaze I sank back into the shadows.

"The value of her statement could be questioned only", said Bob slowly, "if any witness could be found to prove that Rhoda was exercising her undoubted influence on Mary right up to the end. You may say that was impossible. We were all present at that last scene, and Rhoda was certainly not in the room. But one thing I noticed when we rose from our seats to sign Mary's deposition—a curious thing. I noticed a mirror which hung at such an angle to the sofa that it must have presented a view of the formal garden and the shrubs to anyone lying on the sofa. If one of us had seen Rhoda watching the scene, if any of us had reason to suppose that the presence of Rhoda in the garden was even up to the last menacing her aunt, if it was because Rhoda's eyes were upon her that Mary was induced to sign that confession, I suppose we should have grounds for re-opening the whole case and questioning the validity of Mary's last statement."

Again Bob's eyes sought mine and still I sat motionless. Out of all the conflicting emotions of the day only one determination remained supreme in my mind. Never again should the life of any other human being depend on the evidences of my senses, never again should any evidence of mine help to place a captured human animal in a trap. You may say it was a most unworthy conclusion of the matter for a lawyer's wife, but my mind was made up for life.

"On the other hand," pursued Bob, "any such witness, if one there had been, might well conclude that Fate had provided a fit vengeance for Rhoda in full measure. It seems doubtful if she will recover, still more doubtful if she will ever regain her full faculties again. Any of us who saw her to-day might well consider that she had had her punishment, and wish to say nothing which might involve that most unhappy family in further suffering and disgrace."

The silence which followed was broken by the telephone bell and I rose to answer it.

"Mary's gone!" I said, turning round after listening to a few brief remarks from the other end of the wire. "John, I think I'll—I'll go to bed now."

"Indeed you'd better, you poor child," agreed John. "But, my dear, we can only thank Heaven for the news."

"Yes," agreed dully as Bob went to open door for me. "There's nothing more to hear now, is there?"

"Or to say," said Bob a little questioningly put out my hand to wish him good night.

"No, nothing!" I shook my head determinedly.

"Then the rest is silence," said Bob slowly I left them.

CHAPTER XVI
THE END

WARRIELAW HOUSE stood empty and desolate for several years after the tragedy of that July day. Mary had made no will, in spite of Rhoda's persistent entreaties to her to do so, and the estate passed therefore into the possession of the four surviving Warrielaws—Cora, Neil, Rhoda and Alison. It was, John said, characteristic of the family that they would not meet to discuss the fate of the house itself, or of Rhoda in her long and miserable confinement. Alison made all arrangements for her sister with the firm to which Rhoda had entrusted her affairs, and went off to live with relations in Glasgow. Without a word of farewell to her relations or to us. Cora recovered her health and spirits with surprising rapidity. Charles Murray feared that she might wish him to buy out her relatives' shares, and establish herself in the home she had loved so passionately, but, fortunately for him, she turned from any thought of the place with horror, and persuaded him to retire and settle down to hunt near Melrose. With the astounding adaptability which one or two of her family possessed, she became a county lady with a profound interest in poultry, pedigree stock and race-horses. Neil had a theory that she gave up all evening entertainments when he categorically refused to give her the fairy jewel. Charles, he said, had trouble enough without that, and he handed it over to the safes of the British Linen Bank.

Neil himself was no less anxious to shake off his connection with Edinburgh. He went off to Italy, where he purchased an island and married a cheerful colonial widow to whom Warrielaw, and all it meant in his life, was unknown. Before he left he had exerted all his influence successfully on Rhoda's behalf. Her position was indeed a curious one. No charge could be made against one in her condition, and yet on her recovery she might be found guilty as accessory to Mary in the matter of Jessica's death, and the suppression of the truth, in Neil's trial. By medical advice and legal influence, however, she was placed in a private nursing-home. Thence, just before the War, she was sent to Switzerland for a cure. There, we heard, she was making a complete recovery, and from there in 1915 she made her escape and disappeared, leaving a curt letter in which she renounced all her claims to the Warrielaw estate in favour of Alison. In that action the more charitable of us might trace some sign of penitence, but Rhoda remained a mystery to us all to the end. We never heard of her again.

It is usually sad to round off stories which took place before the Great War, but our lot was singularly fortunate. John went out with the Royal Scots and returned in eighteen months with a wound severe enough to keep him at home till the Armistice, and no eventual disability. Neil considered himself the worst sufferer from the European upheaval, for he was refused for active service and spent his time in one of the new Ministries in Whitehall, a victim to a regular life and the inanity of incompetent and fluffy typists. Only Charles Murray went out never to return, and not a few of us felt that a hero's death in Flanders was better than life with Cora. Dennis, being Dennis, went through the War without a scratch.

Alison vanished out of our life till the War. She and Dennis had never met since that dreadful day in July until my brother appeared in Edinburgh in September, 1914, with a commission in the Black Watch. He was, he told me, Scotch by adoption, and if he had to risk his life in any old war would like to do so in the company of men like my husband and Bob Stuart. Next day he met Alison in Princes Street: she had, it appeared, a job as a V.A.D. and he brought her to see us in Moray Place, looking prettier and more fairy-like than ever. A month later, without a word to anyone, he married her in the true war style and introduced her to us proudly as Mrs. Dennis Howard.

No one could have welcomed a marriage into that family, but life in those days was so precarious, happiness so rare and snatched at so readily, that we accepted the accomplished fact with fewer misgivings than we might have known in ordinary times. The only cloud on their happiness was the occasion when Alison received a registered parcel from Neil as a wedding-present, and opened it to find the fairy jewel. Not a few of us gave way to foolish superstitions in those days, and I urged them to throw the thing away at once. But Alison was more practical. The jewel was sold at last for a marvellous sum, and set aside for the education of the future little Howards. Her John and Dennis are, I must add, exact reproductions of their father, and even her fairy-like little girl has Dennis's eyes. It is only when my children really want to annoy them that they denounce them as "Black Borderers" and "Fairy Freaks".

In the madness of the War the last Warrielaws met in sanity and friendliness, and agreed at last to sell the house. The park is a golf course now, and the place a cumbrous and inconvenient club house. None of us have ever played a round there, but I hear that the secretary makes up his accounts for green-fees and drinks in the library where the two sisters sat once, in silent hatred, over their interminable embroidery.

THE END